# THE MAN WHO LOVED CAT DANCING

# The Man Who Loved Cat Dancing

MARILYN DURHAM

Harcourt Brace Jovanovich, Inc.
New York

First edition
ISBN 0-15-156940-1
Library of Congress Catalog Card Number: 72-75415
Printed in the United States of America
B C D E F

*For Kilburn*

BILLY BOWAN was dreaming of soft-bodied women with ivory skin and fine dark hair, when the sun cracked the day open and hit him in the eye. The long-nailed fingers that were pulling him into a wanton bed became small bits of sandstone chips boring into his outflung arm. His bed was nothing but the hard ground, mattressed by two sour-smelling blankets.

He groaned for the lost succubus and threw a shielding arm across his face. It brought temporary darkness and the rancid smell of his own body sweat, dried in the shirt he'd worn for a week, but he scarcely noticed that.

He remembered where he was and why he was there. A slow smile nearly split his dry lips. He ran a healing tongue over them and told himself, "This here is the day you get rich, Ass-buster. How about that, now?" He scrubbed at his face with his sleeve, then bunched himself and sat up suddenly with a "Hah!" that startled his horse, sack hobbled nearby.

His breakfast was short—cold biscuits and coffee—because he had work to do. "There's tits to pull and hay to pitch," he sang as he got out his supplies. And a train to stop.

It was carrying a lot of money.

# 1

It was only nine o'clock, but the desert floor around the mining camp was already like an oven. Catherine Crocker finished strapping the bulging carpetbag to her gelding's saddle and glanced around once more to be sure no one was watching her prepare her escape. But all the men were at work on top of the mesa. She had waited in the tent, packed and dressed for two hours, fearing that if she started too early Willard might notice her movements and come back down from the diggings to investigate.

There should be no one left in camp now but herself and that billowing slut he had hired as a cook and laundress, who had returned to her cot as soon as the men were out of sight.

Or perhaps she was hiding from Catherine herself. Well, small need. She was welcome to traipse into the big tent and make herself at home. For all Catherine cared, she could have Willard, Catherine's bed, and anything else that suited her.

Catherine was leaving him again, this time for good. And it would be good. Their life together had often been marred by quarrels, a history of marital bloodlettings, but until this morning it had been a private strife. Now, no more. Let him bellow and weep, as he often did when he was angry. Let him be spiteful enough to cut off Papa's little allowance, or even enlist that weak old man's sympathy against her. Nothing he could do would matter. She'd find work, she'd hide, she'd keep running until she fell off the world's edge rather than give in and relive her morning's humiliation.

She couldn't think clearly about just how she would live when her escape was made, but there would be a severe financial problem. She had packed only a minimal change of clothing, and a sandwich and water bottle. She hoped there was enough money in her secret hoard for a ticket home and a bit left over for food and shelter on the way. Enough or not, it was all she had.

No, there was another thing she had to carry away as a memento, she thought, dabbing at her hot face with a fragile linen handkerchief: the red mark of his hand across her cheek. Hot tears welled again as she saw that moment just after he had slapped her, with his whole slack-jawed crew gaping at them around the breakfast fire.

Whatever she had said to him had been spoken in a low voice so the others couldn't hear. He had no right to shame her that way. Hadn't it been enough that he had dragged her out to this Gehenna with him from Denver, against her wish, with no one for company but that slut of a cook and himself?

She entered the white tent once more and looked about to see if there was anything she had missed. Willard's hat was still on the trunk at the foot of his cot. He had forgotten it, or he hadn't had the courage later to walk into the same tent with her to pick it up. Did he prefer to risk sunstroke this morning rather than her basilisk eye? Wasn't that how he saw her?

And what did she prefer: that he beat her black and blue without compunction before an audience, or that he be afraid to face her anger alone? What did she want? She stood looking at the cream-colored planter's hat a second longer, then her hands clenched into futile fists.

She wanted nothing, except perhaps to fling a lighted lantern at the taut canvas walls and send all that was left in there to oblivion in a flash of fire. But that would bring everyone running, and she needed time to get away.

No one who glanced down would think it strange to see her ride out alone by this hour. It was her only recreation when they were in the field together, to take her daily ride on Captain Lightfoot. Sometimes she carried her paint box or sketching material and tried her meager skill at copying some unusual rock formation or cluster of desert flowers.

If she went quietly, and if she spread her riding skirts carefully over the brightly flowered carpetbag, she would be safe. Two hours north of camp were the train tracks. She had no idea when a train was due, but eventually one would come, and she would make it stop for her if she had to stand across the rails.

She snatched up her parasol and crop and went out to mount the clumsy sidesaddle. The horizon was already undulating in heat shimmer under an implacable sun. But she went in defiance of it, straight backed, tight lipped; encased to the throat in a mouse-gray velveteen riding gown and starched linen; gloved and veiled against sun and dust; her head held angrily high above her immaculate stock.

Jay Grobart snapped open the lid of his big silver watch and glanced at its face. It was ten-thirty. The case of the instrument was plain; worn down to the base metal along the curve of its back rim from years of soft friction against its snug pocket and his inquiring hand. There was no sentimental inscription ornamenting its inner lid. He had bought it for himself, long ago.

Now he let it rest open in his palm after that brief look, while the train he was riding creaked and clicked across the flat red desert basin, and the bright, dead land outside the window slipped past unchanging. He let it go, unwatched. He had seen it too often, lately.

There was still time: ten minutes before he snapped the lid shut, giving the signal to Charlie. Without looking at the dark youth across the aisle, he knew the sullen, impassive face with which Charlie would be scorning the world, sitting in the white man's car as a paying passenger, wearing his white man's haircut and his fancy-beaded, old white buckskin Indian shirt.

There was no feeling in Grobart for what lay ahead of him

and Charlie, and of the two other men he'd involved in his plan, but a cold despair. He had felt the same way about unpleasant jobs many times, in the Army years. But he had never allowed his feelings to interfere with a campaign.

This was his own campaign and he hated it, but that made no difference. He had known officers who wavered when it was too late for doubts. Their own troops were usually the first victims of that moment of hesitation, losing either their lives or their will to fight because of it.

He might, at the moment, think himself a fool, his plan a temporary madness, its results no help to his real goal. But there were three people involved in it with him now. He couldn't stop them all, safely, and he wouldn't stop them even if it were possible. They had their goals too.

Facing him at the other end of the car was Coleman Dawes, large and bearlike. When their eyes met, Dawes smiled derisively. He was the only one of the four with any experience at what they were about to do. He showed his contempt for their nerves by assuming an air of elaborate ease; pretending to nap at Wamsutter Station while they waited for the train; talking to his seat companion; grinning at the women.

Grobart didn't allow the smile to prod him as it was meant to; he kept his hand from touching, self-consciously, the beard he'd recently grown; he let his glance slide over Dawes's thick, heavy features with no more expression on his own lean face than the frown of a man wrapped in thought. In fact, he was scarcely thinking at all, except to keep track of the time. It was too late for thought.

He didn't look at his watch again until he judged that the ten minutes were nearly up. When they were, he closed it with a faint sigh and tucked it away, feeling as he did so the butt of the big revolver strapped up high under his coat.

Across the aisle, the young Indian called Charlie began to rub his hand over his face, moaning softly. The conductor standing at the end of the car came forward, passing him by slowly, frowning. He checked the door leading to the platform, and when he turned, the boy was bending forward as if in pain, face slack and wet. He groaned louder. Several passengers turned their heads to look. There was a murmur from one or two when they saw it was an Indian.

"What's the matter with you, boy?" the conductor asked nervously, stopping by him the second time. Charlie said something in Arapaho. "You train-sick or drunk?"

Charlie shook his head. "Leave me alone," he muttered in English. His breath escaped him in the shallow gasps of acute nausea.

Now. It was time. Jay uncrossed his long legs and stood up, laying a polite hand on the conductor's shoulder.

"Maybe you better get him out of here before he messes up your train. I'll give you a hand."

The conductor looked at the boy in doubt.

"Let me alone, damn you!" cried Charlie in anguish, hands smearing at his face again.

The conductor made his decision. "Here, you! Come along. This gentleman's right. If you plan to get sick, you do it out on the platform, not here. And watch your language! There's ladies in here." He seized Charlie's arm and tugged. Charlie resisted weakly, but with Jay Grobart's help he was pulled from his seat and dragged protesting to the door.

As they went through it, Jay unbuttoned his coat and reached inside it to the Army-style covered holster. He opened it and drew out the old, heavy Remington, using Charlie's body as a shield for his movements. The car door banged behind him and the unmuffled clatter of the iron wheels covered the noise of the hammer as he thumbed it back.

The conductor thrust Charlie roughly toward the steps and turned to find himself at eye level with the muzzle of the helpful passenger's gun, held by a frighteningly steady hand.

"The express-car door," said Grobart.

Straining at the bar, his breath coming in short bursts of complaint from his open mouth, Billy Bowan forced the last spike out of its angle iron in the two joint ties until he could grab it with a spike puller and work it out. Then, reversing the crowbar, he drove its straight end down between the close-set ties and levered it back and forth until they moved apart a little. They had been laid rapidly over the petrified earth without a cushioning ballast, or he would never have been able to shift them. But then, digging under the ballast would have been easier.

When he had opened a space under the rail joint he knelt and emptied out the contents of a saddlebag at his feet. With the reamer of his crimping tool he hollowed out the ends of two gray, waxy cylinders like dirty candles, reached carefully into his vest pocket, and tenderly drew out the caps, crimping them around the fuse ends before pressing them into the sticks. He tamped a stick under each prepared joint and spliced their tongues together with an extra length of fuse that trailed out several feet from the track. With a final explosive "Hah!" he rocked back on his boot heels and viewed his work with approval.

"Little Gi'nt!" he commended them, examining the close fit of the twin sticks of dynamite. He rose, gathering his tools on the way, and gave them a toss that sent them skidding out of sight into a straggle of sage. His horse shied at the sound nearby, then returned to nibbling at a tussock of wiry grass.

Billy stood for a minute, one foot on the gleaming rail, looking and listening, but there was nothing, yet. The train was due. He took off his hat and wiped his white-creased, red face with his shirt sleeve, rubbing it up over the fine, tow-colored hair. He fanned the hat, stamped with "Boss of the Plains" on the sweatband, before resettling it on his head. There was no shade in sight and the sun was nearing its zenith.

He walked to the nearest telegraph pole and sat down to wait with his back against it, hanging his arms out over his propped-up knees.

He shifted uncomfortably and fished a pair of wire cutters from his other back pocket where they were cutting into his rump. After that he leaned back and closed his eyes.

He must have been more nearly asleep than he thought, because he wasn't aware of the horse until it was close. He struggled to his feet, one hand nervously near his gun, squinting to make something out of the unfamiliar outline of the rider in the bright sun.

It was a woman, dressed in some kind of city woman's idea of riding clothes. She seemed to be chillingly faceless until she pulled the smoky veil up over her little plug hat. That's what it was: an honest-to-God plug hat, on a woman! She waved at him awkwardly. She was fighting a little parasol in her reins hand.

"Hello! Is this where the train stops?"

"Ma'am?"

"You're waiting for the train, aren't you?" She trotted in, as exotic, to him, as something out of a marvel show.

He was still collecting his wits for some word that would send her off when he heard the train at last. He grinned. It was still miles away, but he had one more job to do. He turned and made a jump for the telegraph pole, shinnying as far as the first spike, then climbing hand over hand quickly, up to the wires.

"What are you doing?" she called, tipping back her head to watch him. "Do you work for the telegraph company?"

He reached up with the cutters and severed the lines. "Yes Ma'am." He laughed. "The wires has gone bad on us. Have to cut 'em off and put up some new ones." Anybody who would ride sideways on a horse would believe anything. He dropped back to the ground and threw away his cutters, grinning at her. "You from around here, Ma'am? I don't recollect a house or ranch for fifteen mile."

"My husband has a camp back there"—she gestured south—"near Diamond Mesa. Isn't it unusual to take down the wires when you don't have any more to put up in their place?"

He snickered in spite of himself. "Yes Ma'am. Well, you see, that train that's coming down the line is going to stop here and throw some more off, along with my crew. We'll start stringin' her then."

Diamond Mesa? He'd heard a rumor that a couple of old slickers were supposed to have salted the place with something.

"What you say your husband's doing over at the mesa?"
"Conducting a mining survey for some Eastern clients."
"They rich men? What they lookin' for?"
"I'm not supposed to say." Then she shrugged, looking away toward the train sound. What difference did it make now? "Precious stones. Rubies; diamonds; things like that." She hoped this cowboy would go away soon and tell everybody he knew about it, so Willard would wake up tomorrow surrounded by greedy faces. She smiled, thinking about it.

"I don't want to seem un-hospitable, Ma'am, but my work crew is a bunch of big, rough-talking men, and not used to seeing a lady like you, specially in an old out-of-the-way lonesome place like this. You'd be doing the right thing if you just rode back the way you come, before they get here. Some of their ordinary talk is enough to peel the skin off your pretty little ears. Pleasure to have met you, Ma'am." He touched his hat with a dirty finger while the other hand fished in his pocket and brought out a match.

"But I want to catch the train."

He knelt by the long fuse, timing the train. It was in sight now, the column of smoke from its high stack flowing like a ragged scarf behind it.

"The train don't stop here! You better get along down to Bitter Creek; catch the stage."

"But you just told me—what are you doing? Oh no! Dear Lord!" She understood, and tried to pull back, but her nervous jerk on the gelding's mouth only made him rear and try to sit down.

Billy touched the match to the sun-fired railhead and lighted the trailing fuse. He ran to his own horse and jumped him. The woman's provoked animal was still backing and snorting under her mishandling.

"Better get him going back the other way, lady, or you're gonna lose your hat!"

She looked around at him wildly, her mouth open to scream. She had lost her stirrup and was slipping from the saddle, hands frozen to the reins.

"Je-SUSS!" he swore, disgusted with her ineptness as much

as her presence. The train was a quarter of a mile away when the charge blew a geyser of rock, dirt, and rail-tie splinters fifty feet in the air. Both of the horses leaped, and the train brakes and the woman began to scream at the same pitch. Billy grabbed at her horse's head, and missed, and she slid to the ground. Then he had other things to do.

The fireman had a carbine in his hands already, as the train screamed to a halt on the safe side of the wrecked track. Billy shot him before he got it aimed, but its blast tore by so close he could hear it fry the air as it passed. The fireman fell out of the cab backward, and the engineer disappeared from view.

"Get out where I can see you!" Billy yelled. The man crawled out slowly. "Get down there on the roadbed on your belly, and stay there! And if you think about movin', well, I hope you been Saved!" He saw the brakeman stick his head out of the caboose, and drew his second gun, leveling it at the man at arm's length. "Hop down and join him, unless you want to see me kill him!" The man obeyed. "Hey, Jay!"

The door of the express car slid open and a guard, the conductor, and the mail clerk were pushed out one by one by a slight figure in dirty white buckskin, who followed them with a gun. "Hey, Charlie!" Billy sang out again cheerfully.

Tall and bearded, Jay Grobart appeared in the door of the car. "When you get through calling the roster, Bigmouth, you can get our horses off the cattle car and throw the bags up here! The boy can watch the crew." Billy flushed at the rebuke, but he obeyed without hesitation, while the Indian saw to it that the remaining crew was spread-eagled beside the engineer.

As Billy passed the passenger car he glimpsed a half-dozen or more scared faces at the windows and waved to them. He knew Coleman Dawes was in there keeping them in their seats. And picking their pockets, probably. "Damn," he said. "Everybody is working in the shade but me."

He lifted the bolt on the slat car door, climbed in, banged his knee, and cursed; wrestled the ramp into position and slid it out. The work cost him considerable sweat, but he had always been proud of the strength in his small body. The horses were packed for a long trip, and there were empty saddlebags, which he gathered and ran down to give to Jay Grobart before leading out the horses.

Everything was going smoother than a dance, he thought. It was a hot day's work, but it beat bustin' horses. After today, he'd never have to suffer another stove-up tail from coming off a saddle ass-over-ears. Excitement bubbled up in him until he had to laugh, even while he fixed the bits and tightened the saddle girths. Charlie looked at him sourly, and Billy laughed again, defiantly.

"What's it take to make an Injun smile, Charlie?" he called.

Jay tossed down a packed saddlebag that caught Billy off guard and nearly knocked him flat. Charlie smiled. He had a long jaw and prominent teeth.

"When are you going to stop yelling out names?" Jay snarled from the car door. For a moment Billy blinked up, surprised, into a pair of savage, steady eyes that had more power to silence him than another man's fists. But Jay switched his gaze to a movement out on the flats. "Where'd that horse come from?"

Billy's head swiveled around in amazement. He had forgotten the stupid woman. "Yah—well. That belongs to some dumb woman who rode up just before you come. She's out there somewhere, I guess. She fell off when the dynamite blew."

"Just rode up? From where?" Jay scanned the empty land for her. "Where is she now?" He threw down another saddlebag.

"Don't know. Horse might have kicked her brains out when she fell. Be a shame, if he did. Pretty little woman. Rich too, from the looks of her. Not smart though."

"Where did she come from, damn it?"

"Back by Diamond Mesa, she said. Her husband's over there doing a look-see for some rich men back east." He snorted. "Them two old goats that salted the place really pulled a slick one. I been all over this part of the country since I was a kid, and I'd bet my share of what we got in here that there's nothing natural in the ground up there but prairie dogs."

Jay finished stuffing the last bag, tossed it down, and eased over the edge of the door himself. He dusted off his clothes with habitual care. "Well, I've got to hand it to you," he said. "I left you out here, fifteen miles from noplace in all directions, with nothing to do to get rich but cut a wire, pull a few spikes, and light a match. And you dug up a witness to the whole thing, with a ready-made posse to hang you for it a couple of miles off."

"Hell's fire! It ain't my fault she showed up when she did," wailed Billy. "Anyway, it's more than just a couple of miles over there. It's more like seven or eight. She said she come out here to catch the train. Maybe she's runnin' off from her old man back there."

"So much the worse. They'll be out looking for her. Maybe they're on the way right now."

"Well, what do you want me to do, go find her and shoot her? She don't know who we are. She never saw any of you, and she didn't see my face too good. I saw to that."

"Congratulations."

"Well, I'm not stupid!" He turned and searched the brush for her, but the gray, dusty-woolen sagebrush and her fancy getup were much the same color, he remembered. Her horse was lurking behind a clump of brush not too far away. He had drifted back cautiously after his fright passed, attracted by others of his kind.

"What do you want me to do?" Billy asked again. He had already placed an estimate on the horse's value to him, minus the ridiculous saddle.

Jay had too. "Get him," Jay said. "We can use all the extra legs we can get. And it'll hold up any search party for a while. They'll have to pack her back to their camp first." He turned his attention to the Indian and his horizontal captives.

"All right. Get them into the boxcar, then tell Daw—tell our nursemaid in there that he can come out."

Billy mounted and trotted off, rope in hand, to get the stray horse as Jay strode toward the engine. Passing the prisoners, he stopped, counting them. "Where's the other one?" he asked.

Charlie shrugged and grinned, making a pistol out of his thumb and forefinger and letting the thumb-hammer fall. Jay scowled.

"He's on the other side," said the conductor in an angry, old man's quaver. "He fell out when your partner gunned him. I think he's dead."

Jay pulled himself up into the cab and looked down at the fireman sprawled on the other side. The man's eyes were closed, but twitching; a heavy vein on his forehead was jumping noticeably. His coat sleeve was bloody over the elbow. Jay sighed a mild obscenity to himself and climbed down to lift the man's thin, dry body without much effort and carry him around to the passenger car. He whistled sharply, and Coleman Dawes's thick-featured, heavy face appeared at the landing. Jay set the man on his feet on the first step and Dawes gathered up his coat at the neck in a ham-sized hand, hauling him the rest of the way up into the car.

Jay ran back to the engine, his long legs easily making the jump to the cab again. When he heard the cattle-car door slam he looked out the window until Charlie stepped back and raised his hand. "Hold the horses!"

He looked into the firebox, fed it another shovel of coal, and slammed the door. He checked the water gauge, then threw the reverse lever and slowly opened the throttle. The engine jerked back from the ruptured track like a horse smelling a mountain lion, butting into its tender and train with a slam. The wheels shrieked and slipped on the hot track. The engine slammed and slammed again, with less resistance behind, as the explosive movement began to smooth into an orderly retreat. Jay tied the throttle open and left the cab, sliding over the side into a stumbling run that brought him up to Charlie and the horses.

Dawes was close behind, puffing, and they mounted together.

Swinging his horse's head around, Jay looked back for Billy and saw a struggle that had escaped his attention until then.

Billy had the fancy animal by the reins, but the woman, struggling up out of the anonymity of the brush, had firm hold of the saddle and was striving to remount. They were going in a circle as Billy tried to shake her loose, but she hung on, miraculously. She had managed to get her foot in the stirrup, but she couldn't pull all the way up to a seat.

"What in hell's that?" asked Dawes.

Jay shook his head slowly, a reluctant smile twitching his mouth. Beyond them, the train was slipping away faster, carrying off a string of tiny, featureless white faces, pressed to the windows of the coach.

"Come on, squaw fighter!" yelled Jay. "We haven't got all day! Bring him along! She'll fall off after a while!"

Billy jerked his mount into line behind them and they headed northwest into the vacant, red wasteland that lay veiled in heat waver and dust on the other side of the track. The woman still clung to the saddle, flung face down over it now, like a dead body. The wind tore at her hat, snatching it away, and her hair covered her face, blinding her. But her hands were endowed with the strength of terror. To fall off now, from this position, might mean certain death, dragged at a gallop by a foot caught in the stirrup.

After a quarter of a mile, Billy slowed to a canter as he looked back, surprised to see her still there. He reined in to let her come alongside.

"Straddle him," he advised, and gripped her arm until she could do so. She felt her skirt ripping somewhere. She was shaking with exhaustion and fell over on the gelding's neck. He waited until her fingers had twined into a fresh grip on the mane, grinning at her in admiration.

"Lady, you're some hell of a mess. But you're gonna make a damn fine wrangler one of these days, you keep at it the way you're goin'. Now, hold on there tight, because we got to catch up with old Jay!"

# 2

In THE TOWN called Point of Rocks the grit-whipped single street stood empty while most of its inhabitants took their midday meal. There was some mining and cattle raising nearby, but the town's main reasons for existence were the railroad, two stage companies, and the Wells, Fargo Express Company office, which worked almost as one together, shipping freight through Wyoming Territory.

The stage drivers had gone to shelter in the hay-sweetened darkness of the stables. The stationmaster dozed at his desk. And in the doorway of his office the Express Company's regional agent lounged, waiting for his clerk to return from lunch. He wore a city man's dark vest and neat boots and allowed himself the luxury of standing in his shirt sleeves, hoping to catch a hint of coolness in the arid breeze that only lodged still more sandy dust in the damp and tender creases of his neck.

They waited for a payroll train under Express protection that would bring a warm wealth to every little mining settlement from Bitter Creek to the stamping mills of Atlantic City and Miner's Delight in the South Pass district.

It was twelve-thirty and the train was past due.

No one was concerned about that yet, except the Express agent, Harvey Lapchance. He was brooding over an unvoiced notion that it might not come at all.

He hadn't mentioned it because he despised premonitions of

that sort. They had sometimes caused him trouble, and he had nothing to support this one except a policeman's memory and an uneasy ulcer.

The damned ulcer. He was nervous and hungry. His stomach was beginning to give him the little hot twinges that buttermilk sometimes soothed but whiskey played such merry hell with.

Ed Hape, the owner of the Little Gem Saloon, kept a stone jar of buttermilk cool in the icehouse, just for him. It amused the other steady customers, but sometimes buttermilk and soda crackers made up the sum of his three daily meals there when the thing gnawed him, as it did now.

He wished the damned money would come, and go to be somebody else's bellyache. He wished he didn't feel so strongly that it was going to be his. He had charged his mind with loose conduct unbecoming to a practical man, and his memory with playing tricks with faces just to pass the time. There wasn't much diversion in a place like this, and he had been accustomed to more absorbing work.

Until five years ago he had been an operative for the Pinkerton Agency: a man hunter; a fact finder. Now, though his gut demanded this less aggravating job, he hadn't cured his own pale eyes of examining what others' eyes only looked at, his mind from tabulating small facts and trying to explain little mysteries.

He could trace his latest discomfort back to its source. Three times in the last three months he had seen a man minding his own business. Simple? The business didn't fit the man. Inadmissible? Suppose you saw George Custer dealing faro in a Denver saloon. He had seen the forgotten hero of Black Horse Creek buying drinks for a saddle tramp and trying to pass for one of his kind.

Perhaps he would never have noticed the man at all if he hadn't met him first, ten years back, in a more professional way. He carried a memento of that earlier meeting on his own skull: a narrow scar and a slight dent near his receding hairline. On that occasion they'd both been involved in business closer to their natures. Former Captain John Wesley Grobart had been killing people, and Harvey Lapchance had hunted and arrested him for it.

That time, the killing hadn't made him a hero; it had made him a prisoner in the Territorial Prison for ten years, and Harvey as well as the rest of the world had forgotten him.

Then, three months ago in Laramie, Harvey had come out of the Express office and nearly collided with a shabbily dressed townsman who was engrossed in watching the loading of an express car in the train station. The man's face had turned only part way toward him as he muttered an apology, which Harvey had echoed as he hurried away to his own business.

It was only later, while courting sleep in a hot hotel room, that the face passed through his mind's file and he thought it familiar. But he couldn't place it, then.

A month later, Grobart had been a passenger on the train passing through Point of Rocks. He was better dressed, and, though the dark mustache was a new addition, Harvey knew him at once and immediately recalled the Laramie encounter. He didn't speak to him. They had once had time to become acquainted, but they had never approached friendship, naturally enough.

His suspicions hadn't begun there, either, because the man was doing nothing suspicious, only traveling, which he had a right to do. But Harvey had remembered, then, that because of him Grobart hadn't been traveling for a long time, unless it was between a work camp and a prison cell. It was one of the few times that doing his duty had left Harvey less than satisfied with his job. Grobart had been on his conscience for a while.

Finally, last week when he had been sipping his evening buttermilk and sucking peppermint—which made Ed Hape wince and beg him to please sit at a back table where he didn't have to watch him do it—Billy Bowan slipped in through the batwing doors with—"Jay" Grobart.

For Billy Bowan to enter any door quietly was enough in itself to attract attention. He was a feisty little bastard from up Horse Thief Creek, according to Ed, who counted the week a profitable one if Billy didn't show up. And he had been missing for the better part of a month now, Harvey recalled.

At no time had Grobart seen Harvey. He stood with Bowan at the bar. They talked sparingly in low tones, bought and swallowed a bare two drinks, and went out as quietly as they had come.

They left town leading a pack horse. Harvey watched them go from the shadowed boardwalk in front of the saloon as they followed the rails past the gray ledges of porous rock that named the town. He was puzzled because there was nothing else in that direction for miles, except the rails.

"What was Bowan being so quiet about, Ed?" he asked when he returned to the bar.

"Nothing much that I could hear. Something about an Indian."

Harvey smiled doubtfully. "Billy whispered about Indians? He must have lost his voice."

"I wish he'd lose his ass and never come in here any more!" Bowan hated Indians with a fervor that approached a mania, and Ed was half Indian himself.

"Where's he been the last few weeks?"

"I think he's gone to prospecting. I heard he quit his job, and last week him and that feller he was just with came in with a wagon loaded with barrels and filled 'em up with water to take out someplace."

"Which way? Out by Bitter Creek?"

"No. Seems to me they headed up north towards Superior or thereabouts. Superior can have him, the little runt."

Harvey shrugged at the discrepancy and said good night. He walked back to his office, which was also his home, if a cot, a slat-backed chair, and a row of clothes pegs on the wall make a place a home. After the forge-bright August day the night air was sweet, so he lay on his cot in nothing but his drawers for a while, enjoying it. The thought of Grobart and Billy as partners teased him until he grew impatient.

He granted Grobart the right to watch and ride trains, pick up with trash, haul water, hunt gold, lead pack horses off into empty wastes—anything. He was a free man now and none of

Harvey's business. He ordered himself to stop prying for reasons in all these actions that did not concern him and concentrate instead on the pleasant thought that he would soon be getting his leave and could spend it in some civilized place like St. Louis or even Chicago. It would be good to see old friends there again.

He was half-asleep when his mind commented, almost like a voice in his ear, "There's nothing else in that direction for miles, except the rails."

"All right," he said aloud. "If there's nothing out there, they can't be up to anything with it, can they? Nothing but alkali flats and railroad ties. What can they steal?"

Then he knew what they could steal.

His clerk returned from lunch and went into the office. A minute later he called out, "Mr. Lapchance, did you know the telegraph was dead?"

Harvey looked at him blankly, then he suddenly swore. "Damn! I knew it. My gut knew it all the time! . . . Come on, boy. Help me get a handcar up on the tracks. Don't stand there with your mouth open like a flytrap!"

They arrived at the scene of the robbery, still ahead of any work crew out of Wamsutter. The dangling wires and ruptured track were being examined by a swarm of civilians who looked like mining types.

Their apparent leader, a big handsome man with a soft face and an aggressive manner, hailed him angrily, waving what looked like a parasol.

"Did you see them?" he yelled. "Did you let them get away?"

Harvey eyed the object in the man's big fist. It was a parasol. He decided to ignore it. "My name is Lapchance, sir," he began, still a little breathless. "I'm the agent in Point of Rocks for the—"

"Crocker. Willard Crocker. Consulting mining engineer. I represent the Great Western Expansion Mining and Development Company. See here, Laschance, there's more here than meets the eye. My wife has been kidnapped! Or else there was some kind of explosion here and she was injured." He outlined his loss, and his importance, in short assertive bursts of nasal Yankee speech, breathing harshly. Harvey listened and examined the evidence of the parasol and the woman's riding crop found on the ground, but reserved most of his attention for the condition of the track and the faint puff of smoke in the distance that told him the train was coming back.

"Well sir," he mused, thoughtfully touching the splintered ties with the toe of his thin, polished boot, "you may be right. It looks to me like she might have seen something here that she wasn't meant to see. Somebody went to a lot of trouble to stop the train here, but it wasn't to kidnap a woman."

Crocker stared at him. "What do you mean? To rob it?"

Harvey's mouth twitched. "Seems like it. And she was here on the spot when they did. That doesn't mean they kidnapped her, necessarily. They might have been interested in her horse, though. They could have taken that and put her on the train." He glanced at the man's baby face. "What was Mrs. Crocker doing up here, so far from your camp? It's a pretty long ride for a pleasure jaunt in this weather."

Crocker drew in his breath. "She was—a little upset, when she left this morning." Belatedly, he tried an indulgent smile. It failed. "We had a small misunderstanding that—well, she was a bit put out with me, I'm afraid. She may not have realized how far she was riding until she got here." Harvey noted all the details of tone and expression that he had been trained to observe in a witness. He concluded that they must have had a major battle. There was as much anger as there was worry for his wife showing in Crocker's face.

Very likely the woman had stormed up here to flag down the train to Rock Springs to take her revenge in a shopping spree. Crocker might think ransom could be cheaper.

The train came, pouring out a voluble crew who confirmed the obvious. They had backed up the line until the engine lost steam enough to move them. When they stopped at the foot of a long grade, the passengers stirred at last to unlock the crew from their prison. Then the train had to be fired up again and returned to Wamsutter to let off the customers, patch up the fireman, pick up a repair crew, and notify all the authorities of town and rail alike.

The work crew set in at once removing track and splicing the lines while Harvey interviewed the conductor and his men. Crocker hampered him with constant interruptions. Although it was determined that his wife had neither boarded nor been put aboard the train, the big man persisted in his own interrogation of each man. But only the engineer thought he had seen her at all, and he wasn't sure.

"The lady to one side for a moment—no offense, Mr.—uh—Crocker—which way did the gang go after they robbed the train?" No one knew. They had been battering at the car door, or trying to stretch their arms out long enough to reach the door bolt through the slats.

The engineer and conductor excused themselves with an enumeration of all their special concerns at the crucial moment. The guard and clerk, both young men and both new on the run, were numbed by the extent of the loss and their own poor showing in the affair.

"How much did they get, anyway?" Harvey asked.

"We was carrying a hundred thousand, not counting bonds and the like. But they didn't care nothing about those."

One of Crocker's men whistled in admiration. Harvey stopped the contemplative pulling of his nose and let his long fingers trail down his vest front to the pit of his stomach, where they rested, pressing in a little.

"How—uh—did they get in?" he asked in a voice of soft melancholy.

"Well sir," said the conductor briskly, "three of them got on at Wamsutter, but they wasn't together. Pretty soon after we passed Tipton this Injun boy that was one of them started looking sick, moaning and holding his belly. The big man, the one who gave the orders later, was sitting across the aisle from the Injun. He acted very friendly to me when I came along to see about it. He called my attention to the kid possibly making a mess and offending the ladies. He helped hold the Injun up so he could walk, which he couldn't hardly seem to do, and then, when we got out between the cars—" His spread hands finished the story.

Harvey nodded. Then he appraised the express-car crew, the guard and the clerk.

"How did they get into the safe?"

"I opened it for them," the guard said reluctantly.

Harvey sucked a tooth. "Just opened it up. Well, that made it all pretty easy for them, didn't it? Could they have opened it, do you think, if you hadn't obliged them?"

"I don't know." The guard flushed darkly. "I don't see why not, if they'd pushed it off the train. But they'd sure as hell have opened us up first. He said so, and I believed him. Mister, have you ever had one of those big old .44 Remingtons put right up in your face, on full cock? It looks like a goddamn cannon! And the party behind it wasn't nervous at all. He didn't even blink, when he told me what he'd do. Then, there was that grinning Indian. I've been with the Company for three years, but this is my first run through real Indian country, and I've been reading the newspapers." He stopped.

"What did he look like?" asked Harvey.

The man snorted. "Why, he looked like a damned Indian! I don't know what tribe!" He looked at the others, outraged.

"No, I mean the other one. With the cannon."

"He was big: maybe two, three inches over six feet. He wasn't young. What I could see of his hair was mostly gray. But he had a mustache and whiskers that was mostly black. He could've been forty-five or fifty, but the way that old boy moved around, he was in good shape." He consulted the others with his eyes.

"He wore a dark blue shirt, a black jacket and pants, black hat—one of those flat-crowned, old ones. He'd have passed for a cattleman or a mine boss. Just ordinary looking," said the engineer.

"Not in the face, he wasn't," said the clerk. "I thought for a minute he might be an Indian too."

Harvey looked at him with interest. "What made you think that?"

"Well, he was pretty dark and his cheekbones stuck up high like theirs. And his eyes, like he told you: they could look a hole through a steel door. But he had this beard, though, and I know Indians don't have much beard. It wasn't long, but it was pretty heavy. Like he'd just started it maybe, a couple of weeks ago." He stopped, surprised. Harvey Lapchance was smiling at him like a pleased baby.

"What about the third man?" Harvey asked eagerly. "Was he a talky little runt with a red face and straw-colored hair?"

"No," said the conductor. "From what the passengers said, he was a big, heavy-set man, about thirty-five or forty. He didn't say anything until I was out of the car. If they hadn't described him, I wouldn't have believed he was one of them. He was real friendly and relaxed looking. He took a gold watch off the man in the seat with him, but nothing else. He just stood in the back of the car and kept them from getting up."

"But that kid out by the line—the one that shot Jim—he was like what you said," the engineer put in. "He was talky. The other one didn't like it when he started calling out—hey, I forgot that! The kid yelled out, 'Hey, Charlie!' then, 'Hey—' what was it? Oh, 'Hey, Jay' it was. And then this big fella comes to the door and bawls him out, but real quiet, about calling the roster."

"That's good." Harvey beamed. "That's just what I wanted to hear." He slapped his own clerk on the shoulder.

"Son, you get your apparatus and shin up that pole just as soon as they splice the line. Send a message to Green River, and tell the sheriff, or whoever's there, that the Union Pacific train was held up and robbed of one hundred thousand dollars this morning by John Wesley Grobart and William Bowan, of this county—" they stared at him "—with the aid of an Indian and an unidentified white man, one of which is named Charlie 'something.' We don't know which way they went, as yet, but Bowan is from Horse Thief Creek near Thayer Junction, and they may have gone there. We might have to call on the troops stationed over at Fort Steele, if we have to search the desert. You may as well send the same message back to the people at Rawlins too, and—"

"What about my wife?"

Harvey turned, surprised, to Crocker. In a matter of minutes, he'd forgotten about the woman.

"Thank you, Mr. Crocker. Son, tell the sheriff that the thieves may have kidnapped a witness too. What's her description, Mr. Crocker?" Crocker gave it to him at some length. "Medium height, slender, reddish-brown hair and eyes, thirty-five years old," Harvey summarized for the messenger.

"Well, Mr. Crocker," he said, turning almost gaily, "I suppose you'll want to get started back to your camp to prepare for the search. You'll need extra clothes, and a bedroll, and plenty of water and food. We may be out for a couple of days —but, I beg your pardon, sir. Do you want to join my party or head up your own? Clerk! Tell that sheriff in Green River that if he wants to deputize me by wire, I'll save him a long trip over here!" He turned back to Crocker to see the big man looking taken aback.

"Laschance, I'm a very busy man; but more than that, my time out here is not my own. I had hoped the proper—uh—authorities would be competent to do the—job." He faltered, sensing the hostility this created in some of his hearers, as well as some open amusement in his own crew. Harvey looked at him patiently, a little smile still on his mouth. He was thinking about Jay and Billy, surrounded before they could get the wraps off the money, but Crocker misinterpreted the look. He flushed and bristled.

"I can assure you, sir, that my hesitation was not due to any fear of the miserable scum who've done this thing, but only to a sense of my obligations to my clients, who are paying these men a good wage for their work here, not for chasing road agents all over the desert." He stared at his crew as if they had already been found derelict in their presence there. "I served in the late war, sir. I am an excellent shot. But I am not well acquainted with the local geography. I simply wouldn't know where to look first. I must place myself and my men at your disposal." His head jerked a token bow, which Harvey returned. "Where do you suggest we meet, and where shall we begin to look for them?"

"Well now, that's a good question, Mr. Crocker." Harvey turned slowly, scanning the barren land on all sides. "You know, the man who planned this has picked a very interesting place. It's a good place—for a crime—because it's so far from help. Not even a ranch or a little mine close by. They didn't know about your camp, of course; but even that's a couple of hours away. It's going to take time for any search parties to get assembled, and meanwhile they can get clean away in any direction unobserved by anybody. Except your wife.

"But: on the other hand, it's a rough place to set out from, just because there's no place to stop, for miles. No water for them, and none for the horses, which is more important. They either have to get out a day or two ahead of us without killing the horses, or they have to go to ground someplace nearby, split their money, and wait until they can slip away separately." He was into his lecture voice by now. Not that he usually had anybody to lecture, but this was the way he reasoned things through aloud to himself when he was alone.

"If it was just Billy Bowan," he said, beginning to pace slowly past Crocker, "he'd most likely hide the money someplace close by, and go home. Then he'd be back out here in one or two days to get it, because he's a very impatient man, and he'd start to blow it right away. He'd be weighing down a rope by next Saturday." He swung around abruptly, nearly running into Crocker, who was following him. "But Billy isn't running this. He didn't plan it, or add anything to it but maybe a little muscle. Jay Grobart planned it."

"You seem to know all about this Grobart. What kind of a cutthroat is he?"

"Not a cutthroat at all. Not, so far as I know, a bandit or road agent either, until now. But he was in charge or he wouldn't have been here." He shook his head at some internal puzzle. "He was a career Army man until after the war; an officer who'd come up from the ranks. If you were in the Army you know what that took. I doubt if he made many friends along the way. I don't know if he had any Indian blood in him, like the boy thought, but he lived with a young squaw while he was up at Fort Laramie. There was some kind of trouble about her there, and he quit the Army and went to work for the railroad, bossing a road gang at first, then acting as a sort of go-between in the run-ins the U.P. was having constantly with his red in-laws." He stopped, shrugged.

"Well, that's beside the point. The thing is, Grobart is smarter than the usual run of thief out here. He knows how to plan ahead a bit. He knows how to lay out a line of supply—when necessary." He stood quite still, thinking about the water barrels Ed had mentioned. There was a shifting veil of dust in the distance, like a dancing woman.

"Of course, the Colorado border is close, if he wanted to trade off the money quick in the mining camps," he murmured, watching it. "But your camp is due south, and if he planned this right, he'd have known about you and picked another spot, maybe." He sighed.

"Well, it's no use guessing. We'll just have to wait and see what we can pick up." He came to himself, briskly. "Mr. Crocker, if you'll spread your men out on both sides of the line and let them start looking for track, I'll just have a word with the conductor about catching a ride back home. It's a mite faster than pumping a handcar. Then, we can talk about when and where to meet." Crocker's men started to move away obediently.

"Mr. Lastchance!" bellowed Willard. Harvey stopped, already several quick strides away. Crocker paused, since his own crew was looking back at him, and waited until they were out of hearing. Then he came forward, pale eyes accusing. "Now, see here, Mr.—"

"Lap–chance."

"Lapchance. Much as I deplore robbery, the loss of your money is of small concern to me. You seem to know the people who did this, although you've never bothered to say how you did. Very well. But, if you do, I want to know right now whether you have any reason to believe my wife is still alive. Are you holding back something from me, sir, just to get the use of my men to swell your posse? Are these men murderers?"

"Mr. Crocker, until this morning, I couldn't have said they were thieves. Well, that's not quite accurate. Billy—"

"Never mind the 'ifs, ands, and buts.' Have they killed Catherine, or worse?"

"I don't think they have, sir. But, what's worse?"

Crocker flushed. "Have they taken her with them to—to abuse her, in any way?" he finished lamely.

"You mean, to rape her? Why, I don't know. I'm not in their confidence, I just entertained a wholly unfounded but, as it turned out, fortunate suspicion about what they were up to. They might. She isn't of any conceivable use to them otherwise. I beg your pardon. But I just don't think they set out to find a woman to 'abuse.' I find myself wondering why they'd want to take her. Jay Grobart could have changed his views on rape, but—"

"Now what does that mean?" snapped Crocker irritably.

"Well, about ten years ago he killed three men in Laramie for raping the squaw he called his wife. Somehow, the jury was heavy with friends of the victims, and they took the position that he was an Indian lover and guilty of manslaughter. They put him in prison for avenging his wife. That's a pretty hard setback for any man's ideals, I'd think. How do you feel about it, Mr. Crocker? Would it make any difference to you? I mean, if your wife should turn out to be alive and safe, otherwise?"

# 3

CATHERINE CROCKER had ample time to regret her moment of recklessness before they came to a halt beside the ruined tumulus of a rust-colored butte that time had reduced to rubble. Its meager shade made only a slight difference in the temperature, but merely to be out of the sun seemed as delicious as a drink from a cool spring. Or nearly so. Her mouth was parched, her skin was abraded with wind-whipped grit. She slid from the saddle and tried to stand, but her legs were boneless. She slumped heavily to the ground as her Captain Lightfoot was led away from her. Now they'll take him, and leave me here, she thought. But she couldn't make herself move, except to stretch out flat on the hard, hot earth and ease her back. She closed her eyes against the glare of the sky and tried to shade her face, throwing one strengthless arm across it.

Around her there was speech and movement without much meaning. She heard the one called Billy say, "By God, Jay, I cussed you when we was hauling these out here, but I'm sure glad to see one of 'em now." Someone answered. Someone laughed. Something about the hall (haul?) and cooling the horses first; talk of a black boot (beaut? butte?) that she didn't care about. She only lay paralyzed by thirst and exhaustion, until she heard herself mentioned.

"Damn fool woman!" was the spoken verdict. Silently, she agreed. There was a crunch of boots approaching on the sand. She kept her eyes closed. The man-smell of sweaty clothes, neat's-foot oil, and leather assailed her nostrils as one of them knelt beside her and slipped a hand under her neck, raising her head a little for the canteen he touched to her lips.

She clutched at the canteen, but he took it away after two swallows. "Don't be greedy," he said. He poured out some of the water onto a grimy blue handkerchief and mopped her face with it, smearing the dirt but bringing a sweet momentary relief to her tortured skin. "Lordy, if you ain't a mess," he whispered, making a last sweep down her breast with it.

She struggled to sit up and opened her eyes to glare at him. It was the towheaded dynamiter called Billy, grinning his infuriating, good-natured grin. He gave her the canteen and let her drink her fill. "But don't blame me if it comes back up again," he warned. When she finished, gasping, he pulled her to her feet and led her over to the others.

She glanced furtively at them—the heavy-armed bear of a man who guffawed at the sight of her, the solemn copper-faced youth who stared without expression—and her back stiffened. She realized that her hair was a snarled mass covering half her face, and that her clothes were filthy and torn. Part of her mind began to recognize her helplessness among such men, and the provocation she offered just by her presence. She was not ready to face that problem yet, and her mind, fumbling for craft, told her to keep silent and let her hair hang.

"Looky what I got me, Dawes," crowed Billy. "Ain't she a beaut?"

"I seen Blackfoot medicine men prettier than that," the bear man growled. But his little eyes ran over her body approvingly. She let herself slump a bit more.

"How old is she, Billy? Have you looked at her teeth?" asked the young Indian softly. "I'll give you a bolt of calico and a trading post skinning knife for her, just as she stands."

"This here's a white woman, Injun. Not one of your damned squaws—" Billy snapped at him.

"Now, wait a minute," said the bear man. "I get a bid in here somewheres before you two start up again."

"The hell you do," Billy scoffed. "Either one of you. This

here's a rich lady. She good as told me so herself. She's worth more than either one of you has ever seen 'til today." He joggled her arm encouragingly. "Ain't that so, Ma'am? You tell 'em. Spit in their eye!" He laughed as he threw his arm around her shoulders and shook her up to him in a comradely hug. "And what's more, she's the finest little wrangler in the Territory, next to me. When we get our split and break up, her and me's going down south and jayhawk ponies off the 'Paches. She can stick on 'em any way you can name—sidesaddle, cross saddle, backwards—shoot! Hey, Jay! What you think about my new partner?" He called to the fourth man, who was watering the horses from a large barrel standing against the rocks. She supposed it must be the thing Billy had cussed to haul and rejoiced to see.

The man called Jay turned, in his own good time, and walked toward them. She sensed that his look of indifference was assumed, and not being easily maintained. He was furious about her presence. He struck some kind of mad, sympathetic chord in her with his grim, stiff-legged approach, so that she was tempted to shout out her like-mindedness on the topic. But she didn't. As he inspected her, she could only look at him nervously through her fallen hair.

He was taller than Billy by a head, and old enough to be his father, but it was obvious he was not. They couldn't have been more unlike. Billy was scarcely taller than herself; straw headed, red, and ignorant; already round shouldered with the saddle slouch of the cowboy.

The man studying her with such ill-disguised disgust was brown, lean, and straight. Even before he stopped in front of her and fell naturally into an "at ease" stance, she could see "Army" written on him. She had seen enough soldiers as a girl in her home town to know. She had few illusions about their gallantry. Nor did his eyes encourage her to hope for it. They were long, brandy colored like his face, and decidedly cold. They took in every detail about her, from the dust-caked, expensive clothes and white hands, to the emerald-studded stock pin and the little emerald earrings just visible through her russet hair.

"Looks like a piece of lace-curtain Irish," he said harshly. "Let's see her face." She tried to pull away, but Billy, still holding her tight with one hand, skinned back her hair with the other.

The other two men came up to see as well, but she was blind to their approach, standing in Billy's grip, and frozen like a snake-charmed bird by Jay Grobart's long, silent interrogation.

"Whooo-ee! Ain't she pretty?" Billy sang out.

"She ain't no girl, but I'm not the boy I used to be, either," said the bear man, Coleman Dawes, grinning at her over Jay's shoulder.

"White women always look like they've been living under rocks," sneered the young Indian.

"What's your name?" Jay asked finally, breaking the silence between them.

"Catherine Crocker. Mrs. Willard Crocker." Her voice seemed faint in her own ears. Don't sound frightened, she warned herself. That's the worst thing you can do.

"Where's your husband, Mrs. Crocker?"

"Back at Diamond Mesa, this morning. Looking for me by now, I imagine."

"How many men are there with him?"

"Twenty-five or thirty," she lied, "and they are all armed, and have horses. They'll be after you. And they know all about this country. They'll find you." With use, her voice was regaining its old assurance.

"Do you?"

"Do I what?"

"Know the country? Do you know where you are now?" She hesitated, not knowing which answer would be to her advantage. He saw the truth in her silence.

"How long were you out from camp this morning? Did they expect you back by noon, or not until later?" She remained silent. "Look in her bag, Charlie."

Charlie did, and brought out the sandwich and the flowered carpetbag with her clothes and money. He opened it and brought out her tucked, ribbon-trimmed bedgown, flourishing it around himself with delight.

Jay smiled faintly. "Looks like you were planning to make more than just a day of it. Going on a visit?"

"No! I was running away! That's the truth! And I didn't tell anyone. So they *will* be looking for me, as I said. Why don't you let me go? Just let me go, and I'll go back the way I came, and tell them I got lost." It was the wrong answer, the stupid answer, and she realized it at once. But would it have been better to let them think no one would be missing her? There was no right answer.

"Ready to kiss and make up, now?" Billy mocked her drooping head. "Ready to tell the old man you been a bad girl, but you'll know who's boss, from now on?"

That was so close to what she would be expected to admit that she was seized with rage against him, as if he had been Willard. "What I say or do is none of your business, you smelly cowpuncher! I just don't want to be here, more than I don't want to be there!"

Something close to warmth invaded Grobart's eyes, but was gone again before she could appeal to it.

"Please, Mr.—I don't know your name. I don't want to, either. I won't tell them which way you've gone. I give you my word. You look like a—a gentleman. Please, won't you take it and let me go?"

But to her chagrin he had lost interest in her, and was scanning the horizon to the south. "Dawes, roll that water barrel over behind those rocks, out of sight. Bring that canvas cover along, though. Mrs. Crocker will be wanting a bed when the sun goes down."

"She can have half of mine," said Billy, his arm still around her. Catherine moved suddenly, taking him by surprise with a swift, hard elbow in the pit of his stomach. Then she was running blindly across the dead land, skirts gathered up in her fists, wild hair flying. Behind her, she heard an explosion of laughter, some of it Billy's. Then the clatter of boots.

She was surprisingly long legged for her height, and fear

made her fleet, but Billy caught her within a hundred yards and brought her painfully to the ground with a high tackle that pinned her arms. She twisted, arched, and kicked, trying to throw him off. He was not heavy enough to subdue her by weight alone, and she freed one hand long enough to claw at his face.

He caught it deftly, crossed her wrists, and whipped his silk neckerchief around them, as he would have tied a calf. She arched up again and again, or tried to slew sideways, but always he slammed her back to earth. His face was scarlet and wet with the struggle and a prominent vein in the center of his forehead bulged and throbbed. But his pale-lashed eyes crinkled in laughter at her furious face when he had her tied fast.

"Whoo-ee! If you ain't a tearer! Here I am tryin' to treat you like a little red heifer—looky there—a silk piggin' string and all—and you go swappin' ends and sunfishin' like an old outlaw horse. Whoa!" As the fight drained out of her, he held her arms to the ground above her head with one hand while wetting a filthy finger in his mouth.

"Now I got you tied, I might as well brand you." In the dust that caked her forehead he drew two spittle-engraved symbols, an arch above a letter. "Bow N. There. Now, you're in the Book!" Then, still holding her down, he kissed her moistly, trying to force her lips apart.

"That's enough," said Jay, above them. "Put her on her horse. We've got a lot of ground to cover before dark."

"I was just getting started!"

"Well, you'll have to start up again when we're out of this frying pan, if you still feel like it after another six or eight hours in the saddle." He looked down at them as they sprawled in the dirt, and his disgust was evidently divided between them. "Or I could leave you here with her and her horse. You'd have a couple of good mounts, but you'd have to forget about the money. Maybe you were never cut out to be anything but a horse thief, anyway."

Billy jumped to his feet, his burned face even redder. "Part of that money's mine! I worked for it, harder than some others."

"I agree. Now mount up."

When Catherine was on her horse again, Jay rode in close and reached for her reins.

"It slows us down to have to pull you along like a dead weight." He handed the reins over to her. "You ride him pretty well. You must be from one of those fox-hunting rich-Rebel families back east?"

She didn't answer, though if anyone else had asked her that question she might have laughed. Her lip was beginning to swell, and a hot murderous rage against the lot of them, and him in particular, almost choked her. If she had had her crop she would have been delighted to play the rich-Rebel belle and slash it across his cold face, whatever it cost her.

He seemed almost able to read her thought and leaned closer, staring her down with a flat look in those eyes that reminded her suddenly of a mountain cat she had once seen captured. "Whatever you have in mind, forget it. If you try to get away, I'll have to kill you, just the same as if you were a man. I don't want you along, any more than you want to be along. If we get to a place where it's possible, maybe, just maybe, I can let you go. Meanwhile, remember that I can let Billy and the rest have you, or I can keep them away. You can behave yourself and live, or not, just as you choose." He slapped her horse on the rump to get it moving. "Stay out in front, where I can see you."

She obeyed.

Mostly, he was furious with himself. Ordering Bowan to get the horse had been a piece of unprofessional spite, to punish him for his loud mouth. He'd yielded to a momentary desire to see the little man in a lather, chasing a skittish horse around in circles for a while.

Even after he saw the woman hanging on, he'd compounded his stupidity and his error by calling out to Billy to bring her along. Well, now he had her along, and what was he going to do about her? Discipline (he still thought of that) would go to hell very quickly, as soon as they stopped for the night, unless he was prepared.

Then what could he do, hold a gun on the randy little runt all the time? Kill the woman? Leave her, which would amount to the same thing? He did not like to admit to himself—did not admit—that he couldn't do this, because it might be the same as admitting he could no longer take a necessary action, however unpleasant, when faced with it. When you admitted that, it was time to hang up the sword and take to earth mucking. But then, he had already done that a long time ago, hadn't he?

In his own eyes he had been acting the fool. How did he look to Charlie's eyes? If the boy should begin to think the same, he might leave before they reached their destination. He knew Charlie's tolerance for him was thin enough to begin with. What was it made of? Gratitude to a dead old man; a desire to show Jay up; a twisted sense of either humor or honor: Jay hardly understood Charlie's motives. Maybe Charlie understood them no better. Well, he mustn't do anything to make the boy examine them too closely.

He intended to keep the group together until he was certain they weren't being followed. The capture of one of these saddle tramps meant nothing to him, unless it jeopardized his own freedom. But with the woman along, trouble was sure to come. The bids made on her at the water stop weren't a joke; and neither was Billy's claim that she was his property. They would be at each other's throats over her.

Yet unless he could reason himself into killing her she must stay with them. If he dropped her at Dub's ranch tomorrow, he might as well stay there himself and save the lynch party a longer ride. South Pass looked like the first possible place to turn her loose where she wouldn't die before she found help, but where she couldn't put the hounds on him at the first scream. Beyond South Pass he could lose himself in the wooded wilderness that led to Washakie's land. But South Pass was a long way off.

The intensity of his anger with her when he had picked her off the ground and put her back on her horse gave its own warning.

Anger was an indulgence he could not afford. He needed

all his wits to accomplish what he had to do. And it was certain that, except for Charlie, his friends in this enterprise were directed more by their balls than their brains.

He wouldn't let his response to the woman happen again. The poor white-faced fool was probably too frightened to open her mouth again after his warning, and he'd keep the others in their saddles so long they'd be too paralyzed to piss when they climbed out of them at night. That's all he had to do. But he could do the rest, if he had to. What he had done this morning was only the beginning of the unpleasant things he must do to achieve his goal. Sometime, between here and Wind River, he had to learn how to be humble.

If he could learn that, he could kill a woman if it became necessary. But it wouldn't be, he told himself, watching her stiff back ahead of him. He was aware of his danger, and she was aware of hers.

IT WAS DARK and there was water. That was all that mattered to Catherine.

They seemed to have come a thousand miles since noon, yet the land was the same. She was paralyzed with fatigue—numb. She couldn't feel her own feet any more. And she was dead to emotion. All morning she had been furious—with Willard, with these barbarians, and most of all with herself for her incredible stupidity in getting in their way.

But while her skin burned, fear came and sucked anger cold until there was nothing inside her that wasn't cold and sick, with a hollow feeling worse than hunger. She had never pictured her own death until she saw it in those leopard eyes. Only fear kept her from crying, until she was too tired to cry. Now all she had left for feelings were thirst and a need for sleep.

The sun had begun to do its work on her by the time they reached the second water cache late in the afternoon. Her hat was gone, her parasol too. Even without that milk-white skin approved by fashion, which she could hardly have, being dragged through camp after camp behind Willard, she was sure to blister and peel after this day in hell.

She could have wept then, thinking of the lotions, the buttermilk washes, and the creams it would take to heal her complexion when she got home. If she got home. Or anywhere, alive.

The man called Jay—the one she hated and feared, when she could still do so, even more than she hated the foul-smelling Billy—had squatted down in front of her at the second stop and examined her face. Then he drew out a heavy-bladed knife from his belt and began chopping at the petrified earth at her feet.

It was impossible to drive the blade into the ground more than an inch or two, but he broke up several lumps and hashed them into smaller and smaller pieces, while she sat watching the moving knife with dumb apprehension.

"Hold out your hands," he ordered, scooping up the broken clay. "Cup them together."

"What for?"

"Do as I tell you. I'm giving you an old Mexican beauty secret. Keep your fingers together." He poured the clay into her hands and uncapped his canteen, spilling an ounce or two of water into her palms. She made an instinctive shudder of disgust. "Rub it together. Make mud. Here. It needs more water."

"What's it for?" she asked again, disdainfully, though she had an inkling.

"It's to put on your face, to keep you from frying. Smear it on. It may not be the right kind of clay, but it will protect you some, and take a little fire out of the burn you've already got."

"It's gritty, not to mention disgusting. It's what pigs do."

"Ever seen a sunburned pig? But suit yourself." He rose and left her. It was a struggle against a lifetime of cleanliness, as well as an inclination to oppose him in anything that wouldn't get her killed. But her hot face contrasted too painfully with her cool palms, and at last she smeared the clay on gingerly, squeezing her eyes and mouth tight shut against it. It felt deliciously cool at first, then it began to dry and pull at her skin until she thought her cheeks would crack.

Billy and the rest guffawed when she was finished. Even Jay looked almost amused. For a moment injured vanity throttled fear in her and her eyes started to fill with angry tears. But she caught them in time. She would not, she must not let them see her cry. Any show of weakness was an invitation to attack.

She sat turned away from them with unblinking eyes, until the tears evaporated in the dry air.

That had been endless hours ago. Her mud pack had crumbled away since, along with her power to feel and think. She realized they had stopped; were evidently making camp. Yet she still sat on Captain Lightfoot until someone came and pulled her off him.

"All right, little mud hen, it's time to make yourself useful." Hard hands held her arms when her legs nearly buckled under her. She looked up. It was Jay. "Do you know how to make coffee?" he asked.

She pulled herself away from him carefully, hoping her legs would hold her. "I don't want any coffee, thank you. I just want to sleep."

"Sleep isn't what you're apt to get. You better try to make yourself ugly and useful." He shoved her toward the small fire the young Indian was already tending. "Charlie, put her to work."

Charlie flicked her a scornful look, mixed with something she didn't care to examine. "Can she do anything?"

She stood stupidly staring at the fire.

"Just give her the stuff, and give Billy a hand with the horses."

She found herself on her knees before the fire with a canvas bag, spilling out bags and canisters of supplies she didn't know what to do with. There was a coffeepot. She filled it with water from a canteen. There was a canister of coffee, with a tin spoon inside. She shoveled it into the water, uncertain how much to use. She had never made coffee in her life, only tea. Coffee had been Rosie's affair. She thought about Rosie; beautiful, black Rosie, and her beautiful, black morning coffee. The sound that escaped her was disgracefully close to a snivel. She stopped it at once.

She was puzzling over what there was to cook in the skillet when Dawes dropped down heavily beside her.

"That pot won't boil, less you put it on the fire, Sis." He moved the coffeepot to a flat rock. "What you got there, a looking glass?" He nodded to the empty skillet in her hand. "Put some bacon in it, woman!" She examined the vile-looking lump he produced from a bag. She would never have associated it with the sweet, moist, melting strips of creamy fat and scarlet lean that she called bacon. She dropped it in the skillet and left it teetering on the hot rock by the coffee.

He snatched it away at once. "God A'mighty! You really are a case of no brains. Dumber than old Joe Clark! I see you never cooked before, but sure to God you must have et bacon! Don't you know you have to cut it up first?" He turned it on end and cut it in thick pieces with a knife he didn't bother to wipe, before or after. Then he fished a fork out of the bag and set about frying the meat, moving it about with delicate little prods of the fork as it sizzled and shrank. It smelled strong, even rancid, but her stomach cramped hungrily at the smell. She poked in the bag, hoping to find something more acceptable.

"You know how to make biscuits?" Dawes asked. She shook her head. "Corn dodgers? Johnnycake? Tortillas? You don't know much, do you, Sis? What you give me, to teach you how to cook?" He mocked her, leaning forward to speak in a heavy conspiratorial whisper.

But she looked at him with sudden hope. "I could give you something to let me escape. Would you? Would you? I wouldn't make any trouble. Just help me, and I'll pay you," she whispered urgently.

"You really a rich woman? You might be." He grinned. "Fancy clothes; white skin; can't boil water. How much money you got, Sis?"

She didn't look at him. Her shaking hands were taking the earrings out of her lobes, the little pin from her dirty stock. "I have these. They're real emeralds. And I have some money in my bag." She held them out, cupped in her hand.

He scooped up the tiny pendants, pinched between finger and thumb, both black. "They sure ain't very big."

"They don't have to be. Emeralds are like diamonds. Even more valuable, sometimes. Will you help me? Just let me get to my horse afterwhile. Just distract their attention. And—and when I ride out, you could be the one who tries to catch me, but you don't." She waited, eyes fastened on him.

He took the earrings and the little pin and put them in his shirt pocket. "What about the money?"

"I'll get it. No. You can get it. It's in my bag."

He let his eyes linger on her, taking in her draggled hair and dress, pausing at her stubborn mouth, and again at her meager breasts. "Tell you what you do, Sis." He forked the bacon absently. "You get out the flour and the sody, and put about four big handfuls of flour and a couple or three big pinches of sody in that bowl there, and we'll make us some biscuits." He winked at her as Jay, Billy, and Charlie returned out of the darkness.

"You trying to steal my girl, Dawes?" Billy asked with a laugh that sounded forced. Jay looked at Dawes carefully, and at her without expression, as he sat down. Billy slumped beside him.

They were all tired, she realized with a sudden renewal of hope. Maybe she could get away. If this greedy animal beside her offered to give chase, would the others be anxious to beat him to it? She bent over the bowl and flour sack, following Dawes's directions as best she could.

When they were baked, or rather fried, in the bacon-greased pan, the biscuits looked like so many lumps of conglomerate rock, but nobody complained. She even felt a touch of reluctant pride in them, because they were edible, and they were her first.

They were nothing like Rosie's butter-brown, cloud-centered perfections, but they were edible. And she hadn't realized, until she found herself wolfing down one of them, wrapped around a strip of the thick, strong bacon, just how hungry she was. She had had no lunch, and her breakfast, she remembered, had been interrupted by the quarrel with Willard.

When they were finished, they left her to clean up. Dawes told her how to scrub out the skillet with the sandy dirt. She was horrified, and glad she wouldn't be around to eat out of those utensils again. She watched him drift away to her bag in the darkness, and took new hope.

Alone after a fashion, she sat sipping the bitter coffee out of the unused side of Jay's cup. After careful thought, she had reluctantly chosen his, because there were no extras. She was still so tired it was an effort to raise the cup to her lips. She wondered how long she would have to wait before she could risk escape; even more, how long she could wait before she fell asleep.

The men were gathered around a spread blanket on the far side of the fire, mostly with their backs to her, opening the saddlebags. No one was watching her. How could they? Even her eyes were drawn irresistibly to the stacks of money packets, the gold coins that flashed occasionally in the red light.

She could use some of it, herself, to get back home; to placate Papa, when he heard Willard wouldn't be sending next month's allowance. Dawes had taken her little purse by now, and she was penniless. How grasping, when he already had a share of all that, and her emeralds as well.

She shook herself, realizing that she had been staring at the money for several minutes. Maybe, instead of trying to escape, she thought bitterly, I should go over there and demand to be cut in as a partner. With the thought came a soundless mirth, because she discovered she had been wiping her palms back and forth on her skirt. They itched, just as they were supposed to.

The time to go was now. They wouldn't be so fast to scramble after her with all that money loose on the ground. A thought occurred to her, and it was valid. She hadn't had a moment's privacy since her capture. The necessity embarrassed her, but it was the ruse she needed to get away from the fire. And not entirely a ruse, either, really.

She got up and began to edge away toward a shadowy tumble of rocks in the darkness to her left, watching the men uncertainly. Just as she reached the edge of the light, Jay turned his head. She stopped and drew herself up, with all the dignity possible to the situation. He had a trick of looking amused without smiling. It was something about the way his eyes were shaped. He looked that way now, then turned his head again, as if he hadn't seen her.

She closed her own eyes in gratitude and hurried away. When she was alone behind the rocks, hitching up her skirts, she wondered irritably why she should feel grateful to a criminal for permitting a decent woman to attend to the unmentionable necessities. A gentleman would not even have turned his head.

The horses were on the far side of their camp. She would have to make a wide detour through the rocks to get to them. She struggled out of her tight boots and tucked them under her arm, to make her way more silently. The hard stones bruised her feet, and once outside the firelight she had to move blindly in the strange terrain. Yet she must move as quickly as possible. Only so much time would be allowed for her absence before someone came to check.

When she had circled far enough downhill to be out of sight, she hurried to the thinly grassed pocket where the horses were. She could see their shapes moving, blacker against the blackness. Captain Lightfoot was taller than the rest, and easy to find.

She stopped and pulled on her boots, hopping frantically to do so, then went toward him. To her dismay, he was unsaddled. Then she cursed her stupidity. Of course he would be unsaddled. Worse, he was hobbled. She could feel the hobble with her fingers. It was a make-do of rope, not the metal cuffs and chains of another she could hear clinking faintly as the horses moved. The knots were intricate and tight.

She tried to work them loose, but the big gelding moved away. She whispered a command to him, soothing his neck with her hand. He dropped his head down to her and blew at her in recognition. She froze, but when there was no response from the others she bent again to struggle with the rope.

She broke a fingernail, and her fingers were sore from the picking when she got the rope loose and pulled it away from him. As she did so, Captain Lightfoot betrayed her. She reached for his mane to lead him away to some rock from which she could mount him, and he shook his head temperamentally and whinnied out the news of his release to his companions.

From the camp, Dawes said loudly, "Sounds like there's somebody down there with the horses. Where's your little wrangler, Billy?" She grabbed at the beast's mane and back, trying to crawl up on him, as Billy's silhouette appeared on the ridge above her, followed by Dawes's.

With a whoop, Billy rushed down the hill after her, jerking her away from the animal and grabbing at its halter. She tore herself free and ran into Dawes. He caught her up in a hug that nearly crushed her, lifting her feet off the ground. She was screaming at him hoarsely, damning him for his betrayal in words too thick with rage and breathlessness to be understood. He was laughing when he carried her back into the light, where a lounging Charlie, and Jay, standing stiff legged, feet braced apart, waited for them.

"Ain't you ashamed of yourself, Sis? Lettin' us think you were over there, makin' water, while you were just trying to spook the horses. Or was you going someplace?" Dawes put her on her feet in front of Jay.

She fell suddenly quiet under his stare, remembering his cold threat. She waited for him to give the word to one of them to kill her now and be done with it. She would have liked to die defying him, at least, but her tongue was stiff in her mouth. Maybe he would kill her himself. His hand was resting on the monstrous black holster at his waist.

But after a long scrutiny he sighed and said, "Fetch me a piece of rope, Charlie." When he had it, he hobbled her wrists, crossing and tying the knots between them so fast she couldn't remember how they went. It was as effective as handcuffs, and more uncomfortable. The remainder of the rope, about three feet, he fastened to his own belt with a square knot. He said nothing to her the whole time.

When he was finished, he turned away and she was forced to stumble along at his heels. He leaned over his bedroll, jerking the straps open, and spread it out on the ground. Then he reached for the canvas barrel cover he had promised her, and spread it beside the bedroll. Each move was unannounced and caused her to be pulled off balance after him. She was particularly anxious not to run into him, or touch him at all.

He separated one of the blankets from his roll and dropped it on her canvas.

When he sat down to take off his boots, she fell on her hands and knees beside him.

Billy, coming back from securing his other prize, stopped at the sight. "What's going on? Now who's got my girl?" He grinned, but his eyes were wide and glassy looking in the light.

"Nobody's got her. And nobody is going to. I'm going to get a little sleep, and I don't plan to have it disturbed by any more hassling with her."

"Well, I'll see to it she don't go nowhere!"

Jay just looked at him while unbelting his gun.

"Now, listen here, Grobart—" Billy began, his good humor beginning to desert him at the sound of Dawes's laugh.

"Listen yourself, Bowan. I said I was going to get some sleep. So are you, and all the rest. We need it, if you don't. You can just plan to do your courting some other time, because I'll be damned if I'm going to spend the night listening to her caterwaul while you try to get into the saddle." Even Charlie burst out laughing, along with Dawes. It was too much for Billy. He blew up red, like a turkey, but he had to let his frustration out in a laugh, to save face.

"To hell with all you killjoys," he said, snatching up his own roll. "Just remember, old man. I'm a pretty light sleeper myself. Don't try to run any of my stock, cause I already put my mark on her, even if I didn't get it in the right place."

Jay allowed himself a grin as he stretched out on his back.

Catherine lay beside him, her face burning with shame and outrage. In spite of all she could do, tears welled and ran out of the corners of her eyes, making cool, clean streams into her ears. She couldn't even wipe them without pulling at her tether and alerting him. She was lying on top of her blanket too, and unable to get it out and cover herself without tugging at him. Well, let it stay there. If she was going to perish anyway, freezing to death in the sudden autumn chill of the desert night was as good a way as any.

She would rather die than break the silence between them to ask him for anything. There was nobody she hated more, not even the traitorous Coleman Dawes. There was nobody she would rather see in jail, or on a gallows. She had always thought it unbelievably barbarous that people out here turned out to see a hanging as if it were a tent show. But if he ever came to the gibbet, and she was still alive, she would be there gladly, to sing hymns and enjoy a picnic lunch while she watched.

"Move your rump," he said in her ear. She opened her eyes, startled. He was pulling the blanket out from under her. "Get off it. It won't do you any good down there."

He freed it and spread it over her, covering her to the chin. As he did, he looked down at her dirty face with the tear streaks, and the baffled, hostile eyes. Again for a second there was the effect of amusement hidden in a solemn face.

"Pleasant dreams," he said to her moist glare.

# 5

When she woke, the sky was like a pink pearl, with no clouds in sight except for a few little pipe puffs of mole gray overhead. She lay looking at them for the short time it took to get her senses adjusted to the fact that she was lying under the open sky instead of the white canvas tent top in camp.

Then remembrance descended on her like the Assyrian host, and she jerked up with a sound of surprise that turned into a cry of pain. Her neck was stiff. Her hands were so strained and sore they felt broken. And they were tied together, though no longer tethered to her captor. She fell back on the hard ground with a groan.

"Sleep well?" That voice had a quality that always seemed to fire her to a sharp retort and quell her tongue at the same time. Still, she was glad it was he who greeted her first this morning. Any of the rest of them would have been sure to laugh, grin, sneer, or make some hyena pleasantry of the sort they were so well versed in.

In the morning she wanted humorless people around her until she had had her coffee.

She rolled her head. He was sitting by a small breakfast fire, cradling a steaming cup in both hands. He looked humorless enough.

"Are you going to keep me tied?" she asked evenly.

"Am I going to have to?" he countered.

She licked her dry lips, smelling the coffee. "No." Stiff as she was, she couldn't escape now, even if they gave her a leg up and a head start.

"Good. Come here." She pushed herself up and held out her wrists. He untied them and coiled the rope in one smooth operation. "Want some coffee?" He refilled the cup and held it out to her. She took it without any hesitation about sharing. The hot tin burned her fingers, and the brew was bitter, but was also good. She sighed into the cup, letting the steam come up and bathe her closed eyes. She might have expected to wake with one of her headaches this morning. It was strange, with all her other aches, not to feel the familiar migraine throb.

"Mr. Grobart—it is Grobart?"

He nodded.

"I know you must be weary of me, and of course you have no reason to believe anything I say: that if you let me go, I won't tell anyone I was with you. But I truly don't think you want to harm me. And I truly did leave my husband yesterday. I have no desire to see him again. If you would just put me down on any stage road, I assure you I would go in quite the opposite direction from him. Although you'd have to lend me the money for my fare," she added, in bitter remembrance. "I used all I had last night bribing Mr. Dawes to let me get away."

He was stuffing a pipe with tobacco while she talked, and devoted another minute to getting it lighted. "I thought you looked a little bare," he said between puffs. "Gave him your jewelry too? That's too bad. It's an expensive lesson. But a good one. Don't try to bribe a man with something he can take anyway. You really didn't have anything to bargain with, and Dawes didn't have anything to sell. What was he supposed to be doing that helped you, anyhow? Looks to me like you went off on your own."

She felt like a child rebuked for believing in fairies. Her own gullibility was more humiliating than her failure. She wished that, for this cool, efficient man, she could at least have been a clever loser. There was no use detailing to him the naïve plot she thought she had concocted with Dawes.

He got up, dusting himself off. He was looking toward a

spur of rock above the camp, where the Indian was standing lookout, a rifle cradled in his arms. At his movement, Charlie came to life and descended from the height with easy goat leaps, then sauntered toward them.

"Coffee, Charlie?"

Charlie opened his canteen instead. "I don't understand," he said between swallows, "how it is that a white man will turn up his nose at a little bitter water, then drink that stuff. Doesn't it tan your tongue?"

"See anything?"

"No. But we'd better break camp soon."

Catherine saw her blanket snatched from her knees. "Better get up and attend to your little affairs," Jay warned her mildly. "There's some hardtack and beef for your breakfast, and you can put the pot and cups back in the cantina when you're finished. Charlie, show her how to make her bedroll tight, and see that she doesn't stray off." He looked down at her. "Your bag is over there, if you want to comb your hair, or whatever. But I hope you don't have any more trinkets to offer. It would be a waste. Charlie doesn't trade for beads much now."

For all his offers of coffee and blankets, and his relative civility, his eyes were very cold when they met hers.

By the time the sun was completely up they were on their way, climbing out of the desert basin into worn, bare hills, blotched with outcroppings of stunted shrubs and thin, shivering grasses. There were armed encampments of the thorny, pungent bush they had dug out of the ground to make their fire. Occasional flashes of color, like liquid sunshine, gleamed from the pockets in the rock. When she passed them, she saw they were common dandelions, bold and glorious.

Little shocks of pain coursed through her thighs and up her back to her stiff neck with every stumble of her horse. Poor Captain Lightfoot, she thought. You've never been worked so hard and rewarded so little.

His ears, which had been laid back in temper yesterday, hung out like a weary plow horse's today. She wondered, with sudden concern, whether he could survive in this new, hard life. If he went lame or worse, what would they do about her then? Leave her in the wilderness with a dead or crippled animal?

But the rest of the party looked subdued too. Billy was silent or short spoken, and Dawes didn't watch her and grin every minute as he had the previous day. Surely their own horses couldn't go on forever with little water and less forage. There would have to be a change of country, or a change of horses, soon.

Changing horses meant meeting people; someone she might be able to leave word with, to send for—whom? The law, of course. And Willard?

By now, he knew—the whole camp knew—she had run away from him. She supposed that someone would eventually link her disappearance with that of the thieves. She must have been seen by someone on the train. By now a lot of people should know about her. There was probably a reward offered for the capture of the men. Would Willard offer one for her?

He would have to. What would he say about her? That she had been off on a shopping trip to Rock Springs with his blessing? That he was desperate with worry about her, longed for her return, and would give good money to have her safe in his arms again? Maybe he would just begin to play the tragic widower at once. How it would suit him! How she would laugh, to see the face he would put on for the world's pity.

And how she would have to crawl, if he got her back. He must be thinking of that moment too, and savoring it. Even now, perhaps. Oh God, how sweet it would seem to him, after his humiliation, to have her in his hands and in his debt again. For her anything would be preferable to that.

Would it? Was her present predicament preferable, after all? It was nothing more than a choice of fires. She had to get away from them both. She was sick of being bullied and threatened. She was sick, entirely, of the tribe of men.

She was also sick of herself, deeply. She knew herself for a shrew, a cold wife, a nagging daughter. She had never wanted to be like that! Who chose to be a scold? But was it her fault? Scolds were not born, they were made, by their alliance with weak, petulant men. Men who, like inept drivers, could not control their teams and blamed the horses for running too fast. Willard and Papa were alike. They had made their own misery, and hers.

While she brooded, they came to the crest of a hill and drew rein. She looked about, puzzled, before she saw the house in the valley below. It was a shanty of a house, with a better-built barn that slanted with the land, and a fenced corral with perhaps a dozen horses.

In the barren yard a line of wash hung dripping. Chickens roamed at large, and she caught the unmistakable odor of a pig.

"We're going to trade horses here," Jay told her. "It would be in your own best interest, Mrs. Crocker, to keep your mouth shut."

Billy said, "I could keep her up here, out of the way."

"I'd rather go down with you," said Catherine quickly.

Dawes gave his dog-bark laugh. "I don't think she cottons to you, Billy boy."

Billy grinned, but his flush was the color of a brick. "She'll change, when she gets to know me."

"I don't know," mused Charlie to himself. "I got to know you."

"Who asked your opinion, Mr. Smart-ass Injun?" Billy snarled. The goddamned high-nosed female was his prize. Dawes had picked pockets and not shared, Grobart got his bonus from bossing other people around, and who cared what a lousy Injun got? She was his, and his appetite for her, whetted by the touch of her body in their soft scuffle in the dirt, had kept him awake long after all the others were asleep last night. That old man had scooped her up and put her in his pocket, and he didn't even want her. Likely wouldn't know what to do with her if he did. "What you gonna do, let her go down there and run off her mouth about us and make us have to kill the whole lot of 'em?"

"You'd like that almost as much as staying up here with her, wouldn't you?" asked Charlie.

"Listen, you goddamned—"

"Shut up, both of you," snapped Jay. "We'll all go down together. Mrs. Crocker will do as I tell her. I said before, Dub thinks you're going to be partners with me on a spread in the north. I've already told him we'd be coming this way from Laramie, and need horses. All you two have to do is act like you're in your right minds, and he won't ask any questions."

"Just a nice little family group!" sneered Billy. "You gonna play Pa? This here must be Ma, and here's Uncle Coleman and Cousin Billy. But who's that sorrel-skinned son of a bitch over there, your boy? Little dark for it, ain't he?"

Charlie's look of triumphant malice seemed in keeping with his disposition, but Jay's reaction to the gibe startled and shook Catherine. With a speed that made his action seem a blur he slammed the back of his right hand into Billy's mouth, nearly knocking him out of his saddle. Billy's lip split on his teeth, and blood spurted from his nose. Straining to keep his seat, the little man still clawed at one of his guns, but before it cleared its scabbard Charlie's carbine was pushing at his ribs from the other side.

Billy froze at the touch of the barrel, then slowly removed his hand from the gun butt and wiped at his nose. Jay was still leaning toward him, strained and rigid. He had made no move to his own weapon. His eyes held Billy's and nobody moved or spoke. After a minute he reached blindly into his own pocket and held out a handkerchief. Billy took it as if expecting it to bite him, and held it to his nose and mouth.

"Bowan, you're going to dig your own grave with that mouth of yours someday, sure as hell," Jay said in a voice just above a whisper. "Don't ever say that again."

"Say what, for Chrissake? I'd like to know what I said! If he's one of your relatives, you didn't tell nobody!"

Charlie was grinning now, but turned his head away as he took the carbine out of Billy's side.

"He isn't a relative, but never mind. How's your nose?"

Billy shrugged. With every emotion his color surged; now he was scarlet. With the removal of the carbine, he relaxed slightly, but the fingers of his free hand still lingered near the gun on his thigh.

Jay unsnapped his canteen and poured water over the bloody handkerchief, and Billy tipped his head back and squeezed it out over his nose, mopping and gasping. Catherine shuddered at the mess he was making of his face with it. In spite of herself she was in sympathy with him. She too wondered what he had said. At last she could watch no longer.

"Mr. Bowan, if you'll dismount, I'll try to stop the bleeding." She didn't look at Jay for approval, but she thought Billy did. Jay nodded slightly, and Billy climbed down, still holding the sodden cloth to his face.

When her own feet were on the ground, she put out her hand for Jay's canteen. She soaked her own little French linen handkerchief with water, then ordered Billy to sit down. Grimly, she ruined the lace-edged square, mopping him clean, then poured water into his cupped palm and told him to sniff it up his nose. This occasioned more mopping, but as they repeated the treatment the bleeding gradually stopped.

She used the rest of the water in the canteen to finish cleaning him up and to rinse out the bloody handkerchiefs. She bent closer to examine his swollen lip, and he looked sullenly at her.

"It needs a cold knife to take down the swelling, or a piece of ice. Maybe they'll have some down there."

"I'm going to kill that old bastard, the first chance I get," Billy whispered.

"Are you finished?" Jay demanded. "If so, get up in the saddle again."

"Hey, nursie, I think I got something in my eye. Come and fix it for me!" Dawes sang out, finishing with another bark.

Catherine returned to her place, as did Billy. She gave the empty canteen back to its owner without a word.

Jay, seeming to want to make some kind of conciliatory gesture, said, "Boy, you get too worked up over things. They must've raised you on chili peppers."

"*I* get too worked up!"

"We've got a lot to stay friendly for, at least until we're further up in the hills. Now, Dub Kelly is an old friend. I knew him in Laramie. He's not too bright, but he's no fool, either. He'll believe whatever I tell him, if the rest of you don't bitch it up. Let's all just tuck in our tempers until we get these horses traded."

He looked at Catherine. "Dub's got a wife and a baby with him." He waited, not enlarging on the observation, until she gave a brief nod of submission. Then he led them down to the lonely-looking shack.

A man came out on the porch as they approached. He was thin to the point of emaciation, with a leathery young-old face and work-corded hands. He wore a faded blue shirt and pants that still bespoke the uniform. The trousers showed faint lines down the side seams where a yellow stripe had been picked away. He raised his long arms in welcome.

"Yo, Captain! I wasn't expecting you 'til tomorrow! But come right in, right on in. My woman'll be right pleased for the company. Our boy's cuttin' teeth, and he's been a trial to her, lately."

Jay helped Catherine to dismount, keeping one hand on her arm firmly and drawing her close. "Dub, you've not met Mr. Dawes and Mr. Bowan, my partners. Mr. Bowan had a little accident this morning. A snake spooked his horse, and he fell off." Billy stiffened at this piece of libel, but shook hands with Dub and endured his sympathy.

Jay glanced down at Catherine. If it had seemed possible, she would have said he looked ill at ease. He drew her under his arm. "And this is—my wife—Catherine."

Catherine was turned to stone. She couldn't even blink.

Dub Kelly beamed at her. "I'm purely pleased to meet you, Ma'am; purely pleased. I've know'd Captain Grobart for right on to fifteen years, and I can tell you, you got a man who can take up for his own. You're gonna be all right out there! And he knows how to pick pretty women, too." He took her limp hand and pumped it, then looked embarrassed and dropped it as if it were stolen. She remembered to smile, before it was too late, and wondered how he had arrived at his conclusion about pretty women. In her present condition she must look a dismal example of anyone's taste in women.

A figure stirred in the dark doorway of the house, and Dub's wife appeared, holding a squirming baby.

"Dub, you remember Charlie, from the Fort? He was a boy then. His father was Standing Horse."

Dub looked at Charlie uncertainly with his faded, wary eyes. Charlie gave him no help. At last Dub nodded. "Yeah. I remember Standing Horse. He was a—good Injun. You was a kid, ten, twelve years old, when he got killed. Charlie. Sure." But he didn't pump Charlie's hand.

The woman on the porch moved again as the baby gave a fretful cry. Dub blinked back at her, as if just recollecting her.

"Here's my missus, now. Sudie, take Mrs. Grobart in the house and make her at home. Mayhap she'd like a sip of cider, or some hot coffee. Whatever we got." He seemed vague about this, and Catherine thought it was unlikely that they had much of anything.

Sudie, his wife, was as thin as he. Her cheeks were already fallen in from lack of back teeth, and she looked any age between thirty and fifty, though the presence of the baby, apparently the only child, made the latter unlikely.

They entered the dark house, Catherine with Jay's hand still guiding and warning her. She wondered if he had ever been married. He seemed undecided on just how a wife should be escorted. Or perhaps he still thought she might bolt for the hills if he let her walk freely. She eased herself away from him with as much nonchalance as she could manage, walking sedately, with her head down, like schoolbook pictures of the Plymouth Colony Puritans going to church.

Coming out of the bright sun, she was blinded in the doorway; when she could see, what met her eyes appalled her with its poverty.

There was scarcely any furniture. A crude table and two rope-seated chairs; a long bench before the fire; a homemade wooden trunk in one corner; and a boxlike repository for the mare's-nest of colorless quilting that was their bed—no bed in sight for the child—were all they had. Along the walls there were shelves and a few pegs for their smaller household effects and their clothes. Neither were very plentiful. It was as poor as the worst slave shanty she had ever been in.

Dub reached up to one of the shelves and seized a small jug. He winked at the men and motioned them back out the door. "I got us something better than cider. Let's leave that, and the chairs, for the womenfolk."

Jay recaptured Catherine's elbow and pushed her firmly to one of the chairs. Mrs. Kelly retreated to the fireplace, where she stood jiggling her baby. "You'll sit here and be comfortable while we do a little business, won't you—Catherine?"

She wanted to tell him what an unconvincing groom he was making, but she only nodded, dumbly. When he was out the front door, though, she started up suddenly and said, "Wait!"

He turned quickly, and it was plain that his assumed solicitude was nearly at an end. She stepped out on the plank porch to whisper urgently, "You're not going to sell Captain Lightfoot?"

"Who? Oh, I see. That's up to Billy. I've already pushed him to the limit. He figures that's part of his take."

"But he's my horse!"

"Take it up with Billy. Maybe he'd be willing to work out some kind of exchange with you."

"Do you ever think of anything else?" she snapped.

"I do. But I sometimes doubt if Billy does."

"Captain Lightfoot's a very good horse. My husband paid four hundred dollars for him in St. Louis last year."

"Then it looks like poor old Dub's finally come into a piece of good luck, because Billy doesn't know a hunter when he sees one. He's about one part quarter horse himself, and he's already got your gelding sized up as nothing but a long-legged buggy puller. Dub can take him down to Denver and get a good price for him. Anyway," he relented enough to add, "your Captain Lightfoot is used to short rides and long feeds. He wouldn't make it, the way we're going, and everybody would be out of luck."

She returned, defeated, to the doubtful company of Mrs.

Kelly. When she was seated again, and gave no further evidence of flying up suddenly, Mrs. Kelly relaxed enough to creep to the corner and deposit her baby on the tumbled bed. Then she approached Catherine shyly.

"You want something cold to drink?" she asked. Her voice was soft and young; a girl's voice in such a worked-out body.

Catherine smiled at her. "Yes, I would, thank you. In fact, what I'd like the most is a big drink of water."

The woman sighed. "Well, we surely do have plenty of that. We got us a good well. It's about the only thing there's plenty of, here. That, and horseflies." There were swarms of flies humming in the room, lured by the sour vomit smell of the baby and the bucket of soaking, soiled infant clouts by the bed.

"If it isn't too much trouble, could I have a little water to wash in?" Catherine added.

The young woman took a bucket off a peg and went out the door, returning shortly with it, brimming. "You just take that dipper and drink all you want, and I'll get a pan and a rag for you to wash with. It surely is dusty, coming up from the south."

Catherine twisted her hair up on top of her head, fixing it with one of her few remaining pins. She stripped off her stock and started to unbutton the draggled velveteen habit, then remembered she had no blouse under the jacket, only a false shirt front. She hesitated.

"Do you think the men will be coming back very soon? I'd like to wash my—my arms and—" She floundered.

"You want to take a spit bath? They'll be out there tradin' 'til they kill that jug, for sure. I'll shut the door, and leave the window open so's you can see. But I'll stand by it, just in case anybody starts up this way. You can take off everything. I won't look."

"Well," said Catherine doubtfully, and longingly. She was nervous at the thought of undressing in this strange place, with a quintet of men likely to burst in. But the bucket of cold water already seemed like one of the perfumed baths of Sheba. She stripped off her jacket and shirt front, and scrubbed herself with the strong yellow soap until she was on fire with it.

"Have you and Captain Grobart been married long, Ma'am?" asked Mrs. Kelly, eyes turned resolutely to the window.

Catherine stopped, fumbling for an answer; wondering if Jay Grobart was answering the same question outside, and what his inventive reply would be. "N-no, we haven't. You might say it was a very recent thing."

"Why, I thought as much! He looked so awkward and put out about leaving you here, like he didn't want to be away from you for a minute. I thought he looked like a man who was new at the job. Then too, Dub didn't mention nothin' about him being married again, since he got out."

Married again. Catherine busied herself, soaping the rag, keeping her back turned. She slipped down her chemise straps to wipe her breasts clean of sweat and sandy dust. She ought to say something.

"Got out?" she echoed. "You mean, out of the Army?" The question fell on dead air. She looked around to see Sudie Kelly surprised and flustered. "What is it?"

"Oh, I didn't mean—when he—I thought you—yes Ma'am." She looked so distressed that there could be only one other possibility, unless it was the madhouse.

Catherine spoke carefully. "Are you talking about prison?"

"Oh, Miz Grobart, I didn't mean to mention it or offend you, I truly didn't. It's just that Dub told me all about it, after the last time the Captain was here last month, and I thought it was so sad."

Catherine was ashamed to let the woman go on thinking she was distressed, but she didn't know what to say. She was suddenly curious to hear what was behind those half-finished sentences that was so sad. It might be to her favor to know some of Jay Grobart's secrets. And the prison part of it was very serious. It would pay her to hear just what kind of criminal leanings predated train robbery with him.

"I'm not offended at all, Mrs. Kelly. It's just—well—that I know so little about him. You'll think me very silly, I suppose, but, although I know Mr.—my husband was in prison, and that he was married before, I don't know many things about it. We haven't known each other very long." She wrung out her cloth, wiping her body clean of the soap. A fresh, purpling bruise marred the side of one breast, and there were two sets of streaked bruises on her upper arms. She examined them, frowning. How do you ask another woman to tell you about your supposed husband's lurid past? Do you sound ignorant, idiotic, shy? In the cool moistness of their afterbath, her small pink nipples began to rise. She covered them hastily with the damp batiste and glanced at Mrs. Kelly for some sort of clue.

The woman's face told her that she was as anxious to gossip as Catherine was to hear. They understood each other at once, though Catherine felt it necessary to offer a few token excuses.

"It sounds awful of me not to know, but I felt he'd tell me all about it someday, in his own time. Of course, I'd never let him find out I already knew."

"Why, you mustn't feel bad about not knowing everything about your man. There's people that know a whole lot less, I expect; like those mail-order brides you sometimes hear about. They come clean across the country to marry a man they never laid eyes on, and little difference it makes in the end. My ma always said, 'Just as long as you know your man's done good by you, it makes no never mind what else he's done.' "

The baby on the bed had been fussing restlessly, and now it broke out in a sudden rebellion against further neglect. Sudie Kelly hurried to it and gathered it up.

"He's hungry," she explained, unbuttoning her dress as she returned to the table. She exposed one small blue-veined breast with a distended nipple. The baby's greedy mouth closed around it immediately. Catherine looked away as she dressed. She put on the same clothes, because her bag was still strapped to her saddle. The baby made desperate sucking noises.

"It's a wonder he gets anything out of me, I'm made so small," said his mother, smiling at him. "But it's like the loaves and the fishes in the Good Book. The more he needs, the more he seems to get." She and Catherine looked at each other, each waiting for the other to begin.

"Tell me—about why he was in prison," Catherine asked.

Mrs. Kelly smiled sadly. "Well, Dub says he shouldn't never to have been there at all. He did what any man ought to do, he says, and mind you, Dub was never much for Injuns. But the jury was mostly friends of the men he'd killed. And then too, there was a lot of them that had lost someone they cared about on account of the Injun trouble that was so bad then. So there was that too. And then they said Mr. Grobart didn't have no proof that those men was the guilty ones."

Catherine was hopelessly lost in this, but she nodded gravely. "Why did he kill the men?" she asked softly.

Mrs. Kelly looked surprised. "Why, because of her. His wife. You know she was an Injun, don't you?"

Catherine nodded again, hoping she wasn't complicating the mystery by her pretended knowledge. Yet she would have to nod at anything Sudie would expect the greenest sort of fool to know about the man she married. She saw there had to be something in the tale about an Indian. It would explain his sudden rage with Billy Bowan.

"I don't want to make you think I'm judgin', because lots of men have done it, and plenty still do, but Dub says she never was his proper wife. He married her in the way the Injuns have. Just paid her daddy whatever price he set on her—a horse, or so many blankets—they never stood up in front of a preacher. But he always called her his wife. I guess I'm not as religious as I ought to be, but I say it was all the more honor to him. Because it didn't make things any too easy for him with some of the others at Old Bedlam."

"Old Bedlam?"

"That's what they called the bachelor officers' house at Fort Laramie. Of course, he had to move out of there once he had a wife, and get them a little bit of a house in the married officers' part of it. But it didn't do no good. It was right after Black Horse Creek, that you might've heard of, and there was nothing but talk about massacres and killing. I was just a girl in those days, and I know my ma wouldn't let me hear some of the stories the menfolk told about the things that was done on both sides.

"His woman was a Snake, a Shoshone; and they was mostly peaceful. The Cheyenne and Sioux and Arapaho was causing most of the fight, but lots of folks didn't make much difference between them."

"So someone killed her?"

"Wait, let me tell you. First, he up and quit the Army. After twenty years, or near to it. And he went to work for the railroad when they was laying the track through to Cheyenne. And while he was on his way to see her one Saturday night, Dub says, for the first time in a long while—and she and her two little babies was alone in the house waiting for him—these three men from the Captain's old company came and killed her after they—you know—did other things to her, first. And he came home that night and found her, right after."

"Dear Lord," murmured Catherine. "And then he killed them. But how did he know about them? Were they still there?"

"She told him who they was before she died, Dub says. Dub went to see the Captain and bring him some fresh clothes when he was in jail, and to hear the trial afterwards. There was some feeling that the jury didn't do right; among the women, mostly. But, like I said, they was lots of them friends of the ones he killed and none of them friends of his. Even so, they didn't call it murder, quite. They said it was manslaughter, whatever the difference might be. And they gave him ten years in prison for giving those woman killers what they deserved."

Only the sound of the nursing baby broke the silence after Sudie finished her résumé. Her eyes were brighter for the telling of it.

Catherine sat reflecting on the savagery and pain still present in this third-hand report of a ten-year-old tragedy.

She could see that Sudie Kelly relished her moment of drama in telling it. She was silent. Even so unskillfully revealed, and to an enemy, the tale cast a pall of pity over the anger and fear that Grobart had aroused in her. What would she have felt if she had really been his new wife, loving him in ignorance?

She frowned, trying to see the cold, harsh-voiced man who

had promised to kill her if she inconvenienced him as a young husband, the lover of a pretty Indian girl. She remembered the tight fury on his face when he struck Billy for a sarcastic remark about a dark-skinned son, like Charlie.

A son.

"The children," she said, more to herself than to the other woman. "What became of the children, afterward?"

"Those poor babies. I feel sorry for them, even if they are savages again, by this time." Catherine watched the feeding infant, waiting. "Their mother's people took them off, while he was still waiting to have his trial. They're up on the Reservation now, I guess, if they're still alive at all. But he never got to see them again."

THE JUG was empty. Billy and Coleman Dawes had swallowed most of the liquor. Dub tried to do his share, but he had no head for it, and even he knew that with his limited wits he should hold off until the trading was done.

Grobart scarcely touched it, after a token sip or two the first time around. After that he only pretended to drink, but let little of it seep through his lips. He was strongly aware that in his present mood the liquor would work against him. Billy drank, burning his torn mouth; regaining his cockiness and trying it out on Jay, but with care.

Dawes drank and grew silent. But then, he was never talkative. He leaned on the corral fence and sneered or grinned at some private joke, or else at nothing at all. Grobart said nothing to either of them. He recognized the limit of his authority, having reached it. He was a drill sergeant without the power to punish; a section boss without the power to fire. And he knew he had made a bad tactical error when he hit Billy.

He damned himself for it, and for letting his surprise and apprehension get the best of him. He had lost face as well as authority, and gained nothing. It showed how much he had slipped in the last ten years.

Billy traded Catherine Crocker's big black gelding for a broad-backed, frisky little dun with a black tail, and was trying him out in the sparse meadow downhill from the barn.

He was showing off for nobody in particular, since Dawes continued to leer senselessly and Dub was busy going over the big black, point by point, wondering if he was wrong about its worth.

Jay cursed himself again. Why had he slammed the kid in the mouth that way? True, for a moment he had misunderstood; thought Billy was letting him know that he'd found out about his boy. But only Charlie could have told him, and common sense told Jay that Charlie hadn't, even as his hand slashed out.

He had been tight as a bowstring even before Billy popped off. Why? He told himself it was the job; the long, careful preparation for it, the long trip yet to be made before it paid off for him as it was meant to. The others had got all they were after as soon as the money was split. His goal was still ahead. His son. The money was a bribe, if you liked; a prize, a present for the keepers, a ticket that would buy his boy's freedom. If it wasn't that, then it was dirt to him.

Charlie had asked him, what if it wasn't enough? What if Iron Knife thought it was blood money and spat on it? If he couldn't buy or beg his son from Iron Knife, what would he do? Fight the whole Shoshone nation? He hadn't answered the taunt, which was what it was, but it stayed with him, still wanting an answer.

He'd had years to think about the day when he would demand his own back from Iron Knife, and there was nothing Charlie could name that he hadn't thought of too: that the boy wouldn't remember him, or that he would and hated him. A recurring nightmare had been that the boy would die, was already dead of some children's accident or disease. But that fear had been laid to rest before he left prison, and he had Charlie to thank for it, because Charlie had looked, and found the boy, and the girl too. Iron Knife had raised them as his own, and they were both alive and well last winter when Charlie returned from his search.

That was one of the unaccountable things about Charlie. He had first visited the prison a month after Jay's father died, to bring him the news. He had been blunt and brief, but Jay and his father had not been close. Charlie had treated Jay with an irritating mixture of envy and condescension during that short visit, then left with no promise to return. Yet he came again, once or twice a year thereafter, with various shadowy excuses for his presence, never staying more than five minutes when he came. And when Jay asked him to make that journey of discovery for him, Charlie had obliged and reported. Jay had never understood why.

He made an effort to shake off his self-accusing mood and pay attention to Dub, who was spieling yarns about people Jay had either forgotten or cared nothing about. But he pretended to remember and show interest, because once this dull-minded wrangler had shown him a kindness. And he hadn't forgotten that.

"Where's Charlie gone to?" Dub was asking now, his pale eyes staring around the yard shortsightedly.

"I sent him along ahead of us, to pick out a camp for the night."

"Why, surely you're going to stay here with us tonight, Captain. If we can't offer you and your lady a bed, leastwise we can provide a roof."

"It's a kind offer, Dub, but we have to move on. We've got a lot of territory to cover, and I have to be in Farson to meet a train of our goods coming up from Rock Springs." It was so easy to lie to Dub. He hated doing it. Suddenly he hated the whole damned thing, and wished the lies could be true. Maybe he should make them true—really buy that spread somewhere and make something of it. Try for the boy later, when he had. Billy would make a good top hand. Or he would have, until this morning.

But there it was again. The boy couldn't be left until later, because soon he wouldn't be a boy any more, but a man. And Billy would never make a good top hand for him, because Jay had humiliated him in front of an Indian he hated and a woman he wanted.

The whole trouble had started with the woman.

Billy tired of showing off his riding skills and brought his little dun back to the corral. His china eyes were overbright when he looked at Jay, and his breath came short, as if he'd been doing the running, but he smiled, stretching his sore lip, when he looked at the older men.

"Got any more in that jug, ol' Dub?" he called. He teetered slightly on his high-heeled boots when he came to a standstill.

"This one's dry. But there's a speck more in another one up at the house. We'll be having supper pretty soon. The woman'll call us. You want to wash up and cool off, first? We'll pass the jug around with the corn bread."

Billy laughed. "That's a good idea, ol' Dub. My ma always told me you should always wash your neck and ears every evening, just so in case you died in the night, you wouldn't be a shame to your friends. Ain't that right, Dawes? Ain't that what they told you?" He hit Dawes playfully in the belly as he passed.

Dawes reached out one bear arm for him, and they wrestled, grunting, until Dawes had him pinned against a fence post. Billy feigned surrender, then popped his fist into Dawes's belly again when he was released. He danced away, a little clumsily, laughing. Dawes started after him, but Jay said, "Dawes," quietly, and he stopped. His eternal grin had slipped a bit, but he put it back on.

"That little banty wants his tail feathers picked," he said.

"Think you can pull 'em, Hoss? You're gonna need a good pair of pliers for the job. I'd lend you mine, but I left 'em back at the train stop."

Grobart stopped walking and looked at him, feeling a galvanic shiver run down his spine and through his arms, but he kept them still. Billy laughed at him, and stayed well behind him all the way up to the house, stalking him unsteadily in imitation of his long-legged, arrogant step.

The Kelly woman brought them water and they washed up on the porch, drying off with coarse, ragged towels that were cleaner than might have been expected. When Jay turned, wiping his face, Catherine was standing in the front door.

It was the first time he had seen her face when it wasn't caked with dirt and half-covered with her hair. She had brushed her gown and dressed her hair into a large, loose braid pinned low on her neck. Her face was shiny and tight with the sunburn and the effect of the strong soap. Her eyes, brows, and thick lashes were all the same rich, reddish brown as her hair. Her shoulders were squared, her body thin and straight as a young lieutenant's as she stood there.

Accustomed, as he had once been, to plump, docile women, he had already been surprised by her temper and spirit. Now he was surprised again. He had thought her too thin and tight lipped and intense for good looks. He was wrong. She was not pretty, but she had a handsomeness, like that of her horse, made of fine bones, grace, and the sureness that came of good breeding. In that sense she was a beautiful woman. And she had picked a poor time to show it.

He heard it in Billy's voice behind him. "Well now. Looky there. If it ain't the Captain's little lady. I almost forgot what a pretty little thing you are. Did you come out here to see if ol' Jay washed behind his ears? Hey, come here and look behind mine!"

She didn't look at him, but turned back into the house. Jay followed her.

"Act easy with Billy, and don't let him rile you. He's had his nose in the jug all afternoon, and he's feeling cocky. I'm going to get him out of here right after supper." He wondered why he was telling her.

"You don't have to instruct me in how to treat drunkards, Mr. Grobart. It's been my bad fortune to know more about them than I ever cared to." She moved away from him a bit. "From the smell of the rest of you, I'd say he didn't drink it all, though."

He took her by the elbow, then released it when he saw Mrs. Kelly looking at them. "I trust you had a quiet afternoon yourself?" he murmured, trying to look as if he had said something pleasant. "No exchanging girlish secrets?"

"Very quiet," she whispered, flushing suddenly. Before he could examine that, she brushed past him and went to help the woman set the table for a meal that was going to depend heavily on corn bread and watered beans.

Dub found an opportunity to speak a few words into his wife's ear that brought a look of astonishment and joy to her thin face. There would be more meat to go with the beans for a while because of Catherine's luxury horse. Jay saw that she had noticed the exchange too, and she glanced back at him quickly. He couldn't tell if she was more content to make the sacrifice, now, or not. He told himself it didn't make a damned bit of difference either way.

Dawes and Billy, walking too heavily and talking too loud, came in and woke the baby, then set about alarming it by their noisy attempts to soothe it again. Mrs. Kelly took it up to pet and Billy hovered close, trying to jolly it and compliment her, until even her pale cheeks were pink from his heavy gallantry.

Dub dragged the bench up to the table for Jay and Catherine to sit on, and a couple of empty kegs for the other two men They ate, making the best of what there was. Jay, watching Catherine, smiled when she found the corn bread too dry to eat properly and finally crumbled it up in her beans like everyone else, the delicate motion of her long fingers turning a necessity into an elegant little ritual.

Along with the meal the jug was passed around. She watched it with such severe disapproval that Jay took a bit more than he really wanted when it came to him. Even Mrs. Kelly took some. It was raw stuff that made her gasp a little, then giggle and blink her big tear-filled eyes. Only Catherine abstained, withdrawing her cup when it was offered to her, drinking nothing but the hard mineral-tasting water.

Billy noticed this. "What's the matter, Miz Grobart? You a Temperance Leaguer, or something? I just bet you are. You gonna make ol' Jay join the Blue Ribbon Brigade?" He ignored Jay's ominous stare and reached out for her cup. She held it back from him. "Now, if you don't let me give you one little bitty snort, you're just gonna sit there looking pruny and spoil everything when everybody else is feeling good. And when we get up to toast the bride and groom, you're gonna have to toast us right back, cause that's the refined way to do." He winked at her as he leaned farther over the table to splash half a cupful of the colorless liquor into her cup and on her dress.

Jay felt himself tightening up, but he only said, "Sit down, Billy. You're dragging your belly through your plate." Billy drew himself up, eyes fastened on Jay.

"Bride?" echoed Dub.

His wife brightened. "That's right, Dub. Mrs. Grobart tells me they just was married before they come up here." Jay looked at Catherine's profile. She was still wiping the whiskey off her bodice and didn't respond.

"*Just* before," Billy repeated solemnly. "We was the witnesses, wasn't we, Dawes?"

Dub rose awkwardly and lifted his tin cup. "Well now, that does deserve a toast, I think, Captain. I didn't know it was so recent." He put himself into a more formal posture. "Gentlemen and ladies, I pledge you Captain Grobart and his bride. Long life and pros—prost—and happiness to you, sir." He turned up the cup.

Jay rose. "Thank you, Corporal. In return, I give you the health and prosperity of your own house, and especially your son." He drank. Catherine sat fiddling with her cup. "Thank you for your hospitality, Dub. It's been a pleasure to see you again. But, if we're going to make any distance before dark, we better be starting."

"Now, wait just a minute!" said Billy. "We ain't through with the ceremonials, yet. Somebody's supposed to kiss the bride, and I aim to volunteer first!" He knocked over his keg standing up and came around the corner of the table to Catherine.

"Billy," warned Jay.

Billy's smile was manic. "What's the matter, bridegroom? I didn't see you kiss her when she got to be Mrs. Grobart. Don't you remember how to do it? Stand back then, and let me show her what she's missing!"

Jay sensed the Kellys' bewilderment. Dub was frowning at Billy.

"Sit down, Billy," Jay said quietly. "The joke's over."

"Why, the joke can't be over until it's told, *Captain.* And they don't know but just a little piece of it, yet." His hunger for a fight radiated like heat from his small body.

Catherine looked swiftly around the table, her eyes coming to rest on Sudie Kelly, the baby against her shoulder sucking its fingers. She moved suddenly, standing up between Jay and Billy. Jay heard her say, "Thank you, Mr. Bowan, for your good wishes," and put her cheek out coolly for his kiss.

Billy took her by the shoulders and kissed her mouth, pressing her head back until her throat was strained tight. A muscle in Jay's jaw began to twitch. When Billy let her go, her cheeks were scarlet, but she wiped her mouth delicately with her fingertips and turned to Dub.

"Best wishes, I'm sure, Ma'am," he said, embarrassed, and pecked her on the cheek.

Back straight, she looked at Dawes. He got up slowly, brushing by Billy to loom over her. For a moment, his smile faded as he looked down at her. But it returned as he caught Jay's look. His kiss was for her lips, but brief. "Happy days," he chuckled.

"Thank you, Mr. Dawes." She turned away, a polite imitation of a smile set into the corners of her mouth, with a bright, bitter look for Jay. He started to draw a breath of relief because she had handled it as well as it could have been handled, when there was a rabbit cry from the end of the table behind him. It was Mrs. Kelly. Dub shot to his feet.

"Well, it's her turn. She don't want to be left out, does she?" asked Billy, trying to hold on to the retreating Sudie.

"Billy!" snarled Jay, and Dub pushed Catherine out of the way, one hand already dropping to the gun on his thigh, but Jay moved faster. Grabbing Billy's shoulder, he spun him away from the woman with one hand and smashed him in the face with the other. Billy sprawled back over one of the heavy chairs onto the rough plank floor and lay still. Jay snapped around to face Dawes, but Dub's gun already held Dawes's full attention.

He held out both hands, fingers spread. "Hey, I'm not in on this. Hold your fire."

Jay took his hand off his own weapon and relaxed warily. Dub's gun wavered, then retreated to its holster again.

"Drag that out of here and cool it off at the horse trough, Dawes," Jay said, indicating Billy. He waited, breathing a little too quickly, until Dawes was out the door. Then, "I'm sorry about this, Dub. We'll be out of your way as soon as we sober him up and get the horses saddled."

Dub protested politely. "Oh now, Captain, you can't get any kind of a start this time of day. The feller's just swum too far down in the jug. He'll be all right tomorrow. Bed him down in the barn and spend the night with us."

"I'm obliged, Dub, but we'd best be traveling." He held Catherine's glance for the space of two breaths, wondering whether she'd tell them if he left her now. Outside, there was a splash and a yell of rage from Dawes. Jay jerked the door open and strode out.

Dawes, trying to force the bucking, plunging Billy head-first into the trough, had found himself cast into it instead, spurred and tripped by Billy's thrashing feet. They were both dripping and locked in each other's grip on the ground when Jay reached the spot. In spite of their difference in size, Billy was on top.

Jay grabbed him by the neckerchief and jerked up and back, pulling him off Dawes like a terrier off a mole.

Slung away, Billy fell heavily on his back. He lay gasping for breath and rubbing his throat. "All right, old man. You're the one I want, anyway," he said, when he could talk.

Dawes was getting to his feet, blood running out of his open mouth. He spat a red gob into the dust and just as Billy was struggling up stepped forward to put a boot under his chin, sending him sprawling again.

"That's enough, Dawes," growled Jay. But as he stayed Dawes with one hand, Billy flung himself off the ground and butted the big man, driving his head in low. They crashed into the trough again, sending it over this time.

"Ah, the hell," sighed Jay as Dub appeared beside him. "Let

them fight it out. Give me a hand with the saddles, will you?"

Mouth tight, he worked at saddle girths, ignoring the sounds of body blows and the short yelps of pain from Billy. When the horses were ready, he led two of them out, followed by Dub with two more, and the pack horse. Billy was flat on the ground by the wrecked trough. Dawes, wet and gasping, hung over him trying to get up.

Jay helped Dawes to his feet, then leaned over Billy. "All right, boy. You've had your bust-out for the week. Let's go." But when he took his arms to pull him up, Billy gave a breathless shriek. Jay let him down more easily and dropped to one knee beside him.

"What'd you try to do, Dawes, stomp him into the ground?"

"He butted me twice with that damn cannon-ball head of his," Dawes groaned, still nursing his groin with one hand.

A pair of soft boots came to a stand beside Billy's head. Jay looked up at Charlie. "Now, why did I come so late?" mused Charlie. "That was something I've been looking forward to seeing. Is he dead?"

"No," Jay said, "but he's out cold. He may have some broken ribs. Help me get him on his horse. We'll have to tie him on. And get his guns. I'll put them in his saddlebag." Together they lifted him out of the dirt and carried him to the saddle. The effort of getting him into it brought him back to consciousness with a cry, but he tried to sit up and seemed more comfortable when he did. "I'll take him from here," said Jay. "Go get the Crocker woman."

"Why not leave her here?" asked Charlie.

"Get her," repeated Jay.

Billy opened his one good eye. His mashed mouth made a motion that could have been a grin. "Hey, Jay," he croaked. "I can still take you, old man. Just as soon as I get strapped up. I told you, that's my stock you're runnin'."

"She's all yours, Bowan. Just as soon as we're clear of here," growled Jay. He took the piece of rope he had used on Catherine and tied Billy into the saddle, passing it around his hips and over the saddle horn several times, and once around the cantle, where he tied it. He expected the towhead to protest, but he was holding on to the horn with both hands now, eyes closed again.

"If you don't think you can hold on, I'll put you up behind me," Jay said.

Billy shook his head. "I can ride."

Catherine came out of the house with Charlie, followed by Mrs. Kelly. Catherine looked as if she expected one of them to begin to batter her. It occurred to Jay again that she had been given the chance to tell the truth about them, and he looked at her and the other woman closely, to see if it showed in their faces. But Mrs. Kelly had hers buried in the child, clucking and soothing it, and Catherine had seen Billy, close. Whatever she may have been showing was erased by the horror on her face at the sight of Bowan's.

Remembering that they must continue to play their parts, he put his arm around her and drew her away from Billy before she could voice the accusation forming on her lips. She tried to pull free, but he held her to his side in a cruel grip while putting out his other hand to Dub—saying goodbye, apologizing, making all the proper noises.

He couldn't tell if they were the right ones or not. In the growing dark Dub's face was dim. He returned Jay's handclasp, sounding baffled but sympathetic, he thought. Not suspicious, not alarmed. If he could get them all out of here without another word or incident he might leave these good, ignorant people thinking nothing more dangerous than that he was a fool who picked drunken saddle tramps for his business partners and couldn't control men any more.

In the turmoil of his thoughts he became aware of the pressure he was exerting to hold Catherine against him. He let her go, abruptly. She had been saying some meaningless thing to the Kelly woman and now, to his surprise, she leaned forward, gripping Mrs. Kelly's worn hands in hers, and kissed her thin cheek.

When he put her up on her new horse he could feel his arms trembling in reaction to a sudden fatigue. She felt it, with her hands on his shoulder, and her eyes met his for a moment, baffled. But she said nothing, only sat her mount with her chin stuck up as if she were on parade. He thought she might be exactly the sort of glory grabber who would ride off with a bunch of dazed and drunken maniacs just to keep harm from coming to a dull-eyed ranch woman and her child. But he felt a grudging admiration for her nerve.

They left the Kellys standing close together in the bare yard and rode into the cover of some shallow hills to the north. There was no moon, and the darkness was almost upon them by the time the ranch was out of sight. They went in double file, Dawes and Charlie leading, with Jay and Catherine coming after, Jay leading Billy's horse. Billy needed both hands to hold himself up.

They didn't have far to go. Six miles or less from the cabin, Charlie had established a camp on a flat-topped hill with a natural dip in its crown, like the dent in a hat. It shielded them from whatever unlikely eyes there might be to see them, and would have afforded a view of some distance behind if they had been able to see.

When Jay untied Billy the little man looked sick and sober. He sucked in his breath and let it go in a long gasp of pain while he was being helped to the ground. Then Jay found himself trying to support him without pressing his ribs while Bowan vomited, sobbing with the effort. He half carried him to the fire and let him sink down by it when Charlie got it going. It had already been laid and ringed with rock, with extra fuel laid by.

"My gut hurts," Billy said thickly through his ruined mouth. Jay stood over him grimly, assessing his condition and trying to hold on to his rage. Anger was senseless now, when the crisis was over, but he felt it swelling in his chest like a drowning man's last breath of air. He had no one to direct it to. Dawes had done the only thing that would work with Billy's kind of undersized fighting drunk: stomp him flat. But the boy's face was painful to look at. Catherine in particular looked softened toward him. Her pitying look galled him now as much as Billy's impudence had done earlier.

She unhooked her canteen and opened it, offering it to

Billy, who swished some water around in his sour mouth and spat. Dawes, watching them jealously across the fire, smirked. His unpleasant face, made more so by a swollen and blood-rimmed mouth, mocked her. "Nursie," he croaked.

She glared at him. "Mr. Dawes, I know you must be trying to demonstrate something with that everlasting smile, but I can't decide whether it's meant to convey your brand of low cunning, or just plain stupidity! Not that I care to be enlightened."

"Why, Miz Grobart, Ma'am! I thought after that big sweet kiss you gave me back at the cabin that we was going to be friends."

"Well, we're not. And don't call me that name."

"Why, what name was that, Ma'am?"

"You know very well. My name is Crocker."

"What!" cried Dawes, affecting amazement. "You'd tell me a big story like that after I done taught you how to make biscuits?"

"And robbed and cheated me!"

"You answered to Miz Grobart sweet as pie a while back, and hung on his arm like a little vine."

Jay exploded.

"At ease, both of you! We are not going to start on another goddamned row." He took a breath and said in a more normal voice, "What the hell's got into you, Dawes? Have you gone as crazy as Bowan?" Dawes didn't answer, but withdrew to get his bedroll and saddle. Jay bit off the urge to demand that Dawes answer him as ordered. He would be mad to think there was a place for such brass arrogance here. Catherine's face, distorted by the quaking firelight, seemed to shudder at him.

He needed to get off to himself, or to get a night's sleep. At the least, he needed the control of an occupation, so he busied himself with unpacking and hobbling his and Billy's horses.

"I thought we'd all be better off to stay together until we reached South Pass," he said as he worked. "Maybe I'm wrong. If we keep at it like this, we'll be killing each other soon, and all for nothing. The money's divided. If anybody wants to go, he can just ride out and good luck to him."

He threw Billy's saddle down by the fire and unstrapped the roll, trailing it out smooth up to the saddle. "If you can keep clear of the posse and search parties, and the telegraph offices with our descriptions coming in on the wire; if you can stay out of saloons where you'll get drunk and shoot off your mouths about how rich you are, you might live long enough to get over the border and spend some of it." He looked back at Catherine dabbling at Billy's mouth with a wet rag, and an unreasoning spurt of fresh rage against them both shot through him.

"You've got your walking papers anyway, Bowan. You can get out any time, starting with now. But you'll go without your guns. I'm not going to give you another chance to prove what a smart bastard you are, somewhere behind me with them."

"You think I'm a back shooter? Is that what you think of me?" Billy sounded genuinely grieved.

"You couldn't wipe a flea's ass with what I think of you."

"I never shot anybody in my life," Billy protested, sounding near to tears in his pain. "Anyway, I can't go nowhere, yet. I told you, my gut's killing me. It's worse than busted ribs. I had them before. I think old Dawes messed up my insides some."

"You're just sore from puking up your socks," said Jay, knowing it wasn't true as he said it. But he wasn't in the sympathy business tonight.

"Haven't you got any eyes?" Catherine snapped. "You can see he's really hurt and not pretending."

Jay scowled at her without answering. He watched Billy crawl to his bed and collapse. "What about you, Dawes?" he asked. "Staying or going?"

Dawes was removing his boots. "Staying," he grunted. "Got no special place to go." Then he grinned wolfishly. "Besides, if the little man's as bad off as he makes out, we might have more money to divide pretty soon."

Billy didn't rise to the bait. Jay looked away from Dawes with distaste and met Catherine's white face again.

"What about me, Mr. Grobart?" she asked. "Do I have your gracious permission to go too?" He watched her mouth form the words and set itself stubbornly after the last one.

"Mrs. Crocker," he replied with deadly softness, "you have been the bone of contention through all of this. I wish you'd broken your neck at the start. If we weren't all either worn out or stove up, I'd stake you out on the ground, Indian fashion, and let everybody get their fill of you, since that's all they seem to want. Maybe I should have done it last night, and then left you there."

He regretted the words as soon as they were out. They were inflammatory; he saw the scene he had threatened, and she must too. She lurched to her feet, stepping on her skirt. The part of him that approved of her spirit was appalled that enough fear might have been put on her now to break it. Dawes was staring at her too, and even Charlie seemed to be waiting for one more word to set the seal of approval on an attack.

All his regrets occurred in the second it took her to get up, and then she stunned him. He was saying, "Billy brought you into this. He can take you out in the morning," when she cut in.

"That's what you want," she whispered, ignoring his last words. "You keep blaming it on the rest, but you're the one who's saying it all the time, because that's what you're thinking about all the time, isn't it? Is that what they did to your wife? Stake her out? Tie her to the bed? Do you want to get even for her, by making somebody else suffer what she did? I think you do! Well, do it then, if that's what you are—if that's what you want to be—the same kind of animal that killed your wife! Do it, or kill me, or just let me go, but stop threatening me with every breath, damn you! Stop threatening me!" Her voice had risen from a whisper to a shout, and she must have seen that she had struck something vital, because she stopped, mouth ajar, and stumbled backward into Charlie.

Jay was rigid with shock. If he could have moved at the

instant, it would have been to take that soft white throat in his hands and shut off the voice in it forever. But while he stood frozen, Charlie took her arm and swung her away from him, and she began to sob, dry racking sounds, like any woman. Charlie pushed her away to a spot at a distance from the rest and dropped her roll on the ground.

"Undo it, and get into it, and don't open your mouth again tonight, do you hear?" he whispered, shaking her to attention. "Where did you hear about his wife?"

"M-Mrs. K-Kelly told me." She was trembling as if with a chill.

"Well, you don't know what you're talking about, so shut up."

"I thought it was s-such a t-terrible thing. I felt s-sorry for him. But he—he doesn't—" Her teeth were almost chattering.

Charlie snorted softly. "Sorry for him? White Lady, you sure could have fooled me! Just don't tell him that too, or you might get your wish."

Jay, recovering from his paralysis, snatched up his bed and strode away from the light, through a scrubby growth of bushlike firs embedded in the thin soil of the hill. When he found a level spot next to a straight-sided rock, he threw his blanket up against it and sat down heavily.

After a moment he fished through his well-stocked pockets for his pipe and a light. When he found his tobacco supply, he saw it would be the last smoke he was going to get until South Pass. But he needed it now.

The obvious solution, now that he thought of it, was for him to leave. Why spend another day trying to hold together a band of people over whom he had no authority except that which was always given to an attitude of command?

And what difference did it make about her? Give her a horse, and let her take her chances getting home, or any damn place she chose. What business did he have, playing nurse, referee, and duenna to these people? His real business was north with Charlie, to find his children while there was still time to shape them back into what they were meant to be. He would tell Charlie so in the morning and they would go.

What he needed was sleep. He leaned back on the rock, eyes closed, pulling at the pipe. What he got instead was a vivid image of Catherine Crocker behind his closed eyelids. He opened his eyes and closed them again.

He could see her mouth forming the words "If that's what you are—the same kind of animal that—" and he opened them again.

It had been that way once with Cat. For months, the first year in his jail cell, he had been her prisoner, living over every moment with her, seeing every expression. But he had grown numb to it after a while and had blotted her out so effectively that in time he couldn't really remember her face any more. He could recite her features one by one, but it didn't come to life in his mind. She had faded, like an old tin photograph.

As an experiment, he tried to bring her back now.

Cat. Black hair; smooth, heavy, and straight. Black almond eyes. Warm brown skin like silk, flawless and firm all over her body. Child-woman—laughing, then solemn. Soft, stupid, lovely, docile Cat Dancing.

She would not come.

But someone else did. Nobody walked that softly except Charlie, but even he was only a town Indian. Jay heard him coming through the trees. He waited, not turning his head. He didn't want to talk or listen to any more talk now. Charlie waited too, standing like a dun ghost just at the edge of Jay's vision.

Irritated by the insistence and by his own behavior, he finally growled, "Well, what is it now?"

"Nothing. Just Bowan. I'd make a guess that he's bleeding inside. His belly's like a rock and he's passed out again."

"Christ," said Grobart.

In the morning, it was obvious to everybody that Billy wasn't going anywhere under his own power. He was semicomatose. His face was the color of raw dough where it wasn't purple with bruises. His stomach seemed swollen and rigid; and when they tried to get him on his feet he fainted. They gathered around him as Jay laid him back on his pallet.

"Leave him," said Dawes, after a long silence.

"He needs a doctor!" protested Catherine.

"He can't ride. We'd have to make a travois for him. That would take half the morning," Jay said.

"You spent more time than that picking horses," said Catherine bitterly.

He didn't reply. He was looking up at Charlie.

"If you leave him, shoot him," Charlie said.

Catherine was appalled. She forgot the silence she had enjoined on herself, lying awake in the night. She forgot the fear that had weakened her knees when she had finally stopped her runaway tongue and backed away from Jay's terrible eyes.

"Are you serious? Are you all beasts, like this savage?" she demanded. "Is that what you do for another human; your friend? Is that what you'd expect someone to do for you?"

"That's what I'd hope they'd do, if I was like him," said Charlie, still looking at Jay.

She looked down at him too. "Then you'll all be murderers

as well as thieves. And for all your threats, you haven't killed anyone, yet. You've even gone to a lot of trouble to avoid it, haven't you?" She dropped on her knees on a level with him. "Haven't you?"

"Oh hell, there's been too much talk about it," Dawes grumbled. "Leave him. He's gonna be dead by sundown, if he ain't before, and we couldn't find a doc before then if we tried."

Billy's voice interrupted them.

"Hey, Jay," he whispered. "You don't listen to them. Just tie me on my horse, like you did before. I can make it. I got stomped by a loco, once . . . when I was a kid. I made it, then. Broke six ribs . . . and my arm. Made it, though." He finished on a sigh of breath, and his eyes closed once more. Catherine leaned forward tensely, watching Grobart; waiting for him to speak.

"You can't ride a horse, boy. We'll have to make a travois. It'll take a little time."

She gave voice to her relief in a near sob. The rest shifted away, resignedly. Someone took her arm as she tried to get to her feet. She felt momentarily lightheaded, and for a second she pressed her forehead against the arm that held her. The realization, a second later, that it was Jay's arm stiffened her, and she pushed herself hastily away from him.

"Mr. Grobart, in my satchel I have some medicine that might help him, a little, if the bottle hasn't been broken." She went away quickly to search her bag for the little green bottle she kept for her migraine.

He turned it between thumb and forefinger when she gave it to him. "Elixir of Opium?"

"Laudanum. I have rather bad headaches sometimes, and nothing else seems to help. It's very strong, but of course it depends on how much pain he has, whether there will be enough."

He put it in his pocket and went to help Charlie make a travois out of the stubby scrub that was available. There was nothing of the proper length, and what there was had to be lapped half its length and spliced with all the available rope and all the straps they could pull off Billy's saddle. It was too limber to give good support, but it was all there was.

When it was finished they loaded Billy onto it. Jay had given him twenty drops out of Catherine's little bottle, but still he moaned when they moved him. Charlie, who had rigged the travois but who wouldn't touch Billy, stood by her watching them. She shot him a look of triumph when it was done. He accepted it coolly.

"You'll see, when we start to move, what real savagery is," he said to her. "It would have been more merciful to shoot him."

"Merciful? The kind of mercy you people showed at the Little Bighorn River?" she asked scornfully.

He seemed darkly amused by her example. "Even that was merciful, because it was quick. Swollen up the way he is, every little movement is going to be like a knife thrust. We're going to move him all day long, so he can die slowly, a foot at a time. Butchered alive. The way *you* people killed us savages at Sand Creek."

He was proved right about the travois. The terrain was rough, and they were following no trail. They had been keeping to the skirts of the hills, rather than descending to the stage road. Only Catherine among them was ignorant of the road's existence, but nobody suggested using it.

They made a brief stop at noon to eat and rest the horses. Jay seemed to grudge them even that. They were making a snail's progress. He and Dawes spent most of the time trying to convert the limp travois into a litter slung between Billy's dun and the pack horse, only to take it apart again when it became obvious that it wouldn't work.

When they started again, their way seemed even more twisted through the rocky outcroppings, washouts, and loose rubble from the eroding hills. Billy began to cry like a small child. Such sounds from a man always afflicted Catherine with a smothering horror and anger not unlike claustrophobia. Her own throat felt clogged with Billy's fear and pain.

"Please, please stop again and let him rest," she begged.

But Jay refused. "He'd be the same when we'd start to move again. And we can't just stay here."

"What's the matter with him?"

"I'm not a doctor. Something's broken—ruptured. His liver, spleen, intestines. I don't know what else there is, but I know that if you put a hole in any of it, you've got a dead man pretty soon."

"If he's going to die, couldn't we just stop and let him do it in peace?"

"That might take a day or two. Besides, you were the one who said it would be—what was it, beastly or savage?—to leave him."

"I meant it would be wrong to shoot him just because he's injured and in pain."

"What if he were a dog who'd been trampled by a horse? Or a horse with a broken leg? How long would you carry a crushed dog, waiting for him to die?"

"Don't! That's horrible." Catherine winced. "And it's different. They're not human. You have to put them out of their misery."

"But a man deserves all the misery he can endure. And it isn't *human* to deprive him of one second of it. Right, Mrs. Crocker?"

"Not at all, Mr. Grobart. A man's life is worth more than an animal's, and for all your cynical show, you believe it as much as I do. You decided to bring him along! You decided to keep him alive! Why did you, if you think his life is worth no more than a dog's?"

"A man's life has no more value than what the rest of the world is willing to pay, in trouble or forbearance, to let him go on living. I don't know what value he could have for you, Mrs. Crocker, but I think you'll be dropping the price before long. You'd like to keep all your little Sunday-school notions about human life, but it costs you too much now to listen to him cry. I think you'll sell him cheap by morning, if not before. You'll be asking Charlie to be a good savage and cut his throat quietly, tonight!"

Catherine flushed, but managed to say evenly, "Very clever,

to turn the argument to what I'd do. I scarcely have the influence to move Charlie to kill a fly. But you do. Charlie said 'shoot him' and you said 'build a travois.' Why? What is his value to you, Mr. Grobart? Did you just bring him along to punish him for his sins? For making trouble for you?"

Jay dug his spurs into his horse's flanks and left her to ride alone. When he was gone she found herself near tears, but she couldn't deny a small feeling of triumph. It was the first time she had been able to put him on the defensive, and he knew it. That made the victory all the sweeter. And he hadn't closed off the dialogue by issuing his usual threats.

Charlie's voice brought her back to herself. "Still counting coup, White Lady?" He came alongside easily.

"Counting what?"

"Coup."

"I don't know what you're talking about," she said distantly, supposing that she was about to become the butt of some vulgar joke.

"Well, it's a kind of test of courage—you might even think it was a game—that some of my savage ancestors thought up. In battle, you see, a brave will sometimes throw away his lance and bow and ride straight for his enemy, with nothing but his coupstick. The enemy is armed and ready to kill him, if he gets the chance. The brave tries to get close enough to him to hit him with his coupstick and still get away with his own life.

"The important thing is to know your enemy. If he isn't liable to kill you when you make your run, it won't count." He paused, his black eyes dancing with malice. "Now, you play the game real good, but you use a different weapon: your tongue. But I wonder if you know how to pick your enemy."

"I hope I haven't any enemies." She wished he'd go away and let her alone.

"You're making a mistake. You need an enemy, to count coup on. Why, you need an enemy like you need a friend. You don't believe that? I knew an old chief once who said that, to make your soul, you must have a friend you would rejoice to die for, and an enemy you would rejoice to make die."

"A very pretty piece of heathen philosophy," she sniffed.

"Thank you. I made it up myself, just now, because I thought you'd like it. Not that it isn't true, for all that."

"Well, I don't like it, and I don't think it's true."

"Surely you've noticed all the people who go through their lives doing nothing but trying to make a lasting enemy?"

"You're thinking of yourself, no doubt?"

He laughed. She was nettled, but then she realized that, for the length of time he had been provoking her, she hadn't been torn by Billy's moans. She had been on the edge of nervous explosion herself, and his petty warfare had steadied her. She appraised him with sudden curiosity. He had been inviting her to direct her "coups," as he called them, at him rather than at Jay. Or so it seemed. Jay consulted Charlie, young enough to be his son, and no one else. Charlie knew when he was needed as a buffer, or a lightning rod, and acted to protect Jay. Yet they scarcely seemed friendly otherwise. It was a curious partnership.

"You speak very well," she said, as a peace offering. "Were you educated at one of the mission schools?"

He snorted. "Heap many thanks, White Lady."

She ignored that. "Were you?" she asked again. She felt he was losing some sort of struggle with himself: the resentment of all the ways of the white man's world opposing the pride he felt in having mastered some of them. Pride seemed to edge out the other.

"I was born at Laramie. I grew up hearing English spoken every day. But I never went to the mission school. I got my schooling from an old white man with an unusual sense of gratitude. My father was an Army scout at the Fort. When I was ten, or thereabouts, he was killed in a skirmish with some of his own people. He might not have died, but he put himself to the trouble of rescuing a white soldier, the old man's son. 'Who, but for him,' as they say in the books, would have died there instead. So the old man took in the little orphan redskin and tried to show his thanks by making a decent, law-abiding, imitation white man out of him. It didn't turn out the way he planned, as you see. But he meant well. White men always mean well. And he was kind to me. Does that touch your heart, Mrs. Crocker, Ma'am?" His smile was twisted, but she saw in it suddenly that he was still very young.

"Yes, it does. Who was he?"

"Why, haven't you guessed? Mr. Dickens couldn't have improved on the choice. Think, now! No? He was Jay Grobart's father."

"What happened to him?"

"He died, while his son was—away. He was very old."

Jay raised his hand to signal another brief rest, and Charlie left her to consult with him. He didn't return to continue the conversation. Dawes rode beside her for a while. He looked red eyed and inattentive. She wondered if he could be carrying something other than water in his canteen.

Billy was unconscious.

The sun had become a sullen red eye that watched them through a dust haze building up in the west when they came upon an abandoned mine and cabin hidden in the hills. The remains of a sluice box told of fresh water somewhere nearby. The litter of rusted and broken tools and the gaping cabin door told them they were free to enter.

Jay slung the food and utensil pack at Catherine's feet without a word and went to find the water, leading away the horses with Dawes's help. Charlie, having inspected the cabin fireplace and found it sound, picked up a corroded ax from the yard and began to pile up an adequate fuel supply, using the sluice box for a start.

Catherine laid out her stores in readiness for fire and water, then went to crouch by Billy. She was both repelled and racked by his condition.

His breathing was stentorian now. His face and hands were swollen and he stank with fever. He bore no resemblance to the cheerful, vulgar, garrulous person who had kidnapped her unintentionally; the agile young blood who had thrown her to the ground and kissed her. She shuddered, remembering. Pity for him swelled in her throat, but there was horror too. So much that, if he had opened those sunken eyes then, she would have fled at once, as from a staring corpse.

Charlie brought her wood, and Jay water. She did what she could with the unpalatable food. Dawes didn't offer to make biscuits again, and she had forgotten the proportions, so she tried to remember how Mrs. Kelly had made her corn bread, since it was fresher in her mind. The results did not displease her. Her coffee smelled delicious and tasted almost as good as it smelled. She put out of her mind the thought that she had fallen in very readily with Grobart's decision to make her their chief cook and skillet washer, when she had sworn to oppose him in anything that wouldn't get her killed. She shrugged. If she had to do anything, she liked to be able to say she did it well, that was all.

After the meal she sat with drawn-up knees before the fire, half-asleep. Jay put a can of water on the hearth, and when it began to steam he produced shaving equipment from his kit, including a small mirror. He removed the short, heavy beard, wincing at the pull of the big razor. He left his mustache, trimmed with a little pair of scissors, and had just finished smoothing his grizzled hair with a flat military brush when he noticed her covetous concentration on the mirror.

He packed the brush and mirror back into the leather box, then held it out to her. She snatched it eagerly, and set about warming water for herself.

"Hey, what are you dudin' up for?" rumbled Dawes from the door. "Sis tell you she didn't like chin whiskers?"

"They served their purpose," said Jay. "I'm going to try to find a camp or settlement down along the road, and I figure to have better luck if I don't look like the man the stage drivers will all have a description of by now." He unrolled his pack, and took out a clean shirt of a different color and a canvas jacket.

Dawes blinked at him in disbelief. "A camp? What in hell do you want with a camp?"

"To see if there's a doctor anywhere near."

"I'll be goddamned! You'll go down the road and find a

doctor for a man that's just as good as dead right now, and the doctor'll go back and tell everybody that there's four strangers and a draggle-assed city woman up here, where nobody's supposed to live. You really think shaving off your whiskers will put him off the track?"

Jay shrugged. "If I find a doctor, you'll hear me coming back with him before he can see you. You and Charlie wil take her and the three horses and hide in the mine until he's gone. I'll get him to drive a wagon up here so he can take Billy away with him. You'll have plenty of warning."

"What about her, meantime?"

"Charlie's going to watch her, meantime." Catherine stopped brushing her hair. Charlie was outside someplace.

"*Charlie's* going to watch her," repeated Dawes, with a heavy inflection of irony.

"That's what I said."

"Well, does he get any other special privileges you might have forgot to mention?"

Jay continued to give his attention to his shirt buttons. "Nothing I can think of," he said imperturbably. "You take care of the horses; he'll take care of her; she'll watch after Billy."

"I don't like the arrangement."

"It'll work out. Those horses won't give you a bit of trouble."

"That ain't what I mean, and you damn well know it."

"I know what you mean, Dawes. Mrs. Crocker is going to stay in the cabin, with Billy. Charlie is going to sit outside and watch, or catch up on his sleep. I imagine you'll go fair shares with him on that. Because if you have the energy for anything else, by God, you can take the ride down the road. That might be the way to do it, at that. After all, you were the one that put Billy in the shape he's in now."

"And leave you and your Injun blood brother to take off with the money as soon as I'm out of sight?" Dawes complained at once.

"Take your share with you."

"Yeah, well . . ." Dawes was at a loss for a second, then his little eyes lit up again. "But if old Billy dies, there'll be more to divide up. And I want my fair share of that."

"Then I guess you better get out there and sit on the damned saddlebags while Charlie guards the horses. That way, nobody can get away with anything."

"Damn right I will! Can't trust a damn Injun like that!" He withdrew from the doorway with a look of such determined vigilance that Catherine smiled in spite of herself, and found she was sharing her moment of amusement with Jay.

"Dawes gets his head turned around pretty easy," he said. "I trust you'll remember that and not get in a panic if he comes back. You can always latch the door, but it might be better just to look calm and talk him dizzy. You've got enough gall and brains to hold off a dozen Daweses."

"Thank you very much."

"I meant it as a compliment. I'm not against women with backbone."

"Can't I come with you?" she asked suddenly. He didn't seem to consider the question worth answering, because he knelt to strap up his pack again, then reached for his shabby black hat. Without the beard he looked less grim to her, but older and more tired. His skin seemed too tightly drawn, and there were lines of strain or bitterness around his mouth that hadn't been visible before. She wondered how old he really was. He looked closer to fifty than to forty now.

Billy's heavy breathing filled the silence between them as her question went unanswered. He stood up, settling the dusty hat. "I'm flattered that you prefer me to Dawes."

"Do you ever really intend to let me go free?"

"You're an inconvenient guest, but I can't part with you—yet."

"Or ever?"

"Well, prospects look good for South Pass, if we don't run into anybody before then. Cheer up. We'll be seeing the last of each other in three or four days, and you'll go home with a story you can tell over the teacups for the rest of your life."

"Yes, of course. Billy's death will make such amusing table talk. How shall I end the tale, do you think? 'And they were all captured and hanged from the nearest telegraph pole'? Or 'Mr. Grobart was sent back to prison, to spend the rest of his life'?"

"Which would you prefer?"

"Neither. I don't wish you any harm. In your own way, and considering the circumstances, you've shown me more courtesy than—well, I'm just tired of being—baggage. I want to go home, to my own home, and have some peace." He didn't reply, and after a moment brushed past her and out the door. She ran to it.

"When will you be back?" she called. But he didn't answer that, either. In the twilight, he mounted his weary bay and, after a few words to Charlie that she couldn't hear, turned downhill and was lost to sight beyond a stand of dark pines.

How seldom he answered her questions. Now that she considered it, he seldom answered anybody's questions, or spoke at all, except to issue orders. Yet they seemed to have said more to each other than she could account for. A moment ago it had been on the tip of her tongue to tell him something about Willard, even to compare them. She had never gossiped about her life with Willard to anyone, not even her father. Even if she had been so inclined, Papa would never have stood for a word against his meal ticket.

She realized that Grobart never asked questions that were meant to be answered, either. They were often only ironic or sarcastic punctuations to other people's speech. But she had seen the questions once or twice in those attentive eyes that examined her, yet wouldn't comment on what they saw.

Did he despise her, see her for the shrew she was; compare her with his stoical Indian wife? He had said he wasn't "against women with backbone." Did he admire her, then?

A hot wave of shame surged through her suddenly, scorching her face and making her heart pound. What a pitiful thing she must be—how poor in love indeed—if the approval of a bandit could move her so.

She busied herself with examining Billy. He was in a deep coma. She felt his forehead gingerly and found it hot and dry with the fever. She rinsed out the piece of flannel she had used as a washcloth and soaked it with cool water from the canteen to mop his face and throat, then laid it across his brow. He didn't respond to her touch at all.

In a way his lack of response relieved her, because she had no idea what else she could do for him. He was beyond needing opium now. Even if Jay Grobart could find a doctor, he would scarcely be able to do anything except join the rest of them in watching Billy die. And she didn't really believe there was a doctor to be found. Except for the Kellys, she had seen no sign of people living in this waste. There had been no rooftops, no chimney smoke, no fences. What doctor lived where there were no patients?

Why had he gone to look for one, then? So he needn't watch Billy die? To prove to her that he wasn't a "savage"? Absurd. He didn't have to prove himself to his own prisoner. To himself, then?

What if he wasn't coming back? What if he just meant to leave her here with Dawes and go on to whatever he had for a goal? Maybe Charlie would slip away later and join him, and she'd be left here with a dying man and a—what? What was Dawes? How was he any different from Grobart? They were the same, weren't they? They were together in all this. What real difference was there between them?

She looked at his pack in the corner. Of course he was coming back. He hadn't taken that with him, or the money.

She was ashamed of her fear and even more ashamed of the relief she felt to know he would return.

She busied herself with cleaning up the supper things, then settled by the hearth to take what comfort she could from brushing her heavy hair as she waited, until it began to feel like silk again instead of snarled yarn.

Coleman Dawes didn't bother her, being occupied with watching and taunting Charlie. When she finished braiding her hair there was nothing else to do, so she made her bed on the floor in front of the fire and curled up on it to watch the flames.

Oddly, she felt relaxed. Her mind, for once, wasn't running in circles of despair, looking for a way to escape. Nor did she think of Willard, or what she would do if she was ever free of him. Left to drift, her thoughts came to rest on Jay Grobart again, and she was content to let them dwell, in a not unfriendly way, on some of the many puzzles he presented. She fell asleep.

When she heard the voices she thought Grobart had returned, and marveled that he had made the trip so quickly. She didn't feel as if she had been asleep long. Had he found a doctor so easily? The country must be more heavily populated than it looked.

She started for the door, but as she reached it some sense of caution made her pause before opening it and listen again. Then she knew that, whoever it was out there, he was unexpected, unwelcome, and drunk.

That slurred, wheedling tone was unmistakable. How many times in her life had she heard it? Her father had used the same voice to wheedle household money out of her pocket, or to protest his sobriety as she more than half carried him up the stairs to his bed before Willard came home.

But these voices—and she had realized by now that there was more than one of them—familiar as they were, were not speaking in English. She put her eye to the crack of the door.

There were four Indians standing in the yard, between Dawes and Charlie. The wavering light of the campfire before them threw such shadows across their faces that they seemed to be changelings, their features shifting from goblin to human and back as they swayed and gestured.

She held her breath against an outcry, and felt blindly for the door latch. It was undone. She slid it into place with all the care she had once given to slipping the key out of her father's bedroom door. Then she pressed against the door to watch and listen.

They talked, swaying and snickering. Charlie answered at some length. It was all no good. She couldn't understand a word. What did they want? Dawes, she noticed, said nothing at all. He stood licking his lips nervously under the scrutiny of one of the braves. She could see the sweat glistening on his face, and the knowledge that he was as frightened as she did her no good at all.

The Indians were all carrying rifles, she noticed belatedly. As Charlie spoke to them, perhaps inviting them to sit down, for he did so himself, they began to wander around, examining the yard debris, poking at the saddles and packs with their gun barrels. When they came near Dawes, he backed up a step and sat down on the saddlebags containing the money.

Perhaps he had only lost his balance, but it was the wrong move. They fell on him and the bags with loud cries that nearly drowned out his own.

"Let it go! Don't fight them!" shouted Charlie over the rumpus. Dawes went as limp as his shirt when one of them poked a rifle into his belly. They pulled the bags out from under him and tore one of them open, like children with an eagerly expected gift. They were disappointed.

Surely they knew what money was, thought Catherine. Even a renegade Indian knows money when he sees it. But if they knew, they weren't pleased with their find. Yelling whatever words expressed scorn, disbelief, and disappointment in their tongue, they threw the money in wads at Dawes. Then, tearing off the paper bands, they threw the loose bills up into the air and broadside into the fire.

Dawes yelled like a maniac and tried to snatch back what he could, but they tripped him up and rained more money down on him, until one of them found the gold.

Gold was more to their taste, though they continued to search for something else. But they stuffed the gold coins into their leather pouches by the handful, while Dawes crawled on his knees after the fluttering paper. Suddenly she heard him say something that froze her. Charlie got slowly to his feet at the words, still looking unconcerned.

"Listen, boys! I know what you want! Listen. I got something better for you! You didn't expect to find it out here, either. Go in the house!" Still on his knees, he stretched out one long arm, pointing. "The cabin! It's in there! Better than bullets or whiskey! Go on!"

"Dawes, shut up. You're going to get us killed for sure, if they find her." Charlie's voice was a little ragged, but still he tried to keep the fear out of it. "Put that finger down, or stick it up your nose, you bust-head bastard," he grated. "They're just having a little fun with us. When they see we don't have any whiskey or ammunition, they'll steal a little food and go away."

But one of the young drunks had made sense out of Dawes's stabbing finger and turned to the cabin curiously. Charlie shouted to distract them, and one turned casually and fired at him, belly high. Charlie fell, and Catherine tried to stifle her cry, but the brave outside the door heard it. His shout of discovery silenced them all. He repeated the word. She couldn't quite grasp the sound of it, but she knew it meant her. There was soft laughter after the word, and pressure against the door.

Catherine stepped back from it and looked around for a weapon. She felt cold, almost calm. Her mind seemed to be turning over very rapidly, while her body moved very slowly, like someone in a bad dream. She looked for Billy's guns, but they were gone from his holsters. There was a stick or two of kindling, but nothing else. If she were to kill herself, she would have to do it with a rusty can, a tiny fire, or a hand mirror. No. The razor. It was in the same box. She picked up the box and opened it as they battered at the door.

She touched the razor reluctantly, wondering, if she slashed her wrists, would she be dead before they got to her? In the upturned mirror beside it, she could see her own blank eyes.

The banging stopped. There was a pause, then a crooning voice called to her entreatingly. The others laughed. The voice continued in a singsong, provoking outbursts of raucous merriment from its audience with every phrase. Obscenity, like drunkenness, sounded the same in any language.

There was a bare whisper of movement to her right. She turned her head and saw the little shuttered window at the back of the cabin; the only one. The small noise was repeated. One of them had found the window. He would burst in the shutters and be in the room in a moment. There would be no need to break down the door. Without thinking, she stooped and picked up a piece of the kindling, letting the forgotten razor box slip from her fingers.

The young brave pushed open the shutters and grinned at her. She was holding the stick of wood hidden in her skirt at her side. She moved toward him carefully, to his delight. He saw that he would be first, while his companions were still working at the door. He didn't make any noise; only put his foot up on the narrow sill. As he bent his head, gaining leverage to hoist himself in, she hit him with the stick as hard as she could, slamming it down with both hands on the left side of his head, behind the ear. The dull sound of the blow sickened her.

He hung over the sill with both hands, neither in nor out of the room. She hit him again, tight lipped, and again the blow was the only sound between them. He didn't make a cry as he fell in on the floor.

But when he slowly rose to hands and knees and began to crawl to her, one hand raised in defense or appeal, she lost her nerve and began to scream. She had struck to kill; she had thought she killed him. His insistence horrified her. It was like smashing an insect and watching its legs and antennae continue to imitate life.

Her screams brought a renewed ramming at the door, until the latch gave way and the three other assailants half fell into the room.

In a sweeping glance they took in Billy, herself, and their comrade, now slumped on the floor. The stunned brave got three hoots of derision for his trickery. Billy's life did not outlast their surprise at finding him apparently asleep in the midst of such clamor. The one who had aimed his rifle at Charlie so carelessly fired again, into the blanketed bundle, and Billy screamed for the last time.

Catherine screamed with him, in anguish, as she was caught up by one of them. She tried to beat at his face, but he pinned her arms to her sides with one long arm and pulled her head back by her long braid until she thought her neck would break. She quit struggling and he carried her outside. The others ransacked the tiny cabin.

He would have torn open her jacket with one hand, but the sturdy buttons were too tightly sewn. She began to fight again as soon as he released her arms, and he was obliged to throw her to the ground and straddle her before he could use both hands on the cloth.

She felt the jacket burst open and her jabot ties rip. Her stock was caught on his fingers and nearly choking her. He pulled the false shirt away and tore her chemise down to the hem. But her corset stopped him. He tugged at it, but it was laced in the back, and the stout double seams and stays were adamant.

As she kicked and struggled to free her hands, he chuckled at it, puzzled. Then he reached back for his knife to slash it through. She jerked one arm away from him and clumsily hacked at the knife with her open hand, thinking he intended to kill her with it. For a second, he was clumsy too, and it went spinning out of his hand. He raised himself off her, stretching to reach it, and blind reflex drove her knee hard up between his legs.

He cried out and fell off her, and at the same time there was a sharp crack. Catherine had an instant vision of the assassination of Charlie by a cracking rifle, and the same blind instinct for survival rolled her over and brought her stumbling to her feet, running. Sightless, mindless, she ran; her clothes fluttering in tatters around her bare breasts, her mouth open for screaming, but with no breath for it. She could only run, away from terror, butchery, and death, into the darkness, for her life.

She heard but made no account of the rapid crack and whine of a repeating rifle, or the rough yells of surprise and confusion behind her, tearing her clothes and her flesh on invisible thorny bushes that sprouted from the cracks and low places in the ground.

She climbed, not knowing she climbed or thinking about how to make her escape, except that it was the safe, dark, quiet way to life. She left the grove of thin pines and clawed for a hold on a steep slope festooned with the briery growth that might have been wild rose. At the top of the incline her strength began to give out. Shock was setting in; and after another forced scramble up a gentler rise, she found nearly level ground and stumbled along it crazily until her legs buckled under her and spilled her into a shallow trough hollowed by the wind and filled with twisted, dessicated junipers. She pitched into it, rolling to their roots, and lay still.

The twin talons of fear and fatigue gripped her. A thousand painful contractions tore at her muscles. They passed beyond her control. She couldn't move from where she lay under the leggy shrub. Breathing took her entire strength. She fainted, or fell asleep in little snatches, and woke still helpless. If they came they could kill her now, while she looked on with dazed, blank eyes. But there were no following feet. Down below, all the noise had stopped. Blackness.

Her father leaned over her, watery eyes awash with self-pity, and accused her of some trivial deceit. She struggled to defend herself, but his complaint turned wide and general, embracing all her faults. She needed to tell him something very important if he would only let her, but it wasn't until he turned away that she could remember what it was. "Wait!

Papa, wait! Help me!" she cried—thought she cried—but he was gone, and her voice was frozen in her throat. Blackness.

She was dry, so terribly dry she couldn't swallow, and Willard wouldn't give her a drink. "Clean yourself up, first," he said, drinking from the side of the cut-glass pitcher that had been Mama's. She saw he was drinking sand. "You've been down in the gutter, rolling with your father, I see. Just look at you!" She looked, amazed. He knew that she always tried to keep herself clean. Clean and decent. Now she was torn and disgraced. "You made me this way!" she cried. "You made me do it! I never wanted to be this way!" He looked at her with such petulance that she screamed, scarlet with rage, "He's better than you! Even a savage is better than you! I wish he'd rape me naked in the middle of the street, with all your friends around to see. I'd tell them all, even this is better than Willard!" Then she broke, and pleaded with him. "Oh, please, Will, I'm sorry. I'm sorry. Please come and help me, please, help me, please help me or I'll die!"

He was gone, leaving her shaking with dry sobs, for what she couldn't remember. There was someone else she could call, but she couldn't remember who. No, there was no one. They were all gone or dead.

No more phantoms came. She lay forgotten, quivering from time to time with cold and sobs as her nerves slackened their hold on her body.

Her hands found her nakedness and she covered her breasts; but not because they were naked, only because they were cold. She slept, or died; hours of oblivion drugged her. She could no longer move.

When she heard her name being called again, she didn't want to answer. The new voice seemed harsh and stern. More accusations? No, thank you. Don't call me.

"Catherine!"

"No," she whispered.

"Catherine!" He was closer. He saw the pale flutter of an edge of torn ruffle signaling weakly from the ground.

"No," she said again. There was a scraping of boots on rock, and someone above her. She squeezed her eyes shut.

"Catherine." He took her wrists and began to pull her out of the hole. Dried juniper foliage rasped across her face, making her fight at him, weakly. But he pulled at her until he had dragged her to the edge of the hole, then grasped her arms and drew her up to him.

She opened her eyes reluctantly and knew his face. Her mind fumbled for his name and found it. As he held her against him and she clung to him, she whispered his name over and over, as a talisman against the dark, her face pressed tightly into his shoulder.

He had water for her tortured throat, and after the hard security of his arms water was the only thing she wanted. As soon as her throat was eased she reached out for him again, to be wrapped in the blind safety of that embrace.

He held her for a long time that way, rocking her a little, until his knees ached from kneeling on the sharp pebbles under them. When he moved to relieve them, her arms relaxed their hold and slid away from his body. He looked down at her.

"My God, if you're going to sleep, we might as well crawl back in your den. I could use a little of it, myself."

He eased her back down and slid in after her, cushioning her against him and making a pillow for her of his one arm. She drew the other securely about her again before she slept.

There were no dreams at all.

Harvey Lapchance's request for temporary authority to conduct an investigation of the robbery from the point of its occurrence was granted three times over his expectations. He was a little taken aback at his sudden eminence, and more than a little amused by it.

From the Carter County sheriff came a wire making him a deputy on the spot, with full powers to act in the absence of the sheriff, who was obliged to appear in court the next day in Rock Springs as principal witness for the prosecution.

The sheriff, unable to get the immediate aid of the Army, had taken the further precaution of wiring the Territorial Governor, advising him of the crime and of Harvey's new capacity, and requesting that he lend Harvey any such assistance as was available and/or should be deemed necessary.

The Governor promptly wired the Express agent, informing him that he was to consider himself forthwith a United States Deputy Marshal, acting on the Governor's behalf, with full powers, etc. Confirmation to follow.

The Express Company, mindful of Harvey's past experience with the Pinkerton Agency, was happy to consider him its detective-in-residence, the regular holder of that position nearest to the spot being laid up in a St. Louis hospital at the moment with a fractured femur. Harvey was warmly regarded and offered all possible assistance at the soonest date by all three sources. Only the railroad held its own counsel.

Thus it was to be Caesar, he thought; in Point of Rocks, Wyoming Territory, population fifty-some odd, and a few drifters.

He carried all three telegrams over to the Gem and laid them on the bar in front of Ed Hape. It was very doubtful whether Ed could actually read, as he pretended to, but he heard the general import of the three directives gravely.

"Well," he said, "it looks like you've become Head Tumble Bug of the Shit Works around here. Do you mean to keep on drinking clabbered milk after all this?"

"I believe I'll risk a small beer. Where's Crocker?"

"Upstairs asleep, I guess. Listen, Harv, does he have to stay here? Crying drunks are hard on business. And there's always the chance that somebody will get mean and try to shut him off the hard way. He was sobbing in the corner until after the sweeper left last night. I had to put him to bed."

"Well, he's had a few bad shocks. His wife seems to have run off and left him, and that morning, even before he knew about her, he discovered that his back-east clients had got fooled out of close to half a million dollars by those two crooks that showed him the mesa. They salted the place with every kind of gem stone you can think of. Sprinkled ruby chips in all the prairie-dog holes. Cheap stuff. He caught on when one of his crew found a piece that already had facet cuts on it. He thinks now they probably picked up the stuff in Europe somewhere; Holland, probably. It was real sucker bait, and it seems that his clients had accepted it on the strength of his own report, and he hadn't actually been up to the place when he made it. He'd just seen some of the better 'samples.' So he's got to tell them, now."

He regretted having strong-armed Crocker into helping form the first search party. The man was going to be trouble, and now that he had this additional reason to make himself scarce for his clients, there was no way to get rid of him. For the first twenty-four hours in town, Willard Crocker had had the ear and sympathy of everybody, as the story of his stolen wife was told. His loss was magnified in his own mind by their concern. Whatever private quarrel had sent her flying was forgotten. She was his beloved, his peerless treasure, the epitome of womanhood, torn away from him by the lawless scum who had robbed the U.P. train. No wonder he wound up the second night crying in the beer his audience provided. And no wonder the sympathy of the town withered. Most of them had a more direct interest in the stolen money. The hills were covered now with self-appointed groups looking for some trace of the thieves.

Reluctantly, Harvey set down his empty glass and climbed the stairs to Willard Crocker's room. He knocked twice before there was an answer inside. The bedsprings creaked, and unshod feet approached the door.

Crocker's face was gray under the uncombed hair and the blond stubble that covered his full jaw. He stank, as did the whole room, with beer and stale air. The windows were shut tight. The room itself was a shambles of hastily dumped trunks, equipment, and paraphernalia from the disbanded camp.

Harvey told him briefly about his authorization to conduct a legal search for the criminals. He had been up studying maps of the area half the night, and in spite of the barrenness of the region he was inclined to favor a search of the Red Desert, up to the Antelope Hills, rather than the southern hills leading down to the Uintas. But the Uintas were the sheriff's first choice, and Harvey had no alternative but to follow his orders.

Willard nodded repeatedly as Harvey outlined his proposed

search. His red-rimmed eyes were wide and solemn; his mouth formed a tighter line. A good deal of the pomposity that had irritated Harvey was gone out of him this morning. He was convinced by now that his wife was dead.

"If we find her on the desert," he said, "I'm not sure how the thing is done, but I want to bring her body back and take it home for burial. If there is anything to—I mean, how long does a body last—out there?" He shuddered, sitting on the edge of the bed, his head in his hands. "I can't think about it! I can't bear to think about her out there, somewhere, with the vultures. But that's what I have to know, and prepare for. How do you bring back—what's left?"

"Mr. Crocker," said Harvey uncomfortably, "there's no use getting yourself worked up about things like that, yet. We don't have any evidence, so far, to prove Mrs. Crocker isn't still alive. Since they didn't kill her at once, they may very well—"

"Oh no, Mr. Lapchance! Oh no. She would never allow them to shame her. Never. You see, I know my wife, and I know she would rather be dead than let herself be—I think she might even take her own life, first. Even with me, she's always been—" (cold as a bedbug, thought Harvey involuntarily)—"very modest, very pure minded," Willard finished lamely. He looked up suddenly. "But she will be avenged, Mr. Lapchance. I've promised her that. Look. I want to show you something."

He bent over a pile of miscellaneous equipment in the corner of the room, and dragged from the bottom of it a canvas case for a rifle. From it he drew a strange-looking double-barreled gun with an elegantly carved, slender stock. He held it out to Harvey, who took it, puzzled. Its barrels were one above the other; the top one had a revolving cylinder, like a handgun, and the two barrels were of different gauges. He scowled at its freakishness.

"Looks like one of those fancy-Dan pieces that some of the rich Rebels carried."

"In a way. It *is* a LeMat design, but I had it custom made for me in Paris, by his gunmaker, Girard, after the War. It carries nine shots for the rifle in that cylinder; .44 caliber. The barrel underneath is a .60-caliber smoothbore that can be loaded with ball or shot. It's a combination of every kind of weapon you can shoot. I've used it for hunting. It's a splendid weapon, once you get the hang of it. Notice, it has a single hammer and trigger that fires either barrel."

He took it back with grim pride. "Yes sir. My wife will not go unavenged, if fortune puts me within range of the men who took her." He slipped the gun back into its case, which was banded with scarlet leather on the white canvas and had a carrying handle of the same material, and threw it on the bed.

"Would you like to see a picture of Catherine?" he asked suddenly. Harvey nodded with more enthusiasm, because he was curious to see what kind of woman would be stupid enough to pick Crocker for a mate, and still spirited enough to leave him out here. Willard opened Catherine's trunk and took a gray cardboard folder off the top of a pile of lavender-scented garments. "I was looking at it last night. She had it made when we were in Denver earlier this year, to send to her father, but I guess she forgot about it." He passed it to Harvey.

"Harv!" came Ed's voice from downstairs. "There's another telegram for you, from Rawlins, the kid says. It's still coming in. You want him to bring it here, or you want to hustle over and answer it right away?"

"I'll go get it myself, Ed, thanks. Be right down. Excuse me, Mr. Crocker. When you're dressed and have had your breakfast, come over to the office and we'll talk about equipping our party. Good morning, sir."

He clattered down the stairs and ran back to his office, where the operator handed him a message advising him that searchers from Rawlins were on the lookout for the fugitives as far north as Muddy Gap and as far south as Sulphur Springs, with no word or sight of them as yet. Several parties of ranchers and even a few miners from the area had volunteered to comb the southern hills.

He sent his acknowledgment and thanks in return, and walked into his back-room home to organize himself for travel.

He was not disappointed by the lack of success the various groups of searchers were having. He would have been disappointed if Grobart had picked any of those well-traveled routes for his escape. Anyone, with a little luck, could rob a train and get away safe for a while. The interest lay in such a person as Grobart having done it, and in discovering what sort of orderly retreat from the crime his nature would have demanded.

Besides, he wanted to take Grobart himself.

When he was in his room, he realized that he still had Mrs. Crocker's picture in his hand, unexamined. He sat down on his cot to look at it. He looked at it for several minutes.

She wore a high-necked summer dress of some white stuff, tucked and ruffled down the front like a baby's gown. Her hair seemed darker in the picture than its description. It was softly dressed, with an artful back lighting by the photographer bringing out an aura of fine hairs straying from the body of it. Her eyes were wide spaced and dark lashed; very level and a bit haughty. Her mouth had a child's look, though, in spite of her maturity. It was full, but firm pressed, yet the corners of it looked as if they had been willing to smile if the occasion had not been so solemn.

She was too thin for fashion. Her cheeks were flat and her chin pointed and singular. She looked like a very firm-minded young woman; far too sensible to think of killing herself to preserve her honor, as her husband had insisted. But, of course, pictures were no infallible guides to character. She could easily be a fool.

He wondered what Grobart was doing about her.

# 9

"YOU'LL HAVE to move your head. My arm's dead from the shoulder down," he murmured when he felt her to be awake. She leaped a little, nevertheless, and scrambled away over him, out of their earth bed. She had been awake just long enough to realize her disheveled condition to the fullest. She huddled away from him, feeling repulsive and filthy to the limit of her imagination. She plucked the remnants of her jacket around her as he crawled out after her and sat with outstretched legs, rubbing his numb arm. He didn't look at her.

"If you'll just help me get out of this jacket," he remarked, "you can wrap it around your maidenly modesty. Otherwise I don't see how the hell you're going to get down the hill again." She blushed, but laughed, and accepted the jacket gratefully. He concentrated on flexing his arm and hand until she was buttoned up; then he stood, pulling her after him. "Come on. Let's find the coffeepot and the skillet."

Halfway down she stopped, remembering some of the past night. "Jay, what about the others: Mr. Dawes and Charlie?"

"Dawes ran out last night when the shooting started. Grabbed up a saddlebag and hightailed it."

"Shooting?"

"You were in a hurry, weren't you? What do you think became of your visitors?"

She tried to remember what she'd thought, and couldn't. "No, I didn't even wonder, I'm afraid. You killed them?"

"I saw them when I was a couple of miles from camp, and fell back to see which way they were going to go. I could tell their blood was up about something. From what I found on them, I guess there are a couple of dead miners or saddle tramps somewhere between here and Farson. They saw the smoke from Charlie's fire coming up over the trees. I'd seen it too, but this time I hadn't thought it would matter. I left my horse a half mile from camp so I could come in quietly. I should have come in like a troop of cavalry."

"What about Charlie? I saw him fall."

He started downhill again, ahead of her.

"Charlie's dead."

The camp appalled her. The bodies of the four Indians sprawled around the yard like actors in the last scene of some old tragedy. Only Charlie was missing from his place. There was a long bundle wrapped in a gray Army blanket lying at the entrance to the hillside mine. She heard a harsh croak overhead as she was looking at it, and a heavy-bodied brown bird swept across the clearing above them. She shivered.

"Let's just get the things we need and leave here," she begged. "Even a mile away, and the coffee would be bearable." She started for the cabin but he caught her arm.

"You stay here and I'll get the packs. It isn't very pleasant in there."

When he was at the door she called out quickly, "Jay, I need clothes—not mine—something practical. Could I use Billy's? I mean, his extra ones, if he had any?"

He nodded and went in. So she was spared seeing the things that had been done to Billy's body. She stood listening to the flies singing their hymns to the dead.

They packed their immediate necessities back up the hill over the mine shaft to the tiny spring-fed rivulet that had once fed the sluice box. The horses were already there.

While Jay sat cleaning and reloading his rifle and checking the unused revolver, she put herself to the task of making breakfast with such a pleasing efficiency that she found herself humming under her breath as she worked. She stopped guiltily when she realized it, and darted a quick look in his direction to see if he had noticed the lapse.

When they had eaten, he left her and returned to the camp below. "This will take a while," he said.

As soon as he was out of sight she began to strip off her torn, filthy clothes. The possibility of being seen nagged at her needlessly, but the purling water was a luxury she couldn't forgo. She squatted by the shallow stream with Jay's jacket close at hand for instant cover and lathered herself hurriedly with the strong-smelling soap from his kit.

By the time she was clean, her apprehensions of being discovered had eased enough that she dared to sit on the sandy bank until the sun dried her, while she combed and braided her hair into two plaits and tied it with the ribbons from her chemise, since her last hairpins had vanished during her flight the night before.

Billy's clean clothes still bore a good deal of his odor, redolent of the stable, but they were a reasonable fit except that there wasn't a belt to hold up the pants and her waist was considerably smaller than his. She searched her carpetbag for a pair of stockings she could twist together for a substitute. Looking at her belongings there, she felt a sense of estrangement from them, as if they, and not these faded jeans, belonged to someone besides herself. With the exception of the stockings and her own brush and comb, there seemed to be nothing in the bag the least bit useful to her now.

When she was dressed she bundled up her old clothes, including the castoff corset, and stuffed them under a rose bramble. Billy's blue denim jacket finished her costume.

Even with all his clothes covering her from foot to chin she still felt peculiarly naked. She realized it was because of the corset. She hadn't dressed without one for twenty years. For a moment she was still, thinking of those vanished years that had carried away a childhood that still seemed so painfully vivid in her mind.

Then she smiled to think what she must look like now, and bent over the water to catch a glimpse of herself. But the stream was too swift and shallow to make a good mirror.

After she had cleaned and packed up the kitchen gear there was nothing else to do, and Jay was still not back. She felt unusually energetic, but, having caught herself humming for the second time, she counseled self-restraint and lay down on the bank to wait.

It was unreasonable, even shameful, to feel so unconcerned in her situation, and on such a morning. Whatever they had been in life, there were six young men being buried in the camp below. Dear Lord, six of them. While she ate a hearty breakfast and hummed like a drunken bee over their heads.

You're not happy, you're hysterical, she thought. Because you're safe and clean and rested, and, above all, alive. Because it might have been you being buried down there now, instead of four of them. Nobody's given you any reason to sing. Grateful? Yes. Thankful. But not so idiotically carefree!

Sobered by this self-inflicted rebuke, she lay pulling at her braids until she heard Jay returning. She sat up, putting her trousered knees together, but he scarcely looked at her.

His bleak expression reminded her that Charlie's death meant more to him than she could fathom. No doubt their shared feeling for Jay's father accounted for some of it. But she had felt in Jay a kind of dependence on Charlie that had nothing to do with affection. She tried to arrange her own sympathies accordingly. Though in truth she could not feel much regret for Charlie's absence.

Billy's agony had touched her more deeply. Life had seemed so boundless in his tough young body, and had been so wretchedly and pointlessly crushed out. His rude friendliness had struck a chord in her; or at least the memory of it did, now that she was safe from him.

But Charlie's hostility and cold dislike for her, the feeling that he was laughing at her, bred only dislike in return, in spite of her momentary softening the day before. And his death had been so sudden and unreal, with not even a body in evidence the morning following the nightmare, that he seemed no more a loss than the deserting Coleman Dawes.

Dawes was no loss at all. They were well rid of both of

them, was her private opinion. But it wouldn't do to say so, yet.

Jay sat down near the creek, and after staring into it for a while began to remove his boots and then his shirt. When he stood up to unbutton his pants, he spared her a look of faint amusement.

"I'm going to have a bath. You can either shut your eyes or watch. Or you might do something useful."

"What's that?" she asked faintly.

"Go a little way downstream and wash this shirt. It's got some blood on it. See if you can get it out."

She gave the shirt a great deal of attention, since he seemed bent on a leisurely bath. The strong desire to turn her head put her quite out of patience with herself. She scrubbed and wrung the hapless shirt until her knuckles were tender and she had a broken fingernail for her pains. She used a flat, smooth rock a dozen yards above the stream for a drying place.

She spent a long time arranging the garment, and studying the striations of the rock, and the uninteresting crown of the hill above her. At last she heard his rasping-soft, mocking laughter.

"All right, Kate. You can turn around. You've missed another head-in with a fate worse than death."

She turned stiffly. "I don't know what you're talking about."

"Tch, Kate."

"I think you must have a very sordid imagination. And, please, don't call me Kate, if you don't mind. I'm not a Kate sort of person." She couldn't imagine why she had made such an asinine remark. He seemed to enjoy it. He was stretched out on the bank, just as she had been, semiclad and barefooted, his head pillowed on his clasped hands.

"You don't bear teasing, do you? Well, I don't blame you. I never took to it myself. Sit down. Don't fidget. We're waiting for my shirt to dry." He closed his eyes and was quiet. She sat down a good two yards away and maintained a dignified silence.

Gradually, she began to examine him.

His long-wedged face was extremely brown, making his body seem all the whiter. Even his body hair was gray, but his arms and chest looked firm, if not as heavy as Willard's, and his belly was flat. She remembered that his arms were strong, very steady and comforting. The remembrance made her look away.

She was not a woman who told herself deliberate lies, but, rather, one who had learned not to make unnecessary demands on the truth. Her adult life had been shadowed by the ghosts of deferred ultimatums and snubbed realities. They lingered by her like uninvited guests—unwelcome, unacknowledged, but not unseen.

In such a way she was aware of Grobart now, and of the probable cause of her attack of lightheartedness earlier. She was about to meet something new to her experience; but she delayed giving consent to the introduction.

She did admit to a sense of pique that he had fallen asleep beside her.

When she could no longer sit in the same position she got up to examine the laundry. It was nearly dry. She shook it out energetically, waking him. He stretched and yawned and sat up to put on his boots. Then he rose to his feet in one smooth movement and without a groan, and took the proffered shirt without thanks.

She waited, doing nothing, while he packed the horses. One he slipped the bridle from and let go free. It was Billy's little dun. "Can you ride and lead a horse?" he asked. "The extra might come in handy, and we still need the pack animal. Well, we'll try it. If you can't, we'll let him go."

She was suddenly embarrassed, even a little afraid, when he came to help her mount. But if he noticed her red face and nervous hands he didn't let her see it. He helped her into the saddle and shortened her stirrups, as impersonally as her riding master. Rummaging in the food pack, he extracted a stick of the dried beef and put it in her hand.

"If you get hungry, chew on that. We've wasted enough time already. We won't stop until the horses need it." She put it in her shirt pocket.

As they rode down past the cabin, she could see no signs of the dead. The campfire had been kicked apart and scattered. The money was picked up.

"What did you do with them?" she asked, as he stopped to look over the area again.

"Put them in the mine. Not the sort of burial Charlie's ancestors would have liked. But I couldn't do it right, here. They like to be up high; in a tree or on a platform, so the birds can pick them clean." He stared at the mine opening. "Poor Charlie," he said. "He'd have liked being another Red Cloud. He had the brains and the nerve for it, but there was nobody to lead. He had to be a Laramie Loafer and an imitation white man instead. Now he can't even get buried right.

"Well, maybe I pleased somebody. My old man would have liked the idea. It's right out of one of his damned books." He looked at her. "I put them back in the mine with their guns beside them and their enemies at their feet. Two apiece." He noticed the small shudder she couldn't suppress. "Is that too heathen for you?"

She shook her head. "No. No, it seems—right for them." But she felt cold, thinking of them being like that, always. He nudged his pony on past the clearing and down the hill.

"Was your father a teacher?" she asked sometime later. "Charlie said he educated him."

Jay smiled thinly. "They educated each other. No, my father wasn't a teacher. He owned a hardware store and he taught himself, the hard way, burning his eyes out with books and a candle every night after he closed the store. He knew all about the stars, but he never had time to look at them. He said his grandfather had been an educated man in the old country, and he wanted to make a scholar and a gentleman out of me, but he didn't know how to go about it. So he failed, as you might have noticed. Later, he took Charlie in—did he tell you why?—and he had more patience by then. Anyway, he and Charlie got along better than he and I ever did. But they had some rough times.

"Pa read somewhere that the savage is a natural nobleman,

and he started right off trying to appeal to Charlie's finer instincts. It set him back some when the kid paid his respects to him by bringing him a dead dog for his Sunday dinner. He didn't know the Arapahoes consider roasted dog a delicacy and—" He saw her face. "Here now, don't go green. The old man didn't eat it. He gave it to Charlie's mother. I knew he'd changed a lot when I heard about that. He'd have laid my head open with a boot if I'd come in with the preacher's wife's spaniel skinned and dressed out like a rabbit—"

"Don't," she begged.

"Sorry." He did look a little sorry. They rode in silence for a time. When she recovered, she wondered if he was tormenting or testing her for a purpose, or just glossing over his feelings about Charlie with funeral humor. Perhaps he had been afraid she was going to offer him condolences for Charlie's life, or begin an interrogation into his own past. He liked to keep his distance from other people's feelings, that was certain.

Is that why he'd married an Indian woman? They were supposed to be a stoical race. Or was it because of her that he was what he was now? She frowned, thinking of what he was and what he'd done. She frowned at herself when she considered how little his crime had affected her thoughts since they had wakened this morning.

"What are you scowling about?"

"Why did you steal that money?" she blurted. He looked startled and she was horrified at herself, but the words rushed out. "If you just got out of prison, why did you do a thing like that, when you know they'll be looking for you everywhere now, and if they catch you, they'll—" He still just stared at her. She flushed, but her wretched tongue kept moving. "I just don't understand you. You're not like the others. I heard them talking. Dawes and Billy Bowan were just—white trash. I heard how they were going to use their part of the money—women, whiskey, gamble it all away and be hanged for it, gladly. You never talked about it. You never—I was afraid of you at first, but I never thought you were like them. I—just don't understand," she finished lamely, wishing that she could be struck dumb, or that just once in her life she could say a thing the way she had meant to say it when she began.

"Are you through?" he asked. She shrugged. She heard him snort after a moment, but couldn't look at him. "Afraid of me! If you were afraid of a bear, I guess you'd take after him with a switch!

"Afraid of me, for God's sake! You ought to be afraid! Where do you think you're going? What have you been expecting me to do with you? Leave you at South Pass? What are you going to do then? How are you going to get back to your husband, and how are you going to explain what you were doing out here, straddling a horse in a pair of men's pants, keeping company with a thief? That's what you ought to wonder about!"

"It isn't my fault I'm out here like this!"

"Isn't it? Why didn't you let go of the saddle and let Billy take the horse? Why didn't you yell the truth out at the Kellys'? You had a chance. When I left you with the horses this morning, why didn't you take one of them and light out for home? You should have. Do you think I'd have tried to catch you? It was only a day's ride back to the Kellys' place and another day back to your husband. Why didn't you go?"

"I don't know," she said, tears and hurt making her voice cloud. "I'm just stupid, I guess. And even this seemed better than going back to things the way they were."

He rode in closer and she felt him touch her arm; touch and withdraw. "That's a good enough answer to both questions, then. Yours as well as mine."

She thought about that as she wiped her eyes on her shirt sleeve.

"Do you have any children?" he asked after a pause.

She shook her head. "But you do, don't you? Mrs. Kelly said something about them."

"I begin to see why you didn't have a chance to tell Mrs. Kelly anything," he observed without rancor. He told her something about them then himself, somewhat stiffly and tersely. But she was moved by the telling because she had begun to realize what an effort such intimacy was for him.

Of course, he had taken the money for them. But where did he think he could go with them now and live undiscovered? He seemed to believe they would come willingly, too. But he was a stranger to them. How could he suppose that they would want to leave their own familiar world, however primitive it might be, and live a fugitive existence with a father they couldn't possibly remember? It was a hopeless plan; futile and arrogant. Yet she was once more filled with pity for him and for them, the lost children.

Unaccountably, her spirits revived at the same time.

Because she ventured to complain later about the sameness of the food and her weariness with all the variations on corn meal and water, he slowed their pace to hunt for small game. Firing from the saddle, he missed two sage hens.

"A rifle is not the proper weapon for birds," he remarked shortly. "Or rabbits," he added, when the first cottontail zigzagged away in a panic. They came to a halt, and he ordered her to gather firewood while he stalked the shrubbed desert on foot.

She sat down instead and watched the gloriously coloring sky. Pale streaks of turquoise hemmed the buttermilk cover of pink and apricot clouds blanketing half the overworld. In the low far distance, hiding the sun, there were purple shapes; cloud mountains. Or perhaps they were real mountains. She couldn't tell.

It was growing cold and fading to gray when she heard the rifle crack again. He returned, swinging a rabbit by the heels.

"Where's your fire?"

"I was waiting until you got your rabbit. Besides, I didn't think you'd want to make camp out here in the open."

"Why not? There's no one about."

"It seems so unprotected. We've always gone up on a hill or behind the rocks."

"All right, damn it. Get your horses and we'll find cover."

They didn't find water, but because they had more canteens apiece now it didn't matter for them. She wondered about the horses. He led them away while she tried to amass enough dry brush to cook the rabbit. When he returned he told her, with more than a hint of satisfaction, that it would take twice as much as she had already gathered.

Cooking the beast was a slow and tedious job, requiring constant feeding of the brush-devouring little fire. But she was glad of the activity, because he had fallen silent again and she discovered that silence between them now made her nervous. Perhaps that explained his own talkativeness earlier.

Soon they were both dumb and uneasy. They looked at each other reluctantly and both kept busy, one turning the little carcass, the other feeding the fire. When the meat was divided, it was black on the outside, due to her careless handling of the spit, and questionably rare near the bone. But she ate it, since she had demanded it. There was nothing to go with it but hardtack and water. They left their last measure of coffee for morning.

When their meal was finished the silence between them became more oppressive to her. She had no occupation with which to ease her growing strain. Her wretched tongue was useless at last. Her mind was unable to summon up any sense of the past to reflect on, or an idea of the future to question. There was only the present, the endless present that she was helpless to deal with.

She looked at him as he sat oiling and cleaning his weapons again. It hardly seemed necessary, twice in one day, she thought impatiently. But it gave him something to do, while she could only sit watching him. She took note of the fact that he wasn't at all a handsome man, compared with Willard. He looked shabby, tired, and ill humored. He had nothing to say to her. He was thinking about his children. He would be glad to be rid of her tomorrow, so he could hurry on to them. She felt hollow with loneliness; tearless and remote.

There were one or two small night noises outside the circle of light. She looked around for them, glad for a diversion from her thoughts. He put away his gun and got up, gathering the bones of the rabbit.

"I'll get rid of this," he said. "That was a fox. He'll be in to sniff around when the fire's out. Does it worry you?"

"No," she said. "It doesn't matter."

"Good girl." She looked up and felt such a sudden surge of warmth to her bones she almost shuddered with it, because of what she saw in his face. She wondered if he knew it was there.

He took the bones, along with the skin and head, and pitched them out at some distance from the camp, to discourage the scavengers. When he had disposed of them he squatted down and wiped his hands on a clump of spidery grass, and rose, surprised to find the movement had sent a tremble through him. He looked at his hands, unable to see if they were clean, and wiped them on his pants, waiting for the sensation to stop.

He had a clear enough picture of himself at the moment, as if from outside and at a distance. "You poor dumb bastard," he told the fool, "you're going to make an idiot of yourself in a minute." But the man in the darkness didn't answer.

It wasn't that he was afraid he'd surprise her. She knew all about it. And she wasn't frightened, just uneasy. No—embarrassed. Well, so was he! God, they were both too old for this sort of nonsense. If they had to blunder into it, then they also had to take it lightly. And he didn't think they were going to, because neither of them had that talent.

It seemed that neither of them could accept being either demanded of or refused.

He stayed away from her for ten minutes or more, to give her whatever privacy she might need, and time to get her mind made up. He thought that if he went back and found her buried to the ears in her blankets, pretending to be asleep, it would be a damned good thing. And tomorrow he could drop her. But when he returned to the fire glow, he found the bedrolls spread out on either side of it. She was standing with her back to him, vigorously brushing out her long thick hair. He watched the furious activity, unmoving. She was bent slightly from the hips, her rich hair hanging down over her left shoulder. He took notice of her straight back and firmly set legs. Her shirttail was out, and she was barefooted. He checked the two beds again.

Beside hers were her boots and stockings, and a somehow familiar bundle of gray material, shapelessly tangled. He knew it for clothing. It was, in fact, a snarl of hastily removed long cotton underwear. Billy's. In her own way, she was as efficient as a quartermaster sergeant. The little details didn't escape her notice. Nor did the detail of the carefully spaced beds escape him.

He saw that it was all going to have to be his fault.

When he moved again she stopped brushing and straightened, like an automaton suddenly turned off. Her arms fell to her sides, but she didn't turn. He stood, just behind her, making her wait. But her stillness quickened him.

When he put his hands lightly on her shoulders, she drew in a quick breath and let it go in a little sigh of release, and his fingers tightened, pulling her back. She leaned against him quietly while he found and held her breasts, and put his face into the coolness of her hair, and against the warmth of her throat.

He forgot, then, how he was first going to make her see things for what they were.

He turned her, or she turned into his arms. Her face blurred, but the eyes seemed strangely black and familiar. They closed with moth's lashes as he kissed her, awkwardly at first because it had been so long, then hungrily; stopping her from some last word. And in that sweetly silenced mouth he found his own hunger answered.

When he could let her go, which wasn't easy, he found his fingers made a bad job of undoing her buttons and her silken, knotted belt while she pressed against him with little murmurs, not quite words, whispered against his face between the kisses. Shaken, he swore at the damned knot she'd tied.

He left it to her, easing free of her; avoiding her eyes, he went to pick up her blankets and throw them on top of his own. He started to undress himself, unbuckling the gun belt and laying the burnished holster nearby, but well away from the fire. There was no sound behind him. He took off his jacket and glanced back at her.

She was still standing where he'd left her, barelegged now, in Billy's old flannel shirt; looking as if it were the first time, ever. It was a look like Cat's.

He went to her quickly and picked her up, putting her on their double-thick bed where he could kiss those solemn child's eyes closed—wanting her just like that, with her long, coltish legs around him and Billy's shirt pulled up to her chin.

# 10

The morning after Captain Grobart's departure with his white-faced wife and his quarrelsome partners, Dub Kelly watered his stock and performed his chores, preparing reluctantly to ride down to Superior to do his wife's bidding.

He was a red-eyed, weary man, for she had given him no rest the whole night, and the amount of bust-head liquor he had consumed with his guests had been many times over his usual daily measure. His mouth was as foul as a farrier's boots, and his temples throbbed painfully.

He was purely amazed at Sudie. A woman's determination was a fearful thing, once she got something stuck in her mind. Reasons meant nothing to her. He had known Captain Grobart for years; knew he couldn't be mixed up in anything like kidnapping a woman, let alone that other thing about train robbing. It was nonsense. That wife of the Captain's, if she wasn't crazy, must have been fevered with the heat to tell such a story about her own man.

But Sudie believed it, and had that pretty little gold locket to prove it, she said. Although what that was supposed to prove, beyond the fact that the Captain was good enough to buy his woman pretty things, was more than he knew.

Sudie knew what it meant. It meant that Dub had to spend a day in the saddle with an aching head, riding down to the nearest telegraph office to see if any train had been held up at all, and if any crazy woman had been kidnapped.

She had made that clear as soon as the company left. His head had been a little light then, so he thought the womenfolk had been bibbin' at the jug a bit themselves. But she continued to urge him at ten o'clock, when he was sleepy, and at midnight, when he went outside to be sick, and at one in the morning, when he slapped her in the mouth to shut her up. He was sorry for that, of course .He was still saying so at two, and she was still awake and crying at three, until he gave in, and promised to do whatever damn crazy thing she wanted if she would let him sleep an hour or two.

She was up at dawn, packing his lunch, prodding him out of bed. Himself, he would have taken pity on a Comanche Injun who looked and felt the way he did. But not her. She had him on his way by eight that morning.

He rode at a walk, as soon as he was out of sight of the house; and after a while even that got to be too much of a jar, and he stopped to rest his head, and fell asleep on the shady side of a tumble of sandstone boulders along the way. When he woke, he could tell it was past noon. He remounted, a bit guiltily, and made his way down to Superior at a prudent speed.

Even so, it was early evening before he got his message off to Rock Springs, and found a cheap enough saloon to eat in, and a friendly livery stableman who agreed to let him sleep there in the sweet hay and passed the time with him convivially, talking horses.

He was already asleep for the night when the stableman, accompanied by a kid from the telegraph office, shook him out again, bewildered and growing a mite worried at the sight of their faces.

The kid handed him a piece of paper that he knew was a telegram. He couldn't read it, of course, but he mumbled something about leaving his reading glasses at home, and the boy obliged him by telling him that it was sent by some Wells, Fargo man down at Point of Rocks, who was deputized by the sheriff of Carter County to head up a posse against the *robbers and kidnappers* believed to be headed by one J. W. Grobart and Wm. Bowan of this county. Dub was ordered to wait at Superior for a special stage carrying Mr. H. Lapchance and members of his posse, who desired to question him further.

Dub bowed his head in grief and confusion. He didn't want to be the cause of trouble for Captain Grobart, who'd been more than a little lax at horse trading, and had paid generously in cash for the few other things he took with him. But Dub knew he wasn't smart enough to lie for old Jay. They'd be putting him in jail as a confederate if he tried it.

He damned Sudie for putting him in his predicament.

The stage came in around midnight and he was rousted out of sleep again. The Wells, Fargo man was a tall, thin feller who smelled like peppermint and sounded like a preacher. He paced slowly but continually as he listened to Dub's reluctant account. With him was a big florid-faced Easterner with worried eyes who was the woman's real husband, they said. He looked like a man who generally took charge of everything himself. But, though he opened his mouth once or twice to ask about his woman, he left most of the talking to the skinny Express man. Dub didn't wonder at this for long. The thin man's parson-prim voice and nervous manner didn't cover up the fact that he had a head for figuring like a barracks-room lawyer.

He'd already known about the Captain and Bowan from past acquaintance, he said, and figured them for the guilty parties as soon as he heard of the holdup. He'd even figured old Jay to take the route he took, or something like it, just because it was a hard one and not to be expected of just anybody. But he hadn't been able to convince the sheriff, who wanted the first posse sent down into the Uintas.

What gleamed in Harvey Lapchance's face might have been triumph or zeal for justice, but it looked to Dub more like the face of a kid who'd finally been let into the marbles game after toeing the dirt as a spectator for too long. He sounded friendly, almost sympathetic, when he asked about Jay, causing the woman's husband to snort and get red faced. But Dub felt sorry for the Captain, with that wiry hound on his scent, however mild he talked.

The husband was more of a puzzle. He looked like a big bull getting ready to charge, except that he couldn't seem to keep his eyes fixed on anything for long, so you couldn't tell which way he'd run. He dressed like money and education make a man dress: against all good sense. Dub put him down, tentatively, as a man who'd trade you a quarter horse for a mine pony, then yell he'd been cheated.

By dawn they had it all fixed up between them how to catch old Jay. They'd sent telegrams to every marshal in the county, giving the gang's and Mrs. Crocker's descriptions. They'd even notified the troops at old Fort Brown that they called Washakie now, in the Snake territory, to watch out for them. Dub thought that was a hard thing. If the Captain was going up there for his kids, he'd have a bad enough time without having the dog soldiers set to grab him on sight. A man ought to be able to see his own kids, no matter what else he might have done, and no matter what color they were. He'd never cottoned to Injuns himself, not even the Snakes, who were friendlier than most.

He'd never been able to figure out why Captain Grobart had ever taken up with that little Squawtown runabout, but he had, and Dub supposed that even a squaw's kids were cute to play with and easy to love when they were cubs.

The two men didn't let him alone until dawn. Then they went over to the hotel, and Dub went back to sleep for a while, at last. He'd make a late start going home, and he'd have to hurry more returning than he had going forth. He hoped he'd given the Captain a little time. He hoped too that the damned woman who had caused all the trouble would fall off her horse and break her damned neck. He even felt some satisfaction knowing that Sudie wouldn't get to keep her friend's little gewgaw the way the woman had said she could.

Crocker had snatched it out of his hand when he showed it, like he was no better than a thief, and kept it.

It ate into Harvey's patience that Willard Crocker had to sleep. They were so close to the fugitives; a little more than twenty-four hours behind men who were burdened with a captive, a pack horse, and an injured man. And Crocker had to sleep.

Harvey would have left him snoring in the Superior Hotel and gone ahead on the stage in the morning, but even he was forced to admit that they'd both been up for the best part of the last forty-eight hours; more, he guessed, for Crocker. And if he could run them down along the road to South Pass (because he didn't believe that tale about going to Farson for a minute), it would take more than just him and a Smith & Wesson to stop four men. He must wait for at least two more of his party to come up from the Point. He had already tried to deputize a couple of hang-abouts in Superior, but nobody would have anything to do with the offer.

Crocker had his damned gun with him, and they each had packed a bag of clothes. Harvey suspected Willard had packed something else too. His flushed, bleary look might be due to lack of sleep, but Harvey thought the Yankee had converted his drinking from beer to gin.

It was a damned shame they couldn't leave at once. On the stage, with a fresh change of horses regularly along the way, they could easily beat the others to South Pass, where they'd have to come in for supplies. That would be their fourth or fifth day out. Five days' supply of food for four men would be about right for one pack horse. And they now had an extra mouth to feed. At least, he hoped they were feeding her.

Retired resignedly to a private room away from Crocker, Harvey thought about Crocker's wife. A brave woman; a cool head. Her husband seemed disappointed—no, not disappointed; ruffled up—to hear that she'd let herself be passed off as Grobart's wife to the Kellys. What did he want her to do? Call Grobart a liar in front of two defenseless people, with four guns in her back? She had done just as she should: stayed calm, looked meek, and warned the Kelly woman at the last possible moment, so she wouldn't have time to get worked up and give the secret away until after they were gone.

She had let herself be taken off by them, to keep the Kellys safe. What else could a man ask for in his wife? Crocker began to act as if he thought the poor woman might be enjoying her captivity. Maybe that was the key to their trouble together: jealousy. Because she was not only full of spirit, she was a mighty good-looking woman.

He slipped her picture out of his inner coat pocket and looked at it again. He didn't know why he hadn't given it back to Crocker at once, except that the man hadn't asked for it or seemed to realize it was missing. Now he felt a little furtive about keeping it, but had no intention of returning it unless it was demanded.

It was a good picture; very soft, but clear. She looked straight at him with her serious-child's eyes, as if she would measure him up before she spoke. He thought she would have a low, pleasant voice, with no coy nonsense about it. He would have liked to ask Crocker more about her, but that was out of the question. He was looking forward to meeting her and hearing that voice.

He tucked the picture away again and stretched out on the too-soft bed to wait for the noon stage. He was more tired than he imagined. Sleep took him in minutes.

Willard dreamed of Catherine, and it wasn't a good dream. Of course, his dreams seldom were good. The anxieties and insufficiencies he conquered with bulk and energy during the day took back their own again, vividly, at night.

He thought he had found her with the men in some dark place in the mountains and tried to burst in to save her. But nobody saw him. She and the rest, who were all bearded but faceless, moved back and forth like pacing ghosts, never looking his way, although he yelled at her to get out—get out of the way so he could kill the lot of them. He raised his gun, determined to kill the leader, and she turned her head, frowning as if she'd known he was there all the time and had just been too displeased to acknowledge him.

"Don't, for heaven's sake, Willard. What will people think?" she said witheringly. God, it was funny when he thought about it, because how many times had she said that to him? It would be just like her to say it then.

After that it turned ugly, so he began to know it was a

dream even while he still fought it, because she did what Kate would never do, and who knew better than he?

She wasn't dressed right. She had on that nightgown with all the ribbons that she'd worn on their honeymoon. He'd never forget that one, the one with his blood splashed all over it because she'd hit him in the nose. The faceless man in front of her took this one by the ribbons and tore it down the front like it was paper—and she just stood there and let him, right in front of all the others. She was naked, and *he* was aghast!

The rest was a struggle up out of his nightmare. He was suddenly bound and gagged in a chair so he couldn't move or shout, and she was in a big bed with the man, ignoring him and the others, who were playing cards now. And he could do nothing but struggle to speak, and watch.

When he woke he was soaked in sweat—and desire for her. He thought that if he got her back alive and she had gone through anything like that—not willingly, God!—why, he could forgive it and she would see that their life together hadn't been so bad after all. She might not expect him to want her back after they'd had her. Gratitude might curb that castrating tongue, when she found out. She hadn't always been so sharp, in the first years. God, she'd been so beautiful and soft sometimes that he nearly burst with pride to think that she was the property of big, clumsy, upstart Willard Crocker, whose mother had scrubbed other people's floors and taken other people's charity to put him through school so he could be somebody.

Once, when the old sot, her father, was drunk and locked up in his room, some nosy relative of hers had come to call, making herself pretty nasty, asking Catherine about the old man's "bilious" attacks. Willard had been new enough then to be surprised that any of her kin would be so bitchy, and he'd taken offense on her behalf. He didn't remember what he'd said, but it had been the right thing, for a change. He'd put a fire under the old biddy without breaking any of the rules of etiquette.

She'd been proud of him, and grateful, because her mother's people had always been almost as hard on her as they were on the old man. When they were alone in the parlor, after the old girl had taken herself off, he'd found her looking at him with a kind of soft wonder on her face that turned his heart over. He'd felt suddenly sure, and competent, and the master of the house. He'd picked her up, right then, in the middle of the afternoon, and carried her up to their room. The heavy curtains had been drawn, as they always were, so it was nearly dark. He'd undressed her like a doll, and made love to her there, with the door locked.

Of course something happened soon after to spoil things, and she was back on her high horse. It never lasted long before they were at war again. Soon they were sleeping apart more than together. But still, the memories of the rare moments were enough to spoil his revenge when he was with other women. And he kept her with him, when it would have been easier all around to leave her at home with Papa, only partly to punish her. Her body, so often denied him or given coldly, still held an attraction for him that belied ten years of marriage. She would not accept his love, but she had to accept his authority. When she put on all her little airs of superiority, he liked to have her close, to remind her that his least desire could overrule her dearest wish, because she was his.

He got up and took off his soaked shirt, and bathed and shaved in the cold water they'd given him. His head felt like it had shrapnel sticking to the inside of it. He dressed himself in a clean shirt and collar. He looked like hell in the shaving mirror. His face was swollen from having slept on it. It made him look fatter than ever. He wasn't fat, really; just big boned and husky. His face had always been round and full like a baby's, though, and people thought he was fat.

When he was dressed he took a drink from the bottle wrapped in underwear in his satchel, and went downstairs to see if Lapchance was still pacing up and down the lobby.

He wasn't. He was sitting in the dining room, reading a week-old newspaper from Rock Springs telling about the latest exploits of somebody called Big Nose George Parrett. There was an empty bowl in front of him with a few soggy remnants of crackers in it, and a milk-clouded tumbler. He was sucking a sugar stick, like some half-bright country kid.

Willard sat down and ordered a steak and two eggs, since it was impossible to expect anything decent for breakfast, like poached mackerel, out here. He swallowed two cups of coffee, as hot as he could drink them, and ate his meal in silence, while the great and learned peppermint eater hid behind his paper.

One thing he promised himself. If anybody took Jay Grobart, alive or dead, it wasn't going to be this jumped-up mail shuffler who did it with his little pocket pistol.

With the LeMat he could scatter the whole bunch of them—first a buckshot blast into their horses' rumps, then a flick of his thumb to shift the hammer and he'd pick them off one by one with the powerful rifle. He had the range over Lapchance's little gun, and he had the skill. It was one of the few things he felt confident about. He had been a poor country boy who had to do his share and who couldn't afford to waste powder trying to put fresh meat on the table at home.

When he got her back, she was going to have to admit he was a good shot.

# 11

IT WAS STRANGE. When he woke and felt the woman's body nested into his, he thought she was Cat, and it seemed perfectly normal. So much for the effect of ten years on the tactile sense. His flesh accepted Cat pressed to it again, but his brain had a numbing shock. He drew back with a sudden jerk that woke her.

She must have had a moment of confusion herself. But then she turned slightly so she could look at him. What could have become a smile quirked her mouth and died from uncertainty. He knew she was waiting for him to say something that would make it all right for her to be there, and she deserved reassurance. But the Cat phantom had only just vanished, and he was blank.

In lieu of speech, he touched her. Her hair was loose around her face and one strand of it was caught childishly in the corner of her mouth. He put a finger on it and brushed it away. She took encouragement from the gesture, and rolled over to put her arm over him and ask the inevitable question. "Do you love me?"

Some little stiffening of her body made it plain she was instantly sorry for asking, while he thought in the same moment, Oh Jesus, why do men always have to hear that? It wasn't expected that she should know that any whore in the world could ask the same question and expect the same answer.

What else did they think you'd tell them while you were

in their bed? It was like paying them blackmail, that answer.

So he didn't answer at all. He tipped her face up and kissed her eyes closed again and her mouth, soft and open.

Then he closed his own eyes and made a determined effort to sleep again, partly to avoid her, and because it was still just first dawn. But she was awake and restless. She sighed.

"If it took being miserable with Willard for so long to get me here, I could thank him for it." That wanted an answer too.

But he only murmured indistinctly, after a pause, "Who made it miserable, you or him?"

"He—oh, we both did, I suppose. He never really loved me and I was—very disappointed in him. We never should have married, that's all."

"Why did you?" He saw he was not going to be allowed to feign sleep.

"How many people could answer that question?" Her voice had lost its drowsy murmur; was even a little sharp. "We each wanted something we didn't have, and thought the other could supply it. And we were wrong, and stuck with it."

"What did you want?" He didn't know why he asked, because he didn't want to know. She had put on her shirt again before they slept, for warmth. He unbuttoned it slowly with his free hand.

"I wanted a man. Someone I could lean on, rely on, be proud of. Not like my—not like Willard. He wants to lean too, though he doesn't look it." She whispered a shaky laugh. "We were always fighting for the crutches."

There was honesty in that. It warmed him to whisper, "Poor Kate," as he kissed her mouth again, and the hollow of her throat, and a soft-peaked little breast hidden under the flannel, feeling how the clamor of her heart shook it.

She frowned at the gray morning opening over them. "Well, whatever he wanted, he can look for it somewhere else now. Maybe he's doing that now; saying all the things I'm saying, to somebody. It wouldn't surprise me. He's done it before."

"Kate—"

"Let him do what he pleases. I never want to see him or

think about him again. I found what I wanted. It doesn't seem possible, but it is. It's you. I love you."

"Stop talking so much."

She caught her breath and let it out in a last small plea as he drew her under him. "I do love you. I'm not afraid to say it."

But again he didn't answer.

Later, dazzled awake by the sun, she tried to get her clothes on again without waking him. But when she reached for Billy's underwear it was half inside out, and before she could straighten it she heard him snort.

"Don't look!" she said fiercely. "And stop laughing! I have to wear something underneath!" But he shook with silent mirth, one arm flung up over his face. He had been amused the night before too, and she had laughed with him, in the comfort of her new-found love.

Now, though, when she needed all the tenderness and reassurance he could give to make her feel like something other than a camp follower and dirty gypsy, he couldn't say three words, but he could laugh again.

She snatched up the offending garment and the baggy pants, and stalked out of sight, dressed in her long-tailed shirt; hurting her bare feet on the sharp rocks. Tears welled up when she was behind the rock, blinding her as she dressed. Last night—even this morning—she had counted her world well lost for that moment of their shared need. This second waking found her disillusioned, ashamed, unwashed and smelling of stale lust, and hungry.

How could she suppose he loved her? Why should he? What a vain, gullible, weak idiot she must be. Naturally he would use her, now that he had her to himself. If it hadn't been for Billy's injury and death, the same thing would have happened two nights ago, en masse; and why not?

And what did she see in him to make her demean herself, begging for a word of love, like a child for candy? He was neither handsome nor gallant. He was a thief, and who knew what else besides? He was years older than she, older than

Willard; and looked it, too, this morning. What she mistook for strength was only stubbornness. What had seemed to be compassion was only self-interest. He was nothing. She had given herself cheaply and eagerly, to nothing.

She sank to a seat on the rocks in an agony of tears, the sobs tearing at her throat. She didn't hear him approach. He was just standing in front of her, dressed and silent. She tottered to her feet, wiping at her tears and running nose. Dear God, why did she still cry like a child, with a square mouth and a swollen face?

Other women could shed their tears and pat them away, looking dewy eyed and pathetic, after. The effects of her tears spoiled her face for hours, and made her all the more disagreeable to anyone who noticed it.

He didn't speak (when did he ever?), but offered her a large, fairly clean handkerchief. She snatched it from him, wishing it were possible to refuse it, and mopped and blew, with her back to him. When she was calm enough to speak, she pushed it into her jacket pocket. "I'll launder it for you, if we ever find water." She brushed past him toward the horses, hating him for having a handkerchief and offering it.

He let the silence between them hang and grow as he made a little fire for the coffee and strapped up their gear. She sat, not helping, in the throes of a vexation as great as any she had ever known with Willard or her father. She longed for him to speak; willed it, so she could rebuff him. If he would only dare to rebuke her for her childishness, she would pour out her scorn in a volley of cutting words. If he should offer one token of regret, or that tardy word of love, with what pleasure would she refuse it. Her throat ached with the pent-up words. But he said nothing; and so she was forestalled.

He offered her a piece of the nauseous dried beef. She shook her head dumbly. Even her hunger was precious, as fuel to her fire. When he brought out the horses, he merely handed her the reins instead of helping her to mount as he usually did. In her mind, she had already shoved aside his helping hand. Having lost the opportunity to do so, she swung herself into the saddle, a little ashamed of the tongueless tantrum that was shaking her. She had already imagined drenching him in more vitriol than Willard earned in a month of trying. And not a word of it had been spoken.

She was quite able to see that he was handling her, and successfully. A traitorous segment of her own mind—a part that must grin at bloodshed—applauded him. She followed him down the hill, red faced and sullen with herself.

She was so immersed in her own dislike that South Pass came as a surprise to her. They reached the end of the gray, ridged hills and looked out across a wide desert valley, strewn with occasional solitary buttes and sandy wastes, that reached almost to the limit of sight. Yet in the northern distance there were purple shapes, like storm clouds, but jagged and white topped.

Mountains.

The ground of the valley was rutted and gored in a thousand seams by the wheels of countless wagons that had once passed over it to a greener West. It looked like an incredibly old and unkempt fallow field, scarred forever with the marks of ancient plowings.

He told her its name and she nodded, absently, still looking west for the last of the white-topped wagons. Then they rode down it in an easterly direction until they reached the river.

The horses smelled it first, and their ears pricked forward, their tired legs moving quicker over the road that ran in from the left. When they came to it, Catherine sprang off quickly to help loosen their throat latches and slip their bits even as they stretched eagerly for the sweet water.

It was the Sweetwater from which she drank, and bathed her face in too.

"What are you doing?"

She was unbuttoning her shirt. "I have to clean up before we go into town. Would you please look somewhere else for a few minutes?"

"Are you crazy? South Pass is only about ten miles off. You can have a hot bath there."

"But I can't go into town looking and—and—" she couldn't say smelling—"feeling like this! I can't. Please turn around."

"Get on your horse. In two hours you'll be soaking in a tub full of—"

"Jay, I can't be seen in town like this!"

"Nobody in there gives a damn what you look like, Kate!"

"Well, I care! Are you going to turn around?" He sat down instead, looking at her in mild disbelief. She glared back at him.

"All right, then—watch, if you like," she snapped, and began to snatch off her clothes. She had intended at first to wash only her face and arms, which necessitated removing her shirt. But now, enraged with his obtuse lack of manners, she stripped off everything and streaked for the river, stark naked.

The water was icy, and so shallow she had to dash almost to the channel to find a depth that would cover her to the waist. When she found it, she sat down, suppressing a squeal of agony mixed with rage. His laughter followed her like a rain of arrows. She turned her back, immersed to the neck in her cold bath, lacking soap, cloth, or towel, and rubbed at herself ineffectively with both hands, teeth chattering.

She found that rage, however justified, was hard to keep awake in sudden cold spells. Her convulsive shivers soon stirred up choked giggles as she thought about her predicament.

Last week, Willard must leave the tent while she had a sponge bath. Four nights ago, she blushed to be seen on her way to relieve herself. Now here she was, at her own insistence, bathing in front of a man, naked as an eel, exposed to the world in an arena the size of her home town. What would she be capable of next week?

At that moment she seemed condemned to steep herself in the river until nightfall. But Jay, when he had finished laughing and filling their canteens, called her out. She ignored him, until a handful of light gravel sprayed the water near her.

"I'm not finished."

"You're finished. It's another two hours or better into South Pass City."

"The horses need a rest."

"Well, suit yourself. When you're ready for your little duds, come on into town. I'll hold them for you."

She scrambled out of the river with a war cry and threw herself on him. He already had her clothes in hand, but he caught her up as well, holding her hard against him so her feet cleared the ground. It was a mock struggle. When he kissed her she stopped flailing and clung to him wetly, until she was forced to draw back for breath.

"You really wanted me to try to pull you out so you could throw water all over me, didn't you?"

"Yes," she said happily.

"Well, you did a middling fair job of it this way. You feeling better now?"

"Yes," she repeated, nuzzling in under his jaw.

"I'm glad to hear it. Now get dressed."

"Turn your back."

"Jesus Christ."

"What's in South Pass City besides gold miners?" she asked as they rode.

"A bed for the night, a hot meal and bath. The stage, to take you home."

She heard it, but she thought he was teasing her. Yet no challenging look or grin followed it. Slowly, she came to understand that he meant it. Yet still it failed to shake her. He was only a little provoked with her. More than he would show. He wanted to make her suffer a bit. He knew she wasn't going back, couldn't go back to Willard now. He knew she didn't want to go anywhere except with him, didn't he?

Maybe not. After all, it was only day before yesterday that she had last asked him when he'd let her go, and he had said, "Maybe at South Pass." It seemed an age ago to her, but it had been no more than a day and two nights. He thought—dear Lord—he must think she was only amusing herself while waiting to be released.

No wonder he refused to play a shoddy romantic game and say he loved her, when she seemed to be making a vacation of her abduction. He would expect her to be glad to give up the game now and return to her soft life.

She would make him understand. But she couldn't do it while jarring up and down on an animal several yards behind him. She would have to wait until they reached South Pass City.

On the edge of town they came to a puzzled halt. A strong breeze out of the mountains was beating a loose window shutter on the nearest house back and forth, with a noise like a tack hammer. It was the only noise issuing from a town built to hold four thousand people at the height of its mining boom.

There wasn't a man or an animal in sight. No wagons. No smoke from kitchen chimneys. Catherine watched a tumbling skeleton of dried sage roll away from them down the wide dirt street until it bumped into a porch step and got stuck there. She turned to question Jay.

"I've been out of touch," he said belatedly. "More than I thought. I heard the mines were about played out, but I didn't know it was like this."

"Is it deserted, then? A ghost town?"

"No, there's bound to be somebody left. A few miners would have stayed to pick over the leavings. Let's see if there's any business left."

They picked their way through town in the eerie stillness to the business district, a half-mile stretch of street, extra wide for wagon turnarounds, lined with empty horse troughs and silent, dusty boardwalks. The hotels, saloons, shooting galleries, bakeries, meat and grocery markets were still there, their signs not yet faded, their windows shuttered, their doors boarded shut. A jack rabbit shot out from between two of the false-front stores and darted away at their approach, making the horses shy.

"Look!" Catherine pointed to a small building midway between two vacant saloons. "That one looks open. At least it isn't nailed shut."

It was a general store of sorts. A few canned goods stood on the shelves, a few barrels of staples cluttered the bare floor. There was a large clock on the back wall. It was ticking. But there was no one about.

"Whoever runs it is out working his claim, or somebody else's. He keeps a few supplies for the others like him." Jay looked relieved. "Let's see what else is left. We might find that bed and bath after all."

"Do you think we could take a few things and pay later?" Catherine wondered, wistfully eyeing a bin of shriveled apples and a wooden box of raisins standing on the counter.

"He likely does most of his business that way," Jay said. "Pick out what you want." She found a sack and eagerly snatched at the fruit, and at a withered cabbage and a few limp-looking carrots from the vegetable bin. There was a bar of soap wrapped in a paper showing a child embracing a cat, and a rough towel from the dry-goods corner. She broke off a large piece of brown loaf sugar and tucked it into a smaller sack. She was scanning the shelves and licking the sugar from her fingers when he finally took her arm.

"That's enough for now."

"I need some thread and a pack of needles. And boots. Mine are split."

"Later." He put a dollar on the bill spike and pulled her out of the store.

They loosened the boards on one of the hotel doors and explored. There were odd lots of furniture left behind: loose-legged chairs, a badly cracked mirror, a very crude large table in the kitchen. The stove, of course, had made the trip; still there was a fireplace, and a pan or two, missing a handle or dented to wobbliness but whole. Catherine stopped there, unloading her supplies on the table. If luck was with her she would make soup and apple dumplings. She closed her eyes, trying to see Rosie's capable hands at work over those things, her long, beautiful brown fingers delicately turning the apple as she peeled its skin off in one long, curling strip. But after coming so far for an apple, why waste its skin?

Oh Rosie, she prayed silently, if you can see me up in heaven, don't think too badly of me. And don't let me ruin the dumplings!

"There's a bed upstairs that they must have kept for old Abe himself," Jay reported later. "God knows how they ever got it up there. It must be eight feet high. I guess they couldn't figure it out either, so they left it."

"The pump works. It needed priming, but the water's good."

"Where's that kettle you found?"

"I'm making soup in it. You'll have to wait your turn." But when he was gone again, she discovered a large dump heap of discarded items in the back yard, another kettle among them, and heated water for him in it.

It took a while to steam, and when she climbed the stairs with it, using a castoff woolen hat for a pot holder, she found him stretched out asleep on the bed. She set down her burden and came to stand at the foot of the monstrous bed.

He had tipped his hat over his face to blot out the strong sunlight pouring in through the bare window. He was getting more than a little bald in back, she had noticed, and didn't often remove his hat, even to sleep. She smiled tenderly at the vanity, and wanted to lift the hat and kiss him awake. But compassion stayed her, and she tiptoed away instead, to stir her soup.

She swung through the kitchen door and stopped, frozen. Coleman Dawes was lounging in the open back door, grinning at her surprise.

"Mr. Dawes!"

He detached himself from the doorframe and strolled in, stopping to sniff her soup. "Miz Grobart. Or whatever. Where's old Jay, upstairs asleep? That's a mighty good bed. I used it myself last night." He moved past her to glance into the deserted dining room.

"No. He isn't asleep. He's up there shaving. I'll call him."

He turned quickly and put his hand to her throat, squeezing it just a little. "Don't call him. Just stay down here and let's get reacquainted." He looked at her garb, chuckling. "You sure don't look like the same woman. You and old Jay hitting it off pretty good, ain't you? I thought you would as soon as I seen how particular he was about keeping Billy away from you." She stepped back from his restraining hand, frowning; her mind searching for a way to get around him.

"I figure he's asleep, from his being so late gettin' here. I bet you just about wore him out the last night or two, hey?

Otherwise you could've been here yesterday, just behind me." He laughed outright at her angry blush.

"Don't get mad, Sis. I'm not poor-mouthing your man. That old cougar's still more'n about half rough! But he ain't a boy no more, by about thirty years. He's out for the afternoon."

"Mr. Dawes, what do you want? Whatever it is—money, I suppose—you'll have to talk to Mr. Grobart about it, not me. Please let me by and I'll get him." But she didn't move, and neither did he. Instead, he winked at her.

"I'll talk to him later about money. Meantime, you got the afternoon free."

She took a deep breath and tried to look resigned. She turned casually to her simmering kettles. Then she made a dart for the back door.

He caught her by the hair just as she went through it and dragged her back. His other hand covered her mouth, tipping her head back so she was looking up at him.

"Sis, you don't use your brains. If you make a little noise, and wake him up, he'll come down here without his gun and I'll blow daylight through him before he gets off the stairs. And even if you make a big noise, he isn't going to know whether you burned your little fingers, or seen a rat, or what. I'll still have the advantage. Are you chewin' on that?" Slowly, she nodded as much as she was able. He pulled her back into the room, still holding her hair and mouth.

"That's better. Now, you just keep real quiet and I won't hurt you a bit. Like you figured, I just want my share of things as a fifty-fifty partner, since there's only the two of us left. Half the money. Half of anything else. I been thinkin' about you ever since you give me that big, sweet kiss back at the wrangler's shack."

He backed her up against the huge table, removing his smothering hand only to replace it with his loose, wet mouth. She fought him, silently, until he grew impatient and cuffed her across the temple twice with the heel of his hand. It was like being slammed against a wall.

He didn't seem to find Billy's underwear either amusing or prohibitive.

# 12

CATHERINE retreated into strict silence with Dawes. She hung heavy and lifeless while he struggled with her, cold as a corpse when he kissed her. At last, he pushed her roughly away to the floor with a snarl. She got up slowly, not looking at him, and pulled her clothes together. She was dry eyed and empty faced as she tended her simmering pots. He taunted her, breathing heavily behind her, but he didn't touch her again.

He was working hard to make her cry out in anger, but her dead, unresponding silence had, instead, that effect on him. It had worked successfully with Willard too.

"All right, goddamn you, go on up and roust that old squaw man of yours out of bed, and we'll talk money. If he can stand to look at that sour face of yours all the time, he's welcome to it." As she passed him he grabbed at her braids again, pulling her face around to him with a jerk. She thought her scalp might split loose at the neckline, but she didn't wince.

"I'd like to turn you over to the Cheyenne, by God if I wouldn't," he breathed into her face. "And then stick around to watch the show."

She waited dumbly until he released her and pushed her toward the door ahead of him. He followed her through the dining room and lobby and up the stairs.

Jay was still asleep, lying in the same position, except that his hat had slipped to one side and she could see his face. She stopped in the doorway to look at him, and Dawes pushed her from behind again. What she felt this time wasn't his hand, but the barrel of a gun.

She walked to the bed and leaned across Jay, wondering if she was in line between them. Hoping she was, and that her body shielded her own hand, she reached out and shook him a little, then let her hand slide rapidly down his side to his holster. His own hand came up from the bed and fastened on her wrist as she touched the gun butt.

He opened his eyes, fully awake, and she looked at him hard, her hand still on the gun.

"Mr. Dawes is here to see you, you'll be pleased to know," she said evenly, and withdrew her hand. He slipped the holster latch and sat up.

"Hello, Dawes." He swung his feet over the edge of the bed, unperturbed, and put on his boots. "What brings you back, as if I didn't know?"

"That's right. As if you didn't know." Dawes held his gun loosely at his side, but it was still cocked, Catherine could see, as she sat on the foot of the bed with bowed head. "Our partnership has shrunk," he said. "It's time to divide up our earnings again."

"Earnings!" she breathed to herself scornfully. Neither of them paid any attention to her.

"I thought our partnership broke up when you took off so fast, night before last," remarked Jay, slipping on his second boot.

"I wasn't running out, I was trying to save my skin! I saw what they did to Charlie. If they'd gun down one of their own kind, they wouldn't stick at doing the same to a white man. Does Sis think you're a big hero? Well, you were out in the dark behind a tree with a rifle. I was standing belly up to the light in front of 'em, with nothing in my hands but my own sweat! Damn right I took off when I had the chance. You would've too!"

Jay laughed at him. "You're probably right, Dawes. Though, from what I heard, you brought some of the trouble on yourself. Charlie wasn't dead when I got to him. Not quite."

"Well, he's dead now," growled Dawes, "and I figure half

of what he got is mine. And half of Bowan's too."

"Let's go downstairs and talk about it. Maybe there's some coffee." He looked at Catherine as impersonally as if she were the parlormaid.

"I'll make some," she said through stiff lips.

"Oh, Miss Mousie's been all kinds of busy downstairs, playin' house. Cooking soup, and sugaring apples, and spreading sunshine all around, ain't that right, Sis?" Dawes drawled, his loathsome grin reviving as he watched her. She felt the heat of her hatred for him stain her face, and got up quickly. Jay got up at the same moment, and Dawes lifted his gun barrel in a token warning.

"Put away your piece, Dawes, and let's go have something to eat. Unless you really think you're going to need it." Looking at Jay, Catherine herself thought it wouldn't be needed. He seemed as relaxed and affable as she'd ever seen him. Her heart sank. "Thick as thieves" was the unhappy phrase that came first to mind.

Dawes let them pass in front of him and followed them back to the kitchen. Catherine, moving as stiffly as an enraged cat, set out the meal in tin cups, and took her own out to the back steps away from them. Her soup, seasoned with the last of the jerked beef, was thin and flavorless, but she didn't notice. She poked the bits of boiled cabbage into her mouth and swallowed them untasted as she listened to the men behind her.

Thick as thieves. They settled their spoils problem with no difficulty at all. Jay simply handed Coleman Dawes one of the two extra saddlebags. Dawes, much mollified, nevertheless made some little protest about whether it was the one the renegades had rifled and burned some of. Jay remarked easily that if it was Dawes should take the loss, since he had helped create the trouble. Dawes thought about it, and finally accepted the offer to take either of the extra bags, uncounted, and depend on the luck of the draw for his profit. Catherine ground her teeth.

Her precious coffee, of which she'd scooped up only

enough to put in a twist of paper before being driven out of the store, was beginning to boil. She got up and divided her soupy apple-and-raisin dessert with the little boiled dumplings made from biscuit flour. The little dumplings were like so many droppings of lead-filled gum. She was pouring coffee when Dawes swallowed his last one with difficulty and held out his cup.

"Sis, you got to learn to use a lighter hand when you knead up biscuit dough. I believe if I was to file them little slugs down to .50 caliber, I could shoot buffalo with 'em." He grinned at her. "I really ought to stick around and teach you one or two more things."

A red curtain descended over her eyes. Dawes yelled in surprise and pain and started back in his chair so suddenly that the leg gave way. She knew she had thrown the coffee at him, not caring where it hit, and as he fell backward on the chair she swung the empty pot, missing him, then threw it and herself at him blindly.

Jay caught her and dragged her off, struggling.

"Goddamn!" yelled Dawes. "What did you do that for?" His right hand and face were scarlet and stuck with coffee grounds. Jay, who had shoved Catherine almost the length of the kitchen out of the way, had his gun out before he saw that Dawes was no threat.

"You better get to the pump and wash that stuff off. I believe she's trying to cook *you*." He worked the pump handle for the enraged Dawes, gun still in hand.

Catherine sat on the floor where she had fallen and burst into tears. She drew herself up into a ball of misery, face pressed into her knees, and shook with sobs of fury.

"You need some grease on that. Better see if that store has anything for it."

"She's a goddamn crazy woman! You know that, don't you?"

"Mm. I hope you don't have to draw in a hurry, Dawes. You better get over to Atlantic City and find a doctor for this."

"Damn right. She's crazy. You take her into the Indian country with you, she's gonna get you killed! You know that now, don't you?"

"You may be right about that. Here, I'll bring along your saddlebag. You try that store for some kind of ointment before you leave."

"She needs her tail wore out with a switch! That's a goddamn nasty thing to do, throw coffee on a man and try to knock his head off, just because he said her dumplin's was heavy." They went out the door together, the sound of their voices and boots fading under her sobs.

When they were well gone, she drew a ragged breath and got up. The pump offered her a cooling balm for her eyes and face. She was alone so long she thought they might have ridden away together, and didn't care if they had. She laved her face until it was back to some semblance of normality and she was calmer, though shaky and weak. Her mind wasn't working well. She started thoughts and just let them trail away unfinished as she dabbled in the cold water. Finally she dried her hands on her shirt and sat down on one of the rickety chairs to wait.

When Jay came back, he leaned on the doorframe, watching her. She felt him there, but didn't raise her head.

"Is he gone?" she asked in a disinterested voice.

"He's gone."

"Why didn't you kill him?"

He left the doorway and sat on the edge of the table by her. "Because he didn't like your cooking?"

"You just gave him the money. You just handed it over. If he'd wanted it all, it would've been the same, I suppose. You must think an awful lot of him, or else you're afraid of him." Her voice was husky and flat sounding.

He frowned. "I'm not afraid of him. Nobody ever was. And the money is as much his as mine, and means more to him, past a certain point, than it does to me."

"Then why did you take it?"

"The money doesn't make any difference to you. What is it? Don't I live up to your expectations? Did you want me to kill him just to show you I'm the kind of 'man' you were looking for?"

"No, I wouldn't expect anything like that out of you."

"The hell you wouldn't! You wanted some blood showing on somebody, pretty bad, and it wasn't because of the money. Why?"

"Because he—" She drew in a torn breath.

"Because he what?"

"Because he raped me!" she yelled. "Not that it matters, since it was just good old Dawes!" Her voice woke echoes in the empty building. He sat looking down at her with a blank face. She thought he didn't believe her.

"He wanted fifty per cent of everything, he said, including me! That was reasonable, wasn't it? We didn't think you'd mind! But, just in case you did, he said he'd kill you if I made any noise! Any noise at all. So I let you sleep, and I let him do it here on the end of the table, because I was so stupid, I didn't know that nobody was afraid of Coleman Dawes, because I was plenty afraid!" She put her head down on her arms against the table, not to cry, but just so she wouldn't have to see that blank look on his face any more.

"You didn't tell me," he said to her silence.

"When could I have done that? He was expecting it; you weren't. He said he'd have the advantage."

"So you kept quiet to save me, then jumped him over the dumplings?" He touched her head lightly. "Tiger Heart," he murmured. She thought he was laughing and started to jerk away, hot murder filling her heart. But he caught her arms and gathered her up, unsmiling. She let herself be held, her anger and confusion melting in the hard grip of his arms around her. "Tiger Heart," he whispered against her ear. "I promise him to you, if ever I see him again. I regretted the last four. They really didn't deserve it. But Dawes does, and I promise him to you." He picked her up, over her faint protests, and carried her upstairs. "Shut up. You've had a bad day. You need the rest."

She stretched out on the bed, feeling boneless as he removed her boots and his own, then lay down beside her. She gladly let him hold her, feeling so drained of anger that she didn't need Dawes's blood. His concern had restored her sanity. If he cared about her, even this much, let Coleman Dawes go to hell. She would tell him so, in a moment.

But there was something else, something he had said, that she must ask about. What was it? The strong rhythm of his heartbeat in her ear was lulling her to peace. Four men. He was sorry about killing four men. She didn't think he could mean the four young marauders who'd killed Charlie and Billy.

"Jay? What four men did you mean you were sorry for? Were they . . . not the ones who killed . . . your wife?" Surely not.

He didn't answer for so long she thought he must be asleep. But it didn't matter. In his bloody trade, it could have been four out of many. It didn't matter. She tightened her arm around his body to prove that it didn't.

"There were three of them with her. I made her tell me that, and their names, before she died," he said at last. She opened her eyes slowly. His voice was entirely calm.

"Who was the other?" she whispered, when he didn't continue. Again, she thought he wouldn't answer. Then:

"The other was her."

Catherine felt her flesh cool and prickle at the spare confession. Her mouth made a numb protest. "Mrs. Kelly said the three men—"

"Raped her? No. She went to them willingly, like the Squawtown whore she really was. In front of her own children. And I killed her for it."

She raised her head. His tawny eyes met hers without a flicker. It wasn't a macabre joke. He was telling her the truth —a terrible truth—refuting the lie that had first drawn her to him in sympathy. She groped for something to say to him.

"How—how did you know she did that?"

He continued to look at her in the same cool way. "My boy told me. Johnny. They put him outside and locked the door. My daughter—if she is my daughter—was still in her cradle. Cat—my wife—said the boy was lying because she'd punished him." His voice clouded. "But a little boy wouldn't know how to tell about a thing like that unless it was true. He was big enough to see in through the window." He closed his eyes at last against her stare. His pulse had quickened now. Under the heel of her hand she could feel it.

"She admitted it was true before I killed her, though she tried to hold on to her own story, as long as she could. I had a pretty good idea who they were, the bastards. They'd been gaping and trailing after her for two years, every time she went out on the street. I knew them, I found them, and I killed them. And they didn't have to admit to a damned thing, because I didn't bother to ask them.

"I spent ten years in a cage for killing vermin, and it cost me my boy and my daughter. I was sorry about it as soon as I could think straight again, because she wasn't worth killing for and because they probably hadn't been the first. I got her out of Squawtown; I shouldn't have expected anything else."

"What's Squawtown?" she whispered.

"It's the place where the Laramie Loafers live. The poor damned Indians who can't live off the land any more and depend on the Fort for a handout. They're disgusting and pitiful. Old men, old women, bone-thin children. If there are any young women, they're washwomen or whores or both, to support their men. I thought Cat's family was different. Her father was my scout until he got too consumptive to stay on a horse all day. He had pride and honor. I'd put my life in his hands a dozen times. Her mother washed clothes, but she was no whore. She kept me alive once, when I should have been dead from an arrow some Arapaho put in me. She and Cat." He guided her hand to a spot just under his right collarbone, where her fingers could feel a depressed, puckered scar.

"Cat was their last cub; the child of their old age, and their pet. They had sons, but they were grown and gone. She was the pet of the whole Fort, I guess. She had a tame antelope kid that followed her around when she was little. It'd butt the hell out of anybody who tempted it, but when she'd laugh, they'd laugh. That sounds crazy, but not many Indians laughed around there. Not many whites, either, and when Cat laughed, everybody liked her. But they still let her go on living in that sty.

"I could see she was going to be—beautiful. I had to get her out of there, away from the lice, and her father's cough, and what was waiting for her in a couple of years. So I bought her." He made a faint sound that wasn't a laugh.

"I used to say I married her, but I bought her for a couple of blankets and a pair of skinny worn-out horses that had pulled a wagon across the plains from the East. The old man wanted to go home to his tribe to die, and he drove a hard bargain. She cost me twenty dollars."

"But you said you'd married her. Did it make any difference?"

His mouth twisted at the word. "It made a difference! One day she was the camp mascot; the next, she was that flat-faced squaw pretending to be an officer's wife. I tried to keep her away from all that, to protect her. She was the best-looking female in camp, you know. She had a face like a baby and a voice—" Catherine saw that he actually flushed with the emotion that memory brought with it. She was laden with a sick sorrow for him.

"You loved her very much, didn't you?" she asked.

His response shook her. "No! I hated her guts! Living with her was like being leeched every day!" He shoved her away and sat up on the edge of the bed, away from her searching eyes. There was another silence while she lay wishing she could believe that, and wondering if she dared to reach out and touch him.

"Ah well, what the hell," he said at last. "It must have been tough for her too. I guess she had to do something to regain all that popularity. It was a long time ago. I played my stupid part out to the end and they put me in jail. Not because I'd killed three men who'd slept with my wife, but because I'd made too serious a thing out of three white men taking an Indian squaw. Fornication was as common as saddle sores at Laramie."

"They still thought the other men killed her, though."

"Well, I let them think it. It didn't make any difference to them who killed her, anyway. And I'd already realized I was a damned fool as it was. Worse. Johnny needed me, and I had to play the injured husband and let him get lost.

"Now I'm out, and I want him back because he's all I've got to show for my whole lousy life. His mother was nothing, but he's mine. I know that. And I won't turn my back on the girl. I'll take them up to Canada, then back east after a while. Anywhere, just so they don't grow up like animals on the Reservation, and ride down to some damned fort once a month for a handout of flour and sugar and coffee that they don't know what to do with, and die of rotten lungs when they're twenty. If I can just get to them in time, maybe I can make it up to them a little, for having a whore for a mother and a fool for a father." She moved then, crawling across the wide, sagging bed to him. He took her in his arms and held her while her hands smoothed the hard muscles of his back. He cleared his throat self-consciously.

"I'm gabbing like Billy. I don't tell this tale for free drinks. You're the only one who knows, now. Charlie did. And I wouldn't have told you except you—well, I thought you ought to get it straight in your mind about who you were saving from Dawes this afternoon."

She considered that.

"I knew who," she said. She couldn't elaborate. He was the person who had saved her from the shame her need for love had felt for its own existence ever since she could remember. For that, he might confess to the Massacre of the Innocents and hope for forgiveness. But she couldn't say that to him, or anything like it.

"I'm just not used to maiden sacrifices on my account," he said with a half-smile.

"Well, put your mind at rest there. I wasn't a maiden, in case you forgot."

The smile died. "God Almighty, Catherine, why didn't you call me?"

"I told you why."

He took her face suddenly between his hands and kissed her mouth, bruising it with the harshness of remorse, but she responded gladly, forgetting her fatigue. He wanted her. Her own body ached with his need and could not answer it soon enough. In the bald silence of the barren, dirty room they undressed and touched, moving together on the bed. She surrendered all her old, ingrained qualms and fears, naked and with open eyes, in a sunlit, open room, to a feeling she had never fully known before. It was like drowning, sinking willingly to the death, then finding you could breathe in water.

The glare of the late afternoon dimmed to a false twilight as the sun dropped behind neighboring rooftops unnoticed. She lay in fierce possession of him. His hunger for her banished the last taint of Coleman Dawes and blotted her guilt before an accusing Willard. She clung to him, willing that in the same way she could rid him of the ghost of his faithless Cat.

Later, when he was asleep against her body under a rough blanket, and she could hold him like the child she'd never had, she forced herself to remember the locket she'd given Mrs. Kelly.

It had never been completely out of her mind, only laid aside with other unwanted things. Now she must decide whether to tell him what she'd done. Had the woman sent for help or just kept the locket? Let her keep it and welcome, prayed Catherine. Let her husband not believe her. Let the searchers look in all the wrong places until we're safe and away.

If they caught him, they would kill him. Theft was more serious than murder out here, it seemed. If they did catch him, she would have delivered him to them, and she was the only person in the world now who wanted him alive.

Yet so far there had been no sign of pursuit. She cast her mind abroad superstitiously, feeling for the image of pursuing men: for Willard, a sheriff, or some emblem of the law. In the manner of the Irish in her ancestry, she imagined that if trouble existed for her, she ought to be able to feel it.

She could feel no danger near them.

But she must tell him about the locket, tomorrow. Now, when they were so close, he would be sure to forgive her.

He stirred against her breast and spoke indistinctly. She lay utterly still for a long time after that, watching the dreary ceiling fade in the dying light, but he didn't speak again.

It was possible he had murmured her name, or tried to, half-asleep. Her heart welcomed and urged the possibility.

But, to her undeceived ear, the name he had breathed was "Cat."

# 13

THEY LEFT South Pass the next day on good terms with the prospecting storekeeper, who seemed willing to believe they were also gleaners of abandoned claims. He was a tiny, wizened man, whose lack of teeth and huge, lip-shadowing mustache made him difficult for her to understand. Jay claimed his allegiance just by letting him do most of the talking, while Catherine shopped his meager stores for their needs.

She was obliged to stock up on all the same flavorless things they had been living on before, simply because the choice was limited. But she filled her food bag heavily with apples, raisins, sugar, and coffee. He had a crate of precious paper-wrapped lemons in the root cellar, and she bought three, not quite sure what she ought to do with them in the wilderness, but aware that they were necessary to people on limited diets. Notions of scurvy had begun to occur to her.

She bought and tucked out of sight several yards of unbleached muslin for the kind of emergency that was looked for but never mentioned, and a broad-brimmed hat with a peaked crown for her unprotected head.

Jay surveyed the growing pile and added two more blankets, a hatchet, and a tin reflector stove to it. They left the extra horse with the old man and kept the pack horse.

When they set out at last she was so jubilant she would have sung, if she had ever been able to carry a tune in her life. He shook his head at her when she challenged him to a race out of town. But he let her have her way, and they ran the three surprised, heavily laden animals a short way down the empty street, and she won; knowing that he let her win, but crowing about it, anyway. Her night fears were put firmly away.

Grass-grown placer ditches and dry sluice boxes lined both sides of a creek running northeast out of town. She passed them by, half hopefully looking down for the glitter of some overlooked bit of gold, but of course there was none.

The land began to wrinkle and fold upward toward the mountains, whose pine-shrouded shoulders and snowy heads reared above and beyond them. The lower hills bore clusters of fluttering aspen and a kind of poplar with yellow-olive leaves, glittering like mirrors. Other trees there were, and pockets of wild flowers she couldn't name, nor could Jay when she asked him. He knew the trees and a few edible plants, but that was all.

The air grew more fragrant with the growing things. They paused once to rest the horses, but he wouldn't hear of stopping to eat until they had put at least ten miles between themselves and the stage road.

She was ravenous when he finally called a halt beside a deep-gouged, clear lake cupped in the hills. But she decided to forgo hot food in order to explore the site. They ate dried beef and apples as they walked along the lake's narrow margin, then lay on a bank near it that was covered with grass.

She made much of the grass, running her hands over it in delight, to his amusement. "Ever since I came out here, I've seen nothing but wheat grass, horse grass, ironweed, locoweed, tumbleweed, and briers," she complained. "This is just plain old moist, soft, juicy green *grass* grass. The kind we see so much of at home we don't think anything about it, except that it needs cutting all the time."

He obligingly rubbed her face with a handful of it, and baptized her with some more down her neck, and when she fought back he caught her and pinned her to the ground. She lay suddenly quiet under his long gaze, the laughter fading slowly from her face splashed with the dappled forest light.

"Somebody," he said thoughtfully, "has to lay down a rule or two, or we'll still be south of the Wind River when the first snow flies." He waited.

"What rule do you propose—sir?"

"That we don't inspect any more grass banks while the sun is up."

She considered this gravely, tracing the outline of his mouth with the tip of one finger, until he took her hand away. "That seems like a very harsh measure," she said. "Are you sure it's for the good of the troops?"

"It's meant to insure the survival of the command." Her smile rekindled and she drew his head down. She was beginning to test those powers of soft persuasion that had lain dormant in her for so long. Still, it was she who broke away first, to catch her breath and laugh shakily at her own daring. It was in her heart, and almost on her tongue, to tell him how she loved him, but she could not. That word should come from him now. There was no better time for it. But he said nothing; only kissed her lightly again and let her go.

She got up quickly, brushing the grass out of her collar while he watched her with the now-familiar curious, noncommittal look in those pale brown eyes that moved her so. Her smile was firmly in place as she put out her hands to help pull him up so they could continue their journey.

He was quiet and thoughtful most of the afternoon, though he pushed them along at a moderately swift pace. Her comments on the country went unanswered, and later she had to ride close and touch his arm before he realized she was asking a question.

"I know we're going to the Indian country to find your children, but you said before that Charlie was your guide. If you needed a guide then, how are you going to find them now?"

It was what he'd been asking himself since Charlie died in his arms. He was not well acquainted with the unwalled prison shared by the Shoshone and Arapaho. He had a map, but miles of it were little more than a surveyor's dream, sketched in between known landmarks, and his other information was nearly a year old.

The subtribe to which Cat's people belonged had been living on the Wind River last summer, somewhere between Bull Lake, which was on the map, and the place where Washakie was said to have killed a Crow chieftain, once, and eaten his heart raw. This place was not indicated, and the incident itself might be as legendary as the site.

There was a lot of country to cover unobtrusively before reaching that territory, and by the time he got there they might well have moved on.

The Shoshone were a Plains people, driven into the mountains by wars fought before the coming of the white man. By tradition they followed the buffalo still, but when there was no buffalo they hunted the white-tailed mule deer and the antelope through the high ground. They were diverse and fearless hunters rather than warriors like the Sioux, decorating their satin-fine antelope shirts with elk's teeth, bear's claws, and sometimes painted pictures of the chase.

He was tempted to turn east and try to get word of them near Fort Washakie. Washakie himself still lived, though more than eighty now, and his lodge was said to be near the little fort named for him. He was said to still rule his people with a clear mind, and he still periodically re-enlisted at the Fort as an Army scout. When he did, some officer of more elevated rank than commanded the little fort had to make the trip up there for the ceremony.

Jay had seen him several times at Laramie and other outposts, wearing his general's uniform, which was a gift of the United States government more than a quarter of a century before. Dressed in obsolete regulation splendor, except for the soft moccasins on his enormous feet, he was a withered, oaken old despot who easily outclassed every officer at Laramie, Jay had once thought, admiring him nearly twenty years before.

But Jay had resolved at the beginning to try to keep clear of the Indian police and the tribal government, and deal directly with Iron Knife. And he preferred to assume, while still in white man's country, that his identity might be known, although he had taken enough precautions to keep it a secret. He continued to avoid the easier trails and more traveled roads.

He had no reason to believe he had been identified or followed. He had picked Bowan and Dawes as partners partly for their familiarity with the desert country around the railroad, and their willingness to take some orders without explanations; but also because they had no previous connection with him. Of course Charlie did, but Charlie had been safe.

He had picked a difficult and unlikely place for the robbery, and an unlikely escape route, laying down the water caches across trackless ground instead of taking an easier way into the southern mountains. He had no time to hide in some louse-infected thieves' camp of Billy's choosing.

The false story to cover him with Dub Kelly, the trial run-through of the action on the train, the beard to change his face, the traded horses to confuse the trail. He had been careful.

Yet from the moment he boarded the train he had had a premonition that the enterprise would fail. Before the money was in his hands he had felt certain that it would not move Iron Knife; might even work against him, in fact.

And from the moment Catherine staggered up from the ground, fighting for her horse, everything had gone awry. He blamed only himself for it, not her. She had only been failure's instrument, not its maker. But because of her presence Billy and Charlie were dead, and Coleman Dawes was at large and feeling vengeful, running through heavily populated country with a flamboyant burn, too much money, and a big mouth. And Jay was left in possession of an extra person who didn't figure in any of his plans for his future with the two children. He would have enough persuading to do to get them, without having to explain her. He had a growing fear that she was going to change things there too, just by being present.

That events had a way of shaping well-laid plans, he granted. But he was contemptuous of people who let emotions swerve them from a well-laid course. Catherine was not part of his plan. He would not let her spoil it. He would not allow himself to change it, now that he had come so far.

Yet there was the danger of her becoming important to him, in a way he had never intended to let another woman be. In that desolate hotel last night he had actually let himself think for a moment of abandoning his plan and taking her with him to some distant place of safety, where they could make use of whatever was left of their lives, together.

That he could entertain such a thought put him on the alert for further signs of weakening. He had told her about Cat and the children to strengthen his resolve not to forget them. When he had said he wanted her to know whom she had been saving, he had also meant it as a fair warning that he was not to be dissuaded from his primary target—his son.

They slept without having seen any further traces of human habitation that night, and they saw none the following one as they drew close to the Reservation border. He studied his map again the third noon out of South Pass, trying to establish their exact position.

She was having a meditative period, which matched well with his own mood and pleased him. Her capriciousness was puzzling, when he troubled to think of it; by turns amusing and provoking. He was amused that she could rise from a river, wet and naked, and fling herself on him, then primly require him to turn his back while she dressed. Yet her vanity and self-absorption, which made her so indifferent to anything not concerning herself at the instant, made him impatient and short with her. He sensed in her a yearning to be loyal, a bent for devotion to something or someone, as earnest as that of any young shavetail fresh out of West Point. It was the single most disturbing thing about her. Because he had no belief in the loyalty of women, no experience or expectation of it. And it didn't accord well with her self-indulgence, or with her own history. Wasn't she here now because she had run off from her husband, without a word of warning? And she had never given any reason for the desertion beyond the remark that they never should have married.

She was company; she was beguiling, mostly when she didn't try to be; but she was not to be counted in with the future. Much as she seemed to be enjoying her holiday, she would grow tired of it soon and he would leave her, as he should have left her already except for a moment of weakness.

He returned the map to its case. It was time to turn east, downcountry. If he did, the next stream he crossed should be the Popo Agie, and beyond that was the Reservation border, supposing the map to be accurate.

He started to rise and wake her from her doze when he heard the sound of movement on the trail below them, which they had been following until he led them away from it to rest. There were a number of horses, ten or a dozen, shod, and trotting with a practiced unity as familiar to him as his own pulse. He knew before he saw them that they were a squad of cavalry out on reconnaissance. He dropped down beside Catherine, putting his hand over her mouth before she could speak. Then he wished he could do the same for the three horses tethered and grazing farther uphill. He thought they were well enough hidden from view, but there was a good chance that the scent of their own kind would move one of them to call out.

The ground between was too open to risk moving up to them. He felt Catherine's hand pulling at his, to free her mouth. He released her. Her eyes were more aggrieved than frightened.

"I wasn't going to call them. Don't you know that yet?" she whispered.

"Be quiet." They passed. He could see flashes of blue and brown through the trees. One of his animals, the mare they used as a pack horse, raised her head, ears forward, and nickered. He swore under his breath, but the squad went by, never changing its gait.

When they were gone he said, "Let's move."

She sat up, and he saw that her eyes were full of tears. "They're looking for us!"

"No, they're just out on patrol."

She shook her head violently. "They're after us. It's my fault. I should have told you before."

He smiled a little. "Not to be boastful, but if they're after us, it's more likely to be my fault, don't you think?"

She crossed her arms, hugging herself as if she were cold. He watched her, the smile fading until it was just a muscle tension making his mouth a little crooked.

"You got the word out, through someone."

She nodded. "I gave Mrs. Kelly my mother's locket to go to the law and tell them you had me and which way we were going. Jay, that seems so long ago! Everything was different. I was afraid! I meant to tell you, but every day I put it off it was harder to say." Her tears brimmed over, matting her thick lashes. "So I just let it go." The fat teardrops trembled and winked as she breathed.

He put out a thoughtful finger and touched one of them, making it run.

"All right. You told me," he said at last. "Let's move." He took her arm gently, spoke softly, but she still looked up for some kind of absolution. And he wasn't in the mood for tears and kisses. They were miles from the border, but if the Fort had been alerted to look out for him, the Indian police would have line riders out on it on regular patrol. He would need to watch it carefully from some vantage point of safety, long enough to gauge their numbers.

He thought two patrols would be the most likely. It was a small fort.

They didn't cross over until that night. He would have gone before, but they were pinned to a hillside for half the afternoon by a hunting party on the other side, stalking small game in their direction. They sat in a willow thicket, tormented by mosquitoes and deer flies, while on the other side the quartet of hunters rested and talked, with occasional laughs and gestures that identified the reminiscing hunter and his skeptical audience.

"What are they, can you tell?" Catherine asked, whispering, although there was no need at that distance.

"Arapaho." He slapped irritably at his own swarm of insects.

"Why couldn't we show ourselves, and ask for directions?" she wondered.

"Because they're Arapahoes."

"You said Charlie was an Arapaho."

"Charlie was a different matter. The Arapaho and the Shoshone don't mix, even up here. They wouldn't know, and if they did they wouldn't be likely to spill it to me."

"How can you know that for certain? Besides, you'll have to ask somebody sometime, it seems to me."

He gave her one of his less friendly looks, because she was right. "Damn it, Kate, let me worry about how to get where I'm going. You just tend to your little pots and pans. Anyway," he sighed, exasperated by her hurt look. "I don't speak Arapaho; not more than a few words. And talking white man's Snake to one of them isn't the best way to start a conversation."

"Snake?"

"Snake. Shoshone." He rubbed his itching face tiredly. "Lie back and catch a little sleep, if you can. We're going to be here for a while."

So they waited until the hunters moved on before fording the little river into the territory. He began to miss Charlie more than ever. Even Dawes would have been welcome. He needed someone to keep an eye open for unwanted company at night, and Catherine was no help. She fell asleep every night like someone drugged, even when she tried not to.

He slept lightly, waking often and knowing that such a watch was useless. If anyone was following them and wanted to take them, he was helpless to stop it, unless he was bent on suicide. He was only one tired white man, and getting worse. He was also a trespasser and an outlaw now. Throwing himself on the mercy of a random selection of Indians, even from a traditionally friendly race, went against his grain. Humble pie had never been his chosen dish. But his alternatives seemed few.

The next day he was sure they were being tracked. He said nothing about it to Catherine. Her calm both baffled and pleased him. He had expected her to be full of fears and atrocity stories gleaned from Eastern newspapers. Certainly the Cheyenne and Sioux in recent years had given enough trouble to justify some fear.

But she said little or nothing about such things; only asking something about the Shoshone from time to time. He couldn't decide whether this was a mark of unusual intelligence in an Easterner, being able to make distinctions among savages, or of unusual stupidity, relying on him to save her, no matter what.

In many ways she was more of a puzzle to him than Cat had ever been.

That night they made camp on the south fork of the Little Wind. He spent the evening cleaning, oiling, and reloading the old "New Model" Remington he had carried since the War. He had had it converted, and had purchased metal cartridges for it, and a cartridge belt with ammunition loops sewn on, that was a new thing to him, but was favored by the more flamboyant gun wearers. It made him feel foolish, and he soon put it away and returned his ammunition to his pocket. He preferred to wear his holster high and reversed in the Army style he was accustomed to. The cut-down civilian holsters seemed a desecration of style and good leather. They left the gun flopping uncomfortably on the thigh unless they were tied down, and offered the weapon no protection from the weather. He had never considered a fast draw to be an advantage, because it was usually followed by wild, nervous firing. Rapid fire had far less tactical value than accuracy did. That was tactical gospel, and he had never yet seen it proved other than true.

When he was finished, and had made the customary inspection of his rifle, his animals, and his other equipment, he sat watching Catherine brush her long hair until it snapped fire after each stroke in the dry air and flew out in a thin train after the brush. He liked to see her do this, and to put his hands in the heavy silk mass afterward, but she started braiding it at once, and on the whole it seemed best if she did.

He built up the fire until it was a beacon a blind brave could have found by the heat alone. She looked a bit surprised, because he had been strict about even small fires up to now. They made their bed together, as usual, and he held her close, feeling somewhat more nervous than he liked. He didn't make love to her. He was tired, and she seemed content just to be held. Besides, he was not minded to provide any more free entertainment than he already had for the invisible audience he could feel—almost smell—out there in the dark.

He slept, dreamless as a stone, for the first time since the beginning. When he woke in a milky dawn, they were surrounded by brown faces.

THERE WERE six of them, all young, all staring at Catherine. They were Washakie's people, he saw to his slight relief. He greeted them, still lying on his back under the blankets with her. At his voice she woke, and he felt the beginnings of a surge of alarm in her that was going to take her up off the ground. He tightened his arm around her quickly, pressing her against him, so the movement was stifled before it was well begun.

"Easy," he said softly. "Don't look scared. Don't look anything, understand? They're not going to hurt you, but, from now on, you play idiot. Don't talk; don't look worried. Be a good squaw." Under the blanket her fingers were clutching at him, but gradually they relaxed. When they did he sat up, lazily.

"The Shoshone braves are as silent on their feet as the fox. I didn't hear you until you were an arrow shot away."

One of them grinned down at him. "Then you have sharp ears indeed, white man. But are you afraid of the night shadows, that you built so big a fire?"

"I built it to welcome you. I saw you trailing me yesterday." He hadn't, but he had sensed them, which was the same thing.

"We have trailed you since you crossed the river."

He doubted that, but let it go unchallenged. He decided to remain sitting. A look of ease in a subordinate position seemed like a good idea until he had something to stand up for.

"You are on the wrong side of that river, white man. Are you hunting? Digging for gold? Or lost?"

"None of those things. I am looking for someone."

"Another lost white man?"

"One of your own people. A man named Iron Knife."

"Are you his enemy or his friend?"

"I was his relative." They exchanged looks among themselves. "His sister was my wife. She is dead now," he added, as they turned their eyes again to Catherine.

"I do not know any Iron Knife," said the spokesman, switching his attention away from Catherine, with an air of disdain.

"Last year he was said to be living on the Wind River, above the Lake of the White Bull, but not so far as the place where Washakie feasted on his enemy's heart."

"What do you want with this Iron Knife?"

"It is a personal matter, but I mean him no harm."

"Are you afraid of us, white man?" asked one of the others with mock curiosity. "It seems that you must hold the woman's hand under the blanket." Jay let her go and got up, slowly and easily. When he was erect, he was half a head taller than the tallest of them. He stood loosely, hands at his sides, weaponless.

"I am not afraid of the Shoshone, no. I have eaten their meat and married their daughter. Also, I know that when Washakie pledges the friendship of his people, they keep his word." He smiled. He wondered if he was winning, losing, or breaking even in the exchange.

The first brave changed the subject. "You have a gun and belt like a pony soldier," he said, nodding to where they lay. "Are you a soldier?"

He was winning. "I was. I was at Laramie, when Washakie came there, many times." He was satisfied with the effect the old chief's name had on them, and planned to drop it into the conversation at regular intervals, but the young man took him by surprise.

"It is good that you know Washakie. His lodge is set not far from here. It is just past the time of the Sun Dance with us, and he is still at the dancing ground. If you trespass on his land, looking for one of his people, he will be interested to know of it. Of course, since you know him, he will be glad to see you. We will show you the way, so you won't become lost again."

He was breaking even. He looked down at Catherine briefly and said, "Get up and roll the beds. We have an escort into Washakie's camp." She granted him a particularly idiotic look for the second she had his eye, then turned out lumpishly to obey.

The young men lounged about while Jay and she packed and saddled. There had been no show of force, although the party was equipped with carbines as well as bows and knives.

When they were mounted, Catherine tried to ride close to Jay, but found herself relegated to the rear, leading the pack horse, instead. No one seemed to pay any further attention to her, or feel there was any likelihood of her escape; as, indeed, there wasn't.

Her stomach was heavy with fear. She hadn't been able to understand what they were saying, and she didn't know where they were going now. Had he found his guide to the children so quickly? If they were going to ride through all of the Indian territory like this, she didn't think she could stand it.

But they hadn't far to go. Following the river for only a couple of hours at a moderate pace, they came to an encampment of a hundred or more tepees and circular brush shelters set out along the water. The sun was still making long morning shadows behind them, and the hills rising south reflected it from their sides in Venetian reds and ochers so brilliant they seemed to vibrate in the light.

Cooking fires sent up wispy signals all over the camp. The women chattered to each other and to their children, and filled bowls with a sort of fragrant mush that gave Catherine cause to remember that her only breakfast had been a case of nerves.

They were led through the encirclement to the largest and most ornately painted dwelling in sight. Catherine half expected a palace guard of braves to burst out of it as they did in the wild West shows, to stand with folded arms while their chief made his appearance among them in full regalia, from paint to feathers. She was more than relieved it didn't happen.

Before the tepee was a very old woman, a fat middle-aged woman, and a young boy, squatting by the fire. They looked up, taking in every detail of the visitors with black, unreadable eyes. The brave who had spoken to Jay first approached the fire and in respectful tones said a few words in the direction of the old woman, not looking at her. She in turn spoke to the boy as she continued to scrape the sides of her pot, and he sprang up and went into the lodge.

Jay helped Catherine to dismount. She could feel a barely perceptible tremor running through him as he did. His face was so tight and alive with expectation it hurt her to look at him.

"This may be the easiest way, after all. He's the law up here. He can turn Johnny over to me if he wants to, and Iron Knife can't do a thing about it." He looked down at her. "Afraid?"

"I don't know," she temporized; then lied outright, "No."

"Good girl."

"I wish I knew what was happening, though. Are they here, right now—your children?"

He didn't answer, because the boy came out then and beckoned to the leader of their escort, who went in. They stood watching the opening for five minutes, in complete silence. She longed to ask again about the children, but he was absorbed in watching the lodge door. She realized suddenly that she was hoping they weren't in camp now; that she didn't want to see them yet. She flushed with shame at her selfishness. She didn't particularly want to see them ever. She looked around. The other braves stood like images, waiting. Then the first brave broke through the shadowed hole into the sunlight and motioned to Jay.

He stooped and went in. She followed. Nobody stopped or encouraged her. Inside the house of hide it was dark as a mine after the dazzling day. She felt Jay sit down and groped her way down blindly. Globular blue and yellow sun specters floated before her eyes until they became adjusted to the twilight of the lodge.

Then she saw the old man sitting on his buffalo robes, eating his breakfast from a tin Army plate, and forgot her fear and perplexity for a while in her examination of him.

He sat waiting to give audience like a king, and if she had never before pictured how a king would behave, she saw now.

He seemed to have been made from the bones of the earth. Though he remained seated, she could see that he must be very tall. He was old; incredibly old and wrinkled, but still straight. His hair was thick and white, his hands and feet were immense. His face, very broad at the jaw, with a wide mouth, was like supple, worn leather drawn smooth over stone. His hooded eyes were slow moving and faded, but awake and keen; intelligent and curious.

"Who are you?" he asked in English. She had been prepared for another baffling exchange in the vowel-riddled Snake tongue.

"John Wesley Grobart."

"That does not tell me anything much, John Wesley Grobart. Who are you?"

"A man who has come to claim what was taken from him." The old man waited, unprompting. "My two children are living here on your land. My wife was a woman of the Shoshone, the daughter of an Army scout named Lance Thrower, who served with the troops at Fort Laramie. I served there too, as a captain of Mounted Rifles. When my wife died, her father took my children without my permission, and sent them to his son, here. The son's name is Iron Knife. He's living somewhere up on the—" Washakie held up his hand mildly and Jay stopped as if he had been cut off.

"White men know how to do a great many things. But they have never learned how to tell a thing. You are too impatient. You leave many things out. How can I judge the truth of your tale if you say it, so: 'I was there. He is here. My wife is dead'? Are you hungry? Perhaps you will talk better when you have eaten."

"Yes. Thank you," said Jay without enthusiasm. Washakie

spoke to those outside, and his wish was apparently anticipated, because the fat woman bowed her way in through the door with a steaming bowl of meat and mush in each hand and offered it to them.

"Thank you," Jay repeated stiffly, and Catherine murmured an echo, receiving her bowl from the squaw. The woman looked at her curiously and withdrew as quietly as she had come.

Washakie drank sparingly from a cup by his side and waited in silence while they ate. Jay ate mechanically, with a studied calm. But Catherine knew he was not calm, and she worried about his growing tenseness. She supposed it might be natural, coming so close to his desire after so many years, but it was frightening to feel his uncertainty along with it. His sureness and calm had become rocks of security to her.

She ate her own breakfast with an eagerness she had never expected to feel for native cooking, trying not to wolf it, or to discover what it was made of. Jay had told her the Arapaho ate dogs but the Shoshone did not. She hadn't pressed for any further disclosures at the time, and she was glad she hadn't. Whatever it was, it was hot, tender, and not too strong tasting. She thought it would benefit from the use of more salt.

When they were finished, and were offered water, the old man said, "Do you use tobacco? I hear some white men think it is a vice."

"I have a pipe, but I ran out of tobacco," Jay said, in a more subdued voice than before. The chief reached down among his furs and produced a small pouch of soft white leather, though much soiled, and handed it to Jay. For himself, he brought to light a painted tin canister and took from it an enormous cigar. He spoke another word, and the boy came in a moment later with a burning tinder to light the cigar, and to wait, until Jay had filled and tamped his pipe, to kindle it.

Washakie wreathed himself in aromatic smoke, then held his cigar before him, observing its glowing end as appreciatively as a Virginia gentleman testing his own crop.

"The cigar was one of the white man's good ideas," he

said. "It needs no care, no vessel to hold it, and it is not so soon gone. I remember Lance Thrower. He was of the same age as my first son. They have both been dead now many seasons. And I know of Iron Knife. He has lived a life of honor and peace since he came to the Reservation. He does not deal in stolen children, or in any children, that I know. The youngest one of his family has shed all her milk teeth and will soon marry, I think. Iron Knife has never made known that he had a sister, or a white brother." He drew on the cigar again.

"Tell me your story once more, John Wesley Grobart, and put in more pieces. When did it happen, that you were a captain among the bluecoats, and married this woman?"

"I was at Fort Laramie before the white man's war, and during it. You know why we were kept there: to watch you, and the other tribes." Jay spoke carefully now, with little pauses between sentences. "The girl's father was attached to my company at one time. He was only a few years older than I, I think. But he had a lung sickness that was killing him. He wanted to return to his own people, up here. He had one daughter. She was born at the Fort; grew up there. She wouldn't have been happy up here, penned up—excuse me. I married her."

"You took her, as a kindness to your friend, so she would not be—penned up?" Washakie asked dryly.

Jay faltered. "No. It was for myself too. I was of an age, thirty-three, four, I forget what, but old enough to want a settled life. A wife and sons."

Can't you say you loved her? thought Catherine vexedly. Can't you say it, even about your wife? If not, how will you say all the rest?

Jay cleared his throat. "My son was born the following year; my daughter, two, no, three years after that. In between my wife had a stillborn child. After Sand Creek and the Sioux and Cheyenne wars, mixed marriages were less than popular at the Fort, especially among the white women. I left the Army the year after the war ended and moved my family to the civilian town outside the Fort. My daughter was born there."

"What was the name of this daughter of the Shoshone?" asked Washakie softly.

"She was called Cat Dancing." Jay took a more decisive breath. He was wandering. The history of Cat was unimportant. He was here to talk about his children.

"She died when the second child was born?"

"No. She was raped and killed by a white man. She identified three white men who had been with her, and I—killed them too." His pipe had gone out. He frowned at it, absently. Catherine bowed her head. The way he had said it—he was trying not to lie to the old man.

"I was arrested for killing the men. And while I was waiting for my trial to begin, my children were taken from the town. I was not consulted, or even told where they were."

"But, surely, they needed someone to care for them?"

"I could still have provided for them. And my own father lived in the town. But they were taken without his knowledge too."

Washakie puffed for a while.

"All of this was long ago. Why did you wait until now to seek out your children, if they are here?"

"I was in prison for killing the men. I was released last winter."

"And still you waited."

"I had some affairs to settle. I needed money, to take care of them."

Oh Lord, groaned Catherine inwardly. Washakie sat meditating. Jay raised his head and looked at the old man. He had been concentrating on the pipe in his hands as he talked.

"If Iron Knife took your children, then he must have done it as a duty to his father and his sister. He is an honorable man, and if they are the youngest two of his lodge, then he has reared them as his own. Yet you speak as if you bear him ill will for this act of kindness."

"No," said Jay crisply, "but he did take them without my consent, and in all the years that followed he sent no message to tell me about them. They could have been dead, as far as I knew, until last summer. He didn't approve of my marriage to his sister. I don't know what else he might have felt about me, but apparently he didn't think me worthy of being their father. Whatever his intentions, what he did, in my country, is called kidnapping."

"Much of the white man's thinking is difficult for me. I would have said that whatever his feeling against you, if he had any, he gave the children a home and stood as their father —if he has them. And that being so, they have lived with him since they were babes. How will you know them? How will you expect them to know you?"

"The boy was four years old. His name is John Canby Grobart. The girl was called Elizabeth Carey, after the woman who helped C—my wife, when she was born. She was a baby, it's true. But the boy was old enough. He'll remember."

Washakie shook his head. "I do not think that Iron Knife and his wife call them John and Elizabeth."

"Whatever Iron Knife calls them, that's who they are," Jay said. He caught himself and said more steadily, "I am grateful to Iron Knife for raising them. I mean to show my gratitude, if he will let me, by making a rich man of him."

"They are as dear to him as his own sons, it may be."

"I'm thankful for that too. And I want to repay him. But they are my children. I am able to take care of them now. I can give them an education. I can take them away someplace where their blood won't matter."

"I don't believe there is such a place as that, John Grobart. I do not think you believe there is such a place either, for a mixed blood."

"In the East it's different from here. There, if a man has Indian blood, even a very little, he boasts of it to the whites. Besides, they are mine, and if I say they are white they'll be accepted for that." There was a muscle ticking in the side of his face.

"In the East they have just finished a war among themselves, over the black men. I hear that if a man has black blood, even a very little, he hides the secret from the whites or they will turn away from him, no matter if his skin be as white as yours."

"That is an entirely different case."

Catherine dared to put her hand on his arm to steady him, but he shrugged it off.

"Here, Iron Knife says they are Shoshone, and they are accepted." Washakie noticed Catherine's restraining gesture and Grobart's dismissal. "However, these matters cannot be settled just between the two of us. Iron Knife; his wife, who has been like their mother; and the children themselves—I call them children only because we have been speaking of their beginnings; they are not children—they must all have a voice in this matter too.

"I will send for Iron Knife," he said. "He is not far from here. A journey of one or two days. He was here until then, for the time of dancing. You will have to be patient for as many more days, until he is found and returns. A man of your years will have learned patience if he has learned anything at all. You will be comfortable. There is a good tepee for the guests of Washakie."

He called to those outside. Jay stood up, and Catherine after him. The muscles of his arm, when she touched it, were like stone. He was gripping the pipe in that hand.

"Thank you," she said on impulse to the old man, surprised as much as he at the sound of her own voice. "You have been very understanding."

He looked at her with a light of amusement in his old, filmy eyes. "What are you called?" he asked.

"Catherine Crocker." She felt Jay's scowl burning into her.

"Crocker? You are not John Grobart's wife?"

"No," she whispered.

He nodded, puffing at the shrunken cigar.

"Another piece left out. As I told you, the white man does not know how to tell a thing well. He leaves out so many interesting pieces."

# 15

SHE KNEW she had overstepped some forbidden boundary when she spoke to Washakie. But it was more than that. She realized it when they were alone in the guest lodge. She had blundered onto dangerous ground, and for the first time since the night of Billy's maiming, when she had seen her death in his face across the campfire and stumbled back from it, she was afraid of him.

He remained standing in the middle of the lodge, back to the door, while she hesitated behind him. He didn't speak; hadn't spoken since they left Washakie. He seemed to be looking at nothing. The silence grew. He behaved as if she weren't there, or as if he weren't. It was as if he were gathering himself for some sudden assault, yet he didn't move. It occurred to her that he might hate close, dark places like the cell in which he had been confined so long. Perhaps that was it. After all, what had she done that was so terrible? Spoken her thanks to an old man for his graciousness.

Well, it mustn't go on like this. She would make him speak. Let him reprimand her for disobeying him and get it over. It would ease the tension. She made herself move, walk around him. She made him look at her.

He looked at her. Then his hands came up, on either side of her head, holding it tightly, and he pulled her to him and kissed her.

For the briefest of seconds she thought it was a forgiveness and her arms reached out for him too. Then she knew it was never meant to be that, or to be any expression of love at all, and she began to struggle, hands gripping his wrists, trying to pull away. But his hands were like a vise that only tightened when she resisted, and he was bruising her mouth on her own teeth.

When he was finished there was a spot of blood on his own mouth. He held her head still, long enough to say, "That's what a woman's mouth is for, and that's the only thing it's good for. You'd do well to remember it, next time you're tempted to put it to work on somebody else's business." Then he let her go so suddenly she staggered.

She felt the fear draining out of her as anger took its place, but she tried to swallow it. It wasn't over, yet. There was still hurting to be done, and she didn't want to start it.

"I'm sorry I broke one of your Divine Rules," she said coldly. "I'm afraid I don't make a very good squaw."

"That you don't!"

"Well, what did I do that was so terrible? I said thank you! I told him what my name was when he asked!"

"You told him it was very understanding of him to refuse me what's mine."

"That wasn't what I meant at all! I thought it was kind of him to see you; to hear you out. He seemed to me to be very sympathetic and understanding about the problem of the children. He seemed to see on all sides of it—"

"The problem of the children, as you call it, is my problem. And all his understanding of it was that they were better off left to grow up in bare-assed squalor up here than with me. That's what you thought was so understanding!"

"No! You just want to think that because you—God, Jay, let's not talk to each other. It's none of my business, just as you said."

"In that, you're exactly right. None of your goddamned business. But your opinions are showing, like quills on a porcupine."

"I'm not saying anything!"

"No, but it's so churned up in you you're about to choke on it, like you were the morning before we got to South Pass. Well, go ahead this time. Spit it out."

"You want to fight with someone, but you need somebody else to start it. You don't care what I think."

"I'll give you that, but you look ready anyhow. Fire away! Tell me how misguided I am to want my son."

She saw that he wanted her to hurt him, so he could feel justified in hurting her. It was so much like Willard it made her sick. But the temptation to oblige him was too strong. He had accused her once of wanting to see somebody's blood showing. Very well. There was blood on his mouth now, and it was hers. She raised her chin.

"How old was Cat Dancing when you married her?" she asked.

His eyes flickered surprise. "Fourteen, whatever difference that makes."

"And you were how old? Thirty-three or four, you said. Almost—no—quite old enough to be her father then. Yet you'd never been married before, had you? I wonder why not?"

He scowled down at her. "I don't know. The choice in women was never too great. I was moved around a lot. The pay was poor and there were other things to do. Is that what's worrying you? Whether I had a weakness for little girls?" he asked scornfully.

"She was very young, wasn't she?" Catherine mused with cruel concern. "Three babies in four years, and dead at eighteen. She hardly lived at all. She couldn't have had many thoughts or opinions of her own, or known how to express them if she did. You said you kept her away from others. You kept her busy having babies, but she was just a child herself. And you loved her that way." She was speaking softly so her voice wouldn't carry outside.

"Her people count a woman grown at that age."

"I said you loved her that way! You did love her, didn't you?"

"That's enough," he whispered.

"Why did you kill her, Jay? Because she slept with other men, or because, even before that, she was growing tired of being treated like a child or a pet, and you couldn't just take her up and put her away again like a toy, any more? Wasn't that how it was? She turned into a human being instead of a doll—an impossible child-wife—and did something *you* didn't plan. Not sleep with men, but just think, go out alone, punish her children. And you weren't God the Father to her any more?" She had no idea such thoughts had been working in her brain.

He grabbed her arms and shook her. "Goddamn you, Catherine, I said that was enough!"

"You wanted me to spit out my opinions, remember?"

"Your opinions, hell! Your craziness! You don't know anything about me or her. You never knew her! You're just putting yourself in her place. You're either rotten with jealousy or you like digging up the dead. I don't, so let her be."

"She may be dead, but you've never buried her!"

"I buried her a long time ago."

"Then why are you here?"

"You know damn well why I'm here."

"Oh yes, of course. To rescue your son—and the girl. I've noticed how you always say it that way: 'and the girl.' Those poor little children you love so much and haven't seen for ten years, to save them from 'growing up like animals.' "

"Yes, goddamnit!"

"I think you have another reason." He didn't ask what it was. "I think you want them for souvenirs of the kill."

He snorted in sudden amusement.

"I've been thinking you were out of your mind, but now I see what this is all about. You are jealous, but not of Cat.

"It's the kids. You're in a big rush to jump into Iron Knife's camp before you've even met him, and to make it sound like I'm some sort of lunatic, because you don't want them around. You're scared to death of them."

"No!"

"You think that if he keeps my kids, you won't have any competition while you play at being the little girl again."

"That is not true!" Catherine shouted, her face flushed with guilt.

"Isn't it? Then tell me something. You're a healthy, good-looking woman, and you certainly like what you get in bed. How is it you never had any children of your own?"

"Don't you speak to me like that," she said in a choked voice.

"I say it's because you wanted to be the only doll baby in the house."

"I never did! I never wanted to be that. You think I didn't want babies? I wanted them. I could have used their love and their company these last nine years. But I didn't want them to grow up like I did, in a house full of constant war and hate and shame!

"My father is a drunkard. He drank away his property, his career, and my mother's love, so that she went to the grave hating him. He made me so desperate to get away from him that I married the first man who asked me. And I was an old maid before that happened, because all the boys and men in our town knew about Papa; knew they'd wind up having to take care of him too.

"But poor Willard was a stranger and he had money. He saw me as a proper little lady with a father who must be rich because he never seemed to work; who lived in a big old house, twice the size of the Boston shanty he came from.

"We didn't tell him that the house was all we had left. Or that Papa didn't practice law much because he didn't have many clients. People are picky about being represented in court by a man who forgets to show up on the day, or else forgets their names when he does.

"And nobody else told Willard, I suppose, because nobody liked him very much for being a new-rich Yankee in a poor little Maryland border town. We were on the same side in the War, but God, he was such a *Yankee* Yankee!

"Well, he proposed quick and I accepted quicker and we both got fooled. He didn't get much of a lady and I didn't get much of a man. He settled right into our old house with Papa. He kept him in liquor and bootlicked his rich friends, 'til he made more money. He looks like a man. He's big and strong and hearty. But underneath he was scared to death. Afraid of me, afraid to make a wrong move at the dinner table, afraid to offend people who weren't worth speaking to in the first place. I didn't get a man. I just got another poor, hollow *thing* to take care of and be ashamed of.

"That's the kind of life we've had. That's the kind of home my babies would have lived in if I'd been selfish enough to give them birth."

He shook his head a little at her. She thought she saw pity begin to take anger's place in his face. The certain feeling that she had even been fishing for it was like a gadfly to her pride.

"Don't you pity me, though. I grew up on pity and whispers. You're the one who'll need it if you do what I think you mean to do." The look vanished. "Maybe you did love those babies when they were small. Maybe you do, still, after all this time. I don't know. But I do know you didn't hate that poor girl you married and killed. You loved her, whatever she did, and you want more punishment than you got in jail. Well, if you take her children away with you, feeling like that, you'll get it."

"Don't start on that again," he said huskily.

They were standing very close in the dusky lodge. Suddenly she was exhausted and confused and sorry. She saw from his face that she had made him loathe her; that she had ruined things for herself again, the way she always did. Counting coup with your mouth again, White Lady? Know your enemy. Did she know this one, really? She reached out for him, wanting to undo some of it. What had she said? Everything but what she'd intended. Everything but the important thing.

"I'm not on Iron Knife's side, I'm on your side. I'm not jealous of them; I don't hate them. I love *you.* I want you to have them if you love them, but not just to use, to twist the knife in yourself when you look at them and see her. Don't try to see her in them and blot it out. She's already dead, and that's punishment enough for anybody. If you killed her and her lovers because she wounded your pride—"

"By God, I see I did old Willard a favor when I took you off his hands. You dried-up, jealous bitch, the only thing you're worried about is yourself. You're the one who's afraid my daughter might look like her mother—and put you out in the cold. Or that I might spend some time trying to make things right for Johnny and not screw you every night!"

"You bastard," she whispered, white faced with shock. It was a word she had never spoken before. He jerked away from her hand and left the tepee.

She remained behind, transfixed; hearing the echo of their last words and sucking in the hot, stale air of the place in deep breaths, as if she had been climbing.

Her rage seeped away in the silence, taking the strength in her legs with it. She sank to the ground as if crippled, as she was, with despair and shock. At first, she hoped she wouldn't begin to cry, but the pain she felt was worse than tears. She was miserable beyond anything she had ever known. She ached heart and throat with it, so that breathing was a labor. No encounter with her father, no quarrel with Willard, had ever left her with this heavy fear.

What had she done? Killed herself, striking at him. Was it possible to begin to hate someone while you were trying to tell them you loved them? That's what she wanted to say. What had she said? Something terrible. She hardly knew now. Like a berserker who returns to his senses bathed in blood with no remembrance of the slaughter, she could not recall her exact words. She only knew she had made him hate her. He would turn away from her now, and she would have no one. Why? Why? She hadn't even felt the anger coming until it was on her. That was the way she had often responded to some minor rebuke from Willard.

She had thought herself cured of that when she made her escape from him. Now she had revealed herself again, and this time to the man she wanted more than anything she could conceive of. A harpy in dove's feathers: she had proved she was everything he had said she was. Jealous, selfish bitch.

It must be true. She was jealous. She must be, but, oh God, only because he was still new to her, and precious. Selfish. Yes, but could she be so damned and blamed when she only wanted to keep her first love to herself for a little while? She had waited so long for it, never thought to have it at all, found it in such an unlikely person.

She blamed herself, relentlessly. But still there was a spot of white-hot anger in her heart for him.

Damn him! Damn him, anyway, for that last word; for imputing that motive to her!

No one came near her for all the hours she lay in dry-eyed misery in the lodge. After an eternity of self-condemnation she fell heavily asleep, exhausted by her emotions and enervated by the thick atmosphere of the place.

When she opened her eyes again, he was still gone. The day must be far advanced. She left the tepee, feeling wretched, and went to the river to wash her face. She had a migraine, the first since she had left the camp at Diamond Mesa, and all her medicine was gone. A giant pulse pounded in her head; a pain sharp as a gimlet pierced her right temple. The sun, slanting toward the peaks of the Wind River Range now, blinded her as she stumbled down to the water. There was no one about, to her relief. The women of the camp must be attending to their cooking fires again, this time for supper.

She knelt by the margin of the stream and tried to lean out far enough to get a drink, but her hands sank into the soft ooze at the water's edge, and she stirred up all the mud within drinking range when she pulled them out again.

Wringing out her shirt sleeves, she tried again several yards upstream. She lay on her stomach with her hands under her breast, clutching at a tiny embankment, and stretched her neck out to reach the water, but stopped when something frantic, and nearly transparent, skated past her approaching face on hairlike legs. She pushed herself back from it with a choked cry of disgust. For a time she knelt looking into the water for signs of it. Her mouth was stale, and dry as paper.

On the third attempt she managed to suck up a long draught of the warm, silty water, and a stray piece of grass that nearly choked her. As she gagged and coughed, her face ducked into the river, causing an explosion of water up into her eyes and nose.

"Oh my God! Come and take this before you drown!" The exasperated rasp came from a clump of scrub willow a dozen feet away. He was sitting on a slab of sandstone in the forefront of the shielding thicket, watching her. She wiped water from her eyes and got up, still coughing.

He held out a flat tin box that opened into a segmented drinking cup. She had to wave it away, because she was still fending off a drop of moisture that threatened to spill over the edge of her windpipe. When she routed it, and could speak, she gasped, "How many pockets have you got? You're always pulling something new out of one."

"I've been carrying my house on my back for thirty years. It's all in knowing how to pack it."

Not knowing what to say, she knelt and busied herself with washing her face again, rolling up her soggy sleeves to the elbow. Then she took off her boots and waded in, soaking her feet in the coolness of the pebbly mud and water.

"Feeling like a bath?"

"Yes," she said politely. "I'd love to be able to get all the way in. I smell like a horse blanket."

"Why don't you? There's nobody around but me." She shook her head, wordlessly. She could no more undress in front of him now than if he were Willard. She stepped out and picked up her boots, scuffing her feet in the damp sandy grass to clean them. She was scrubbing at her face with her soggy sleeve, and wishing she could think of a dignified way to leave, when he got up. He took her chin in one hand and mopped her face dry, slowly and thoroughly, as if she were his Johnny or Elizabeth. Her tears came then, at last.

When he put his arms around her, it was as if he had drawn a thorn out of her heart. She leaned against him, thinking of the gratitude of that fabled lion, as his arms barred her back. He didn't kiss her, or speak. She wondered if there was more pity than anything else in the gesture, but didn't care, because it made even her breathing seem easier.

"Jay—"

"Don't tell me you're sorry. I never could apologize, and I don't want to hear you try it, so let it go."

"What do we do, if neither of us is sorry?" She herself had been schooled in the enforced regret.

"Nothing. Let it go."

"I love you. I'm scared because you don't know it."

"I know. Listen, Catherine—" Whatever else he might have said was forgotten because there was a sound of horses on the dirt trail leading to Fort Washakie in the east. He pulled her back with him into the willow thicket.

There were six bluecoats, with brass buttons flashing in the red sun. Their hair was blue-black, their faces were dark, and they rode by, two abreast, less than a hundred yards away.

"Dog soldiers," he said behind her ear. "Indian police." They drew rein at Washakie's lodge and dismounted. Jay continued to watch the spot even after they disappeared inside.

"What should we do?" she asked, after a long moment.

"I don't know. We can't reach the horses from here without being seen. We can't go far on foot without food and blankets."

"Then what will we do?"

"Wait." It was ten or fifteen minutes before the soldiers emerged from the lodge. They walked their horses slowly past the pony corral, examining the stock carefully, then re-formed and cantered off two by two the way they had come.

Catherine struggled into her boots, feeling the sand grit inside them, while Jay stood looking east. When she stood up again and followed his gaze, she noticed for the first time the timber stockade wall and tower of the Fort on the horizon. She had not realized it was so close.

"We're right in their pocket," he said. "And they're no kind of Indian if they didn't see the prints of two shod horses leading right up to Washakie's door."

An early evening breeze sprang up, lifting the thick dust of the encampment common as they returned to their shelter. Washakie was standing by his own fire, wrapped in a blanket as if for the winter. His sparrow-thin old wife still sat tending her pots, as if she hadn't moved all day. He beckoned to them to approach, and when they did he seated himself and indicated that they should do the same.

"The evening meal will be ready soon," he said. "I thought you might have forgotten you were Washakie's guests, and were trying to catch the little brown river fish by hand for your dinner." At his repeated gesture they sat down by his fire. Washakie settled himself cross legged, as Jay was sitting, and put his hand out to the old wife for his tin plate.

"What did the soldiers want?" asked Jay.

The old man smiled, creasing his leather face a thousand ways. "Why, they came to tell me a thing too. But I believe they have been sadly affected by their closeness with the white soldiers over there. They showered names and places on my head like hailstones. I have gathered them up, and when we have eaten our meal you must try to put them all together again for me. If you do not cheat, it will be a good story, I think."

"Why didn't you turn me over to them? What they say is true, and you know it."

"I am not the enemy of the horse soldiers; nor of the railroad, although it has destroyed the buffalo. I am still an Army scout myself, as perhaps you know." Catherine must have looked her surprise, because he wrinkled his old face at her again. "Yes. It is a laugh-making thing. Often, when I think about it, I wonder who has tried the hardest not to smile, the pale colonel, or myself. But it is a way for an old man to keep the peace when fighting is futile. And I assure you, neither the colonel nor Washakie will ever smile into one another's eyes when we perform our duty for such a cause." He smiled at Catherine, who was frowning a little because his words seemed evasive, and she wondered whether it was because he was an old man wandering or an old man playing with them.

"I am not a fool or a senile dreamer," he said to her. "I do the things I must, to symbolize the things that are: the willing surrender to peace of a people who, if they could never hope to win, could yet shed much blood and cause much ruin if they chose to fight. But I am no lackey.

"Your Chief of Chiefs, General Grant, has given me a silver saddle, which is very uncomfortable to ride, because we aided his people in the wars they fought with the Sioux. But we fought because the Sioux are *our* great enemies, not because they are his."

Jay stirred the dust before him with a slow finger. "I have always known that you were a man of great courage and honor," he said softly. "For this reason alone, I wouldn't expect Washakie to tell a lie for me, or for any other man. What did you tell the soldiers who came?"

"To return in two days."

"Is that all?"

"When that is not enough, then I am no longer the chief of the Shoshone."

"Why do you give us two days? One would have been generous enough, when I've tried to deceive you."

"You have never deceived me. And I am not being generous."

Jay lifted his eyes to Washakie's.

"You forget that two days must pass, at least, before the return of Iron Knife," said the old man. "It may be that he will be more eager for your blood in the end than the men who wait in Lander for permission to enter here." He turned his hooded black eyes slowly in Catherine's direction, like a sun-drowsing old turtle.

"The husband of Mrs. Crocker is one of them."

# 16

THEY SLEPT APART that night, and the next, waiting for Iron Knife to come. The unhappiness it caused her was threefold. She felt their estrangement must be a matter of indifference to him, in spite of the return of his gentleness with her. She longed for the physical nearness of his body at night, to give her solace in a strange, lonely place. And she suffered the knowledge that her misery was her own fault, because it was she who had put the bedrolls apart the first night, hoping to be invited to return.

She had not meant to tease, she argued to herself. She had been trying to show him she wasn't expecting to be—she couldn't repeat the word even in her own mind. Well, she had been too subtle for her own good. He didn't understand her motive. Having hurt herself in an attempt to win comfort, she could only feel the more hurt because she was not caught in the deceit.

If he didn't understand, neither did he question her move or lose any sleep over it. He fell on his blankets and into a deep sleep within two minutes at the most, leaving her a yard inside Coventry, uncomforted and awake.

The next day, and the next, she was hurt and polite while he was withdrawn and thoughtful. The days seemed very long. All around them the monotonous life of the camp continued. Their presence was accepted and not much noted after the first day, it seemed. Either the villagers had not heard why Jay was there, or they were as clever as the Chinese were said to be at concealing natural interest.

She stayed with him, sitting outside their tepee or pacing the camp, while he stared at this remnant of Cat's people. He watched the women pounding corn, stirring their eternally simmering pots of mush, skinning small game and stretching the little skins to be scraped and cured.

He stood motionless watching the children too, as they rolled naked in the dusty circle between the tepees, or played their warrior games in the long grass. But when he did that, she turned her head.

When he wasn't roaming the camp, she tried to get him to talk to her, plying him with innocuous questions about his early life, his parents, the geography of the mountains in the distance; anything far enough away in space or time to be safe. She dared not risk offending him now, even unintentionally. She was desperate for a word of reprieve.

He replied to her questions with scant interest. Sometimes, for a moment, he would warm to a memory and enlarge on it without prompting before falling back into his silence.

He told her how he had left his father's house for good after a severe beating when he was fourteen.

"I guess he was trying to pound some fact into my head. That was his method then. He came out west from Pennsylvania before I was born, when Missouri was 'west.' He was self-taught and quite a scholar. He was out here long enough, but at heart he was an Easterner and a city man. He never seemed to realize that I'd never seen the kind of life he thought was important; didn't understand it and didn't want to." He shook his head in mild wonder at himself.

"It's peculiar, isn't it? A man my age, complaining about how his father misunderstood him. It's stupid. The old man meant well, but he was of the old persuasion, that if you didn't come up to the mark on your own, a knock on the ear would put you there.

"I knew, the last time, that if he laid a hand on me again I'd hit him back. I really wanted the chance too, but I was scared, so I ran. I lay awake many a night after I left, though, trying to figure a way to get even with him."

"Where did you go?"

"I joined a company of so-called volunteers headed for Texas."

"Volunteers?"

"For the war with the Mexicans. I was going to be a hero. I walked all the way, so it was mostly over when I got there."

She tried to imagine him in the short jacket and full-crowned cap she had seen on old song sheets, but failed. When he had been walking all the way to the Mexican War, she had been three years old.

"Did you stay in the Army from then on?"

"Oh God, no. I ran out of interest in walking about the same time I ran out of boots and money."

"Didn't the government pay for your—"

"The government didn't pay me a cent. Nobody could decide whether Washington or Texas was liable for our keep, so they both just forgot about it."

"Then you came home?"

"Then I stayed in Mexico City, and my stomach and backbone got to be next-door neighbors until I found a job." He looked at her slantwise under his lashes for a moment before he continued. They were lying on the riverbank west of the camp. Or he was lying, and she was sitting properly, a yard away. "I don't think you'd have approved of my second career, so we can skip forward to the time I discovered I could get paid for sitting on a horse."

"No, I want to hear. What did you do in Mexico City? Whatever it was, I should think it was a credit to a young boy to be able to support himself at all in a strange country."

For a moment he grinned at her, because she had fallen so neatly into the setup. "I washed dishes, swept floors, and ran errands; made myself generally useful—in a Mexican whorehouse."

"Oh."

"The food was good, the bed was softer than the ground, and I learned a lot of practical Spanish."

"And learned quite a bit about women, I suppose," she said primly.

"The only thing I ever learned about women is that you can't learn anything about women. But I studied the subject for three years."

"Did you have a—a girl, there?"

"For a while. I wanted to get married, and she was very agreeable to that. But she was agreeable because she wanted to leave the house and start a business of her own. I was to be her 'manager.' I was still a very dumb, green gringo boy. I couldn't see selling my own wife to other men. So I left," he finished crisply.

"Then what?"

"Went to California. Thought I might find gold too. Couldn't. Got hungry again. Found out they'd let you sit down to travel in the Cavalry. Joined up. Got switched back and forth from hell to breakfast for years, until I wound up in Laramie, and found my old man had moved into the Fort and opened a new store. My mother was dead." Very succinct. He was tiring of the diversion, and they were coming closer to painful things.

"Did you and your father ever become—closer, after that?"

"I guess we did. Not like father and son, or even close friends, but I didn't want to get even with him any more, and if he was still disappointed that I didn't turn out the way he wanted me to be, well, I guess he was at least glad I hadn't done anything to be hanged for."

"But he took Charlie to raise, because his father saved your life, Charlie said. And he was an old man then. It must have been very hard on him. And no one expected him to do it."

"I guess he put up with the racket to have some company. They say aggravation is what keeps you alive when you get old." The answer irritated her. The real answer was obvious.

"I should think he did it because he loved you," she said, putting her hand out to touch him placatingly a second after, for she saw she had found another sore point. The look he gave her was a mixture of guilt and disbelief. Her hand rested on his shoulder unnoticed, until she took it away again.

So he refused to accept that his father had ever loved him. And he took all his notions of women from some Mexican prostitute he had loved when he was seventeen. And his wife confirmed them. No one had ever loved him. No one would ever be allowed to. That way he owed no debts.

But he was here to pay a debt. Apparently his slate wasn't entirely unmarked. He must have accepted love from one person; only one. His son.

Iron Knife and his family returned in the late afternoon of the third day. She had been sitting alone by the river for several hours, just watching the water flow past; not thinking. She didn't know where Jay was. But when she saw the party ride in, she knew he would have seen it too, and she got up.

Washakie met Iron Knife and took him to shelter while the squaws set up his lodge again. She stood in front of their own tepee, feeling conspicuous, and scanning the new faces for the children.

There was no trouble identifying the boy. He was still growing, and still slender armed and soft cheeked with youth. But, however smoother, younger, browner, he was Jay's. His long, brown-amber eyes and thin, arched nose proclaimed it, as well as the cool, searching examination he made of her when he noticed her. He turned away just as she heard Jay's boots behind her.

He saw the boy too, and stopped, frozen, but was wise enough not to speak to him then.

First there was food to be prepared and eaten, and the amenities to be observed in Washakie's presence. They were called, when the time came, to share the pot with the old man and the newcomers. Jay and Iron Knife sat facing one another at a polite distance, with the old chief between them. The young men and boys sat on the other side of the fire in the same circle, and the women and children in an outer ring behind them, coming forward only to serve more food and drink.

Jay had shown her his "unseeing face" again, so she fell back with the women, taking a place where she could watch their faces while they talked. They were speaking, politely and infrequently, in the other language; making dinner conversation. It was not yet time to discuss the other thing.

She ate without paying attention to what it was. Around her, the squaws chatted in quiet voices, and the children clamored for more food. But there were two near her who remained as quiet as she. One was a woman about her own age, though her face showed the premature age that comes with a hard life under the sun. She watched the faces of the three men as carefully as Catherine did.

Beside her was a young girl, with eyes too big in her face, which was like a lozenge of mellowed, sun-browned ivory encased in her heavy black hair. Her body was still straight and unformed, her face too thin from a spurt of adolescent growth; but she was destined to be a beauty for the short time nature would allow her, before weather, hard work, and childbearing took it from her again.

Her mother must have looked like that, two years further budded, when Jay married her. And he would have known the mother when she was still as unknowing and vulnerable as this one. If he should look her way, he would never doubt again that she too was his. It was there in her fine, high cheekbones; in all the bones of her face. It was strange how clear it was, when you looked for it. Yet she must be mostly the image of Cat Dancing.

Catherine bowed her head. Hadn't Jay himself predicted that she would be afraid he'd see the dead mother in the daughter's face? Well, he must see it. And she was afraid.

The young men finished eating and drifted away. The squaws collected the food scraps. Gradually the company thinned until only the three men were left, and the three waiting women, and the boy, who came to sit just behind Iron Knife's elbow and fix his own eyes on the ground.

"Now let us talk of that matter which brings John Grobart and Iron Knife over such long distances to my lodge. Not in anger, which is the speech of fools. Not in the long, windy speech of the treaty breaker or the white man's law readers, because this is a matter that does not depend on laws that may have been broken, or customs that must be kept. It is a matter of the blood and the heart. I will be counselor if you invite me to speak, but I will keep the order of the speaking, as is proper. John Grobart may speak first, since he is the one who wishes for change. Also, because he is the nearer in blood."

Washakie spoke in English again. Catherine was drawn out of her thoughts by the sound. She wondered if he did it in order to make the conversation more private, or for some devious reason. Was it a courtesy to Jay, or a piece of subtle contempt, to show the white man that he could be met and bested in his own tongue?

The time for Jay to make his plea had come, but for another moment he was still, looking past Iron Knife to the boy, who kept his own eyes averted.

"What's your name, son?" he asked the boy, in the peculiar harsh-soft tone that Catherine had learned to identify with his times of emotional stress.

The boy flinched a little, only a very little, at being addressed, and raised his eyes to his father's. "My people call me Dream Speaker." There was even something of the same effect of nervousness on his voice.

"Do you know the name you were born with? It was long ago, I know. But you heard it often when you were small. There was a game you played. You liked to hide from us, and hear your name called over and over, before you came running out to answer. Do you remember that?" The boy was staring at him in doubt. Jay let him be silent.

"There was a thing—like the bones of a big antelope—" whispered the boy. "You could see through its ribs."

"It was a thing called a rocking chair. You used to turn it upside down over you and make a den."

"It had long horns."

"When it was turned over, yes. When it was sitting up it moved on the horns. Your mother used to sit in it with you." The boy gazed at him, frowning slightly. "What was your name then, son?"

"John . . . some other thing . . . Johnny."

"That's right, Johnny. You remembered. Has anyone called you that here?"

"No. I am Dream Speaker. They told me John was your name."

"It is. We have the same name, almost, because you're my son. Among my—our—people, this is often the custom." Iron Knife moved a little, as if he would turn to the boy, but didn't. Jay ignored him.

"Why do they call you Dream Speaker here?"

"It was the name given to me when I first came here." He looked for aid or comfort to the woman who had reared him. Catherine couldn't tell if she could understand what was being said or not. She never moved. "When I came here," he said, "I was like a cub taken from the litter. I had dreams that made me call out and speak wild things, which only my father, Iron Knife, could understand." He shrugged, disparaging them. "They were baby things." But he flushed suddenly and looked down again.

"Do you remember those dreams now, Johnny?"

"No."

"I'm glad you don't, because they were from an unhappy time. But I'm glad you remember the game and your name, because that was from another, happier time."

Catherine was surprised by his whole approach to the boy, and she saw that Iron Knife was too. She had feared he'd be as he was in Washakie's lodge: demanding his son be turned over to him, talking of kidnapping and trying to pay for the boy with the stolen money; alienating him at once. Perhaps Iron Knife and Washakie had expected the same, and had allowed him to speak first and ruin himself at the beginning.

Jay had been able to see his own mistakes and correct them in time. There had been something besides sulking going on during those endless pacings up and down the camp. Whatever his intention with the soft, reminiscing questions—to gentle the boy like a colt to the sound of his voice, or to try to stir up some deciding memory of his lost life—it was having its effect. The boy was not hostile. He was attracted, and cooperating a bit more than he need have, or possibly had intended.

Jay had yet to look at his daughter. Catherine wondered if he could and still work his spell on the boy. The boy was the main goal.

"Johnny, you're not an ordinary person. Maybe you're a fortunate one. You know, most people only get one sort of life to lead. They have no choice. But you do. You have two names; you might have two different lives, and bring honor to both of them.

"I can see you're proud to be Dream Speaker of the Shoshone, who can read the signs of the sky and the earth, and who someday will hunt the buffalo. You owe a great deal to Iron Knife and his wife, for taking you as their own and teaching you the ways that are good to them. I honor Iron Knife for it. I too owe him a great debt, and I wish I could reward him. I was going to offer him something as payment for making a man of you, but I know now I was wrong, and I would be dishonoring him to offer it.

"So I can give him nothing but my thanks for making you Dream Speaker, who walks straight.

"But you're another person too, Johnny, even if you've forgotten most of it. You are John Canby Grobart, and I am your father. I lost you, long ago, but I didn't forget you. As soon as I was able, I came to tell you that I haven't forgotten my son, and that I want you with me again."

The boy started to speak, but Jay went on.

"I know what you're thinking. It would be strange to come with me and leave all you know behind you. And you might not like the other life when you've seen it. You would miss Iron Knife and your foster mother, just as you once missed me. Or you think I would make a prisoner of you, and never let you come back here again.

"But that would not be so. If you came with me, you could try the other life that's yours by right. You could return here and visit when you liked. You wouldn't have to come alone, of course. Your sister could come too, because she owns another name and also has the choice of two lives."

For the first time he looked in the direction of the girl. If Catherine had expected any break in his control, she didn't see it. He let his gaze linger on her for a moment, appraisingly, but he didn't speak to her; only to the boy.

"We would visit the great towns of the white men. Not like Fort Washakie or Lander. Very great places where the people live in thousands. They have many wonderful things to make their lives pleasant there. It would be an adventure worth having, even if you didn't like all of it. There are a thousand things to see. It's a big country. You would ride the train; cross the mountains; see lands where trees grow as the grass does here. I'll show them all to you, if you'll come with me. You and your sister. Will you come, and try it? It will take a brave to do it, a strong heart. But I gave you a strong one, and I don't think Iron Knife has weakened it. Will you come?"

Dear Lord, he's won, thought Catherine. And so easily. The boy, eyes shining, started to speak again, but Washakie interrupted him. He'll say yes, she thought. What little boy could refuse such an offer; such a dare? Especially if he's made to think he'll be brought home safe at the end of it?

"The boy must not speak before the man. Iron Knife will answer now; then the boy."

Iron Knife was a solid-looking man of seemingly massive calm. Not tall, but well muscled, with a strong, creased face that looked capable of laughter as well as sternness. She wished he didn't look so much like a person she could like. She wished he wouldn't speak. Jay had won the boy. He had even won her grudging approval of a thing she had once thought completely wrong. She didn't entirely believe his assurances of freedom, but he had moved her with his gentle handling of Johnny. If he could be like this, if he could change, be more flexible, perhaps he could do something for his son other than take possession of him, after all. Maybe the boy's healthy presence would banish Cat's ghost as nothing else could. She wanted it to be so. Yet she felt sympathy for Iron Knife and his wife.

"Grobart's skill with words confuses me," said Iron Knife. "I am amazed. You were not such a maker of speeches when

I knew you last; although, it is true, you persuaded my father to give you Cat Dancing, against his better judgment."

Jay, if he was tempted to answer, didn't.

"Once you talked more readily with your fists, I remember. You often would not abide to hear the end of a thing before you struck out. I see that you are much wiser now. Prison cannot be so bad a place, if it teaches a man patience and cunning.

"You thank me for taking your son. I might as much thank you, for getting him on my sister. Either way, the credit is not ours, but hers. Because she lived, you sired him. Because she died, I raised him. The son goes with the mother, or with her people, as Washakie knows. For he is the son of a Shoshone mother and a strange father, and yet he has become the great chief of all the Shoshone. It is the right way."

Washakie shifted a little, opening his slow eyes. "We were not going to talk of custom. But I admit the truth of Iron Knife's words."

"Very well. I will speak only of the things concerning Grobart and my sister, and how I came to have their children in my lodge. Today you call your son to you with soft words. And your daughter. I recall that once you doubted they were yours. Have you found some reason to change your mind?"

"They are mine," said Jay shortly.

"Then my sister was faithful to you? A faithful wife?"

Jay seemed to be gathering himself for some blow or defense. "You know about it." It wasn't a question.

"I know very much about it. But do I know as much as Grobart himself, or more?"

Washakie frowned. "I do not understand all this talk about knowing."

"Does the chief know why Grobart was in prison all these years?"

"He has told me it was for the killing of three white men who lay with his wife."

"He has said that one of them killed her after they had lain with her?" Washakie nodded. "He has let you see the shadow of truth, then. But not the truth. He was in prison for killing those men and for trying to kill the man they sent to catch him. He said the men had lain with his woman. He said that she spoke their names to him before she died. It may be that their names were spoken, I do not know. But they did not lie with his woman and they did not kill her."

"I killed her," said Jay, interrupting him. "Because she was a whore. Her own son accused her. And she did tell me they were the ones, before she died." He spoke to the old man in a hard, even voice. "She turned Johnny out of the house so she could let them in. She left her son out in the dark alone while she was in there with them, but he saw them through the window and told me.

"I gave her a house to be safe in, and food to eat, and children to be proud of. What did she give in return? Shame to her people and her children and me, if I'd told about it. Her daughter saw it from her cradle, if she could remember. Her son saw it from the window, but I hope he can't remember."

He looked at the boy, measuring him, appealing to him. "I killed her," he said in a softer voice. "Did I do wrong? How would Iron Knife let a woman live, who did what his sister did? How would any Shoshone? What is the law here, in the matter of whoring and faithless women? Should I have slit her nose and thrown her out in the street to tell everybody what she'd been up to? Would that have pleased you more?" He regarded Iron Knife with confidence, even curiosity. "I admit what you say. But how did you know about it?" Iron Knife didn't answer, only waited, until Jay's eyes glanced away to the boy and registered what they saw there. "How?"

"As you have said. He looked through the window."

A pause.

"No. I sent him to the Carey woman's house, and he—"

"He didn't go." Another silence.

"Johnny?" whispered Jay harshly, but the boy still wouldn't look at him.

"My sister's son is a brave boy, as you have said. But he may be afraid of you, now. He was afraid of you, then."

"No. He was never afraid of me. He knew how much I—" He stopped, still trying to force the boy to meet his eyes.

"He was afraid of you that night because he had told you what was not true and he had seen your anger. He came back to tell you it was a lie, but the door was shut."

"No. I saw him go before I shut the door."

"But he came back, because he had put blame on his mother and he was sorry—and afraid."

The boy put his hands up to shield his face and Catherine wished she could do the same, but she couldn't tear her eyes away from Jay. There was something in his face now, worse than anger, worse than fear. It was growing; it would be more terrible than he could bear. She could feel it herself and wanted to reach for him, turn him away from it, stop him from knowing it, before it was too late. But she couldn't move.

"He wasn't lying! He was too young to know what he was telling me. If a man had told me, I'd have killed him! Why would a child say such a thing if it wasn't so? You are the liar here, Iron Knife! You've made this lie to defend yourself and keep the boy! He couldn't know or remember any of it now, and if he thinks he does it's because you've told it to him so many times he thinks it's the truth!"

"As I am not a murderer, or a thief, or a taker of other men's wives, I am not a liar," said Iron Knife slowly. "I will tell you what happened on that night, and you will see whether I have made a lie. I was not there, but he was, and he told it to me in many pieces, when he first came. Often he dreamed it, and spoke the same things in his sleep. And when he woke, he cried and told me, until the dreams faded and he forgot what he had seen and cried out at, dreaming.

"Other things my father heard, and the woman called Carey. Together they told a tale that says the same thing. There was no one with Cat Dancing that night, or any night. You believed a baby's fright story told to him by the Carey woman. And because it agreed with your own evil suspicions, you took the life of my sister, Cat Dancing."

"IN THE DAYS when the horse soldiers first came to the place called Laramie and bought it from the skin buyers, my father's father made a long fast and saw many visions of dead buffalo and empty lodges in the land. He would have joined even our enemies, the Sioux, to drive these white faces out of our land. But my father and many of the young men said, 'Let us make friends with these bluecoats, for they are the enemies of our enemies. Let us learn their ways and take the gifts they offer. They are rich with the things a man needs: fine horses and fine weapons. These will all be ours too.'

"My father became a scout for the bluecoats. I was a young boy then, with brothers. We were proud of the blue cap he wore and the long gun he carried. We thought he was a great chief, and our great-father a foolish old man.

"I honored my father in his lifetime and I honor him now. But he was not a great chief, and our great-father was not a foolish old man.

"We learned to speak the white man's speech because we were young. He never did. When we were older he saw that we had no wish to be the white man's slave, so he sent us to the old one and his old ways. Our sister was born in the camp near the Fort and grew up there. I did not see her often after I left the Fort, but my father felt a tenderness for her greater than a man commonly feels for a girl child. She was good and beautiful and full of happiness. I think that Grobart noticed her even when she was still a stick-legs with two great eyes. My father was his scout, and the man would often come to our lodge to sit with him and talk. He had few friends among his own people, it seemed. Even his own father was a stranger to him.

"When my father's lung sickness made him too weak, he began to think of spending his last days in peace with his people. There had been a slaughter by the whites of the Arapaho, at a place called Black Horse Creek. Grobart had led it and had been wounded. It was thought by some that he would die. My father sent my mother and sister to care for him, because of their friendship. He was a long time healing, and while he did Cat Dancing became a woman. I think it was then he first wanted her.

"When he was well again, Grobart came to my father's lodge to try to persuade him not to leave Fort Laramie. Then, when he saw this was useless, to ask for Cat Dancing to be his woman. He said that she had pleased him well with her care of him. He also said that he loved her and would treat her kindly.

"This my father believed to be true. Also he was a sick man and needed what Grobart paid for her to make his journey. So they were joined.

"I think Cat Dancing was very glad to stay with him. Do I speak the truth, so far, Grobart?"

Jay's assent was nothing more than a momentary closing of his eyes. He seemed to be scarcely breathing as he endured the retelling of his own history.

"Then I will go on," said Iron Knife.

Washakie nodded, satisfied by the thorough "telling of the thing."

"He gave her a white man's house in the married officers' quarters, and dressed her in the bonnets and the many skirts of the white women. He gave her a pony to ride, but since he also put a child in her, almost at once, he bought a little cart for her to ride in instead. He had a picture made of her on a little piece of tin, and sent it to my father, so we could see how he cared for her.

"But it was not all well with them. Though they did not approve of him, the brother officers smiled at her, as they always had, and she smiled in return, having no fear, as always. But soon Grobart would no longer take her among the officers, because she was big with child, and it is not proper to their ways to show a fertile belly. A strange thing, when every man desires a son. Many of their ways are strange.

"When the child was born, he still kept her at home, allowing her the company only of one or two women who lived nearby. Many of the women would not speak to her now that she was a white man's wife.

"Why he left the Army, I do not know. But he had fewer friends among the officers than before, spending no time of ease with them at all, but only on his duties, or with his wife and son. He was a silent man. When I came to the Fort once, on an errand for my father, and to see the child for him, Grobart said little to me, and Cat Dancing's face was quiet. But I thought them content with each other.

"She was big with another child, and soon after, their second son was born, but did not live. It was then that Grobart left the Army and moved outside the Fort. By the time he decided to help the buffalo killers lay the iron path through our land, they had a daughter. He left the three of them in their new house and traveled with the destroyers of the good lands, as he has said, coming home when he could.

"Once, when he came, it was because of a great feast day of theirs, where much whiskey passed among the guests at the Fort, making some of their men too merry with the women. I heard this gossip from the scouts, later, and cannot say who was to blame, but there was a fight, and many ugly words spoken in anger. And Grobart said, where many could hear, that perhaps his child was not his child after all. He had been drinking much, and that was not a habit with him, either.

"I have said, this was gossip. Perhaps it never happened?" He waited for Jay to deny it, then shrugged at the silence.

"Now, I will speak of the last day of my sister, but first of how the boy came to me. Then, the other. It is here that

Grobart must tell me if I lie, or if I have made a true telling out of many broken stories.

"When she was dead, and Grobart was in bed under guard, with a bullet in him, an old white woman named Carey sent word to my father, through the son of the squaw who did her washing, to come for the children. She had kept them since the night of Cat Dancing's death. My father went himself, though ill, because I was on the northern hunting grounds and my two brothers were now dead. He brought the babies home with him, and when I came he told me of the crying dreams that terrified the boy. I heard them, myself, and many times soothed the child while he babbled his fears.

"I took him to my own camp, and in days after, little by little, I questioned him about this thing or that, as if it were no matter. If I put the pieces together in the wrong way, you shall tell me now.

"He was playing his hiding game with his mother. It is strange that you yourself brought it to his mind tonight. He would hide and she would look for him, calling him to come out. Many times he hid and she looked, until she stopped to nurse her youngest. The boy was jealous of the girl baby, and teased his mother for her attention, until she became impatient with him and sent him outside.

"His heart was very sore with anger against her and the babe. He was used to much attention from his father, and he was lonely for him. He thought of running away to him. He did walk some distance from his home, a long way for a little one, until the woman called Carey saw him and stopped him.

"She turned him back toward home. In the way of old women she tried to frighten him into goodness by telling him that bad men, who carried off children, would get him if he stayed out alone. When she had done her duty, she sent him toward his home, thinking he would go in. But he did not. He crawled into one of his dens, as his father has called them, and daydreamed about the terrible men who would come to his house and get him. He thought they might come and get the girl child, and even frighten his mother. He was pleased with that dream, I think, and thought about it many ways. She would be very glad to see him when he came home and was the only child again.

"He was near his house and she was calling him again. But her voice was still angry to his ears, so he still didn't answer. It was growing dark, and he was frightened, but he blamed her for not finding him. He thought of the men coming to get bad children, and how she would probably welcome them in because she was angry with him. Perhaps she would give him to them gladly, and keep the baby girl. He crawled out of his hiding place and went to look in his window. He saw that she was nursing the baby girl again.

"When the father came home, the boy was weeping in the dark, under the spell of his own badness, his fear, and his dream. He rushed to his father's arms and told him some tangled part of it. He excused his own disobedience by saying that she put him out of doors. Who can say how he told the rest of it? Only Grobart, and he didn't understand it. In his dreams the boy often said that three black men were coming to get his mother because she was bad.

"Even a small child recognizes a great anger, and his father's was terrible as he held the boy. But he put him down and told him to run to Carey, and went into the house.

"The boy knew he had not told the truth about being kept outside, and that his mother would catch him in the lie. He was worried. Even his father would be angry with him for the lie. He wanted to call it back, but the door was closed and locked. He looked in the window again, and saw what was happening inside. No one else saw it, or heard it. Grobart is not a man who shouts his anger, and my sister made no cry. Perhaps it was because she loved him still, or thought to save her life with silence. In the end, who knows, she might have thought to save it with the names of the three men: men whose names she may have heard him speak. Or else his own jealous mind supplied the names, and she only nodded her head, to gain relief from pain. I do not know, but I have often imagined it. Sometimes I have almost seen it, except for that. Which was it, John Grobart? Did she speak before you killed her? What were her last words to you?"

Jay didn't answer. He was like a man turned to stone, looking at the boy, who still sat with his hands over his face. No one moved. Catherine felt a wetness on her face that told her she was crying.

It seemed no one would speak or move again. They would all sit there motionless, like the Seven Sleepers, waiting for the world to change. He would never look her way; she would never find a word of comfort to speak to him, though her heart bled itself white in pity.

Washakie stirred at last, breaking the spell. "This is a terrible tale. But I see the truth of it on all your faces. There is much to pity as well as to condemn. The boy brought about his mother's death, but he cannot be blamed for it. It was done in innocence. He was only a small boy. Even the man must be pitied, though guilty. One who killed what was dear to him, for his honor's sake, and that wrongly—I will say no more." There was another pause.

"It is time for the boy to speak. Dream Speaker, you owe a duty to Iron Knife, for his long care of you, and his love. You are blood of his blood by mother right, and accepted by the people as one of us. If you wish to stay here, no one will try to make you go.

"But you owe your life's beginning to John Grobart. You are blood of his blood too. More than that, you owe him another debt. Though you were only a child, you did him an injury, to his long suffering, and your mother's death. I don't know what comfort your going with him will bring, but he is your father, and he asks for you. Will you stay or go?"

The boy jumped up and ran away, darting between the tepees out of sight. Iron Knife stood up then, and his wife and the girl followed him. He looked down at Jay.

"In the days after I first learned the truth," he said quietly, "I would have had your blood on my knife, for the sake of my father's sorrow. But you were safe in prison. Then my own blood cooled with the years. I see now that this way was both better and worse than the knife.

"I take no pleasure in what I have done today; except that the boy stays with me, as he should." He walked away noiselessly, attended by his women. Jay remained, staring at the place where the boy had been.

Washakie took out a stub of a cigar from his belt and lit it with a grass spill held over the fire.

Catherine suddenly felt she had to get away. She couldn't possibly sit there with him any longer. Nor could she speak, or touch him, until he gave some signs of humanity. If he would only move, or speak, or look at her even with indifference, the floodgates would open and all the dammed-up love and comfort in her heart would pour out. But he sat like a dead man. She pushed herself up and stumbled away, avoiding the lodge they shared. Walking into it would be like going into a tomb. And he would go there if he wanted to be alone.

She looked around, surprised that the day was still bright. In her thoughts it had been night, but the sun was still well above the mountaintops.

She returned to the river and sat down on the flat stone in the willow thicket. Then, assured of solitude at last, she began to cry. Sobs shook her until she doubled over, head on her knees, rocking her body rhythmically back and forth like a child. The well of her grief seemed to have no bottom. She wept for herself as well as for him. But mostly for him: for the mess he had made of things; for the terrible toll his pride had taken of his life, and the pain that he deserved but she couldn't bear him to have.

The sound of a horse galloping away from camp scarcely fell on her ears. She pictured Iron Knife hurrying off, now that his revenge was taken. When she couldn't cry any longer, she sat looking into the brown water, wondering what they would do now.

She had wanted him to herself. She had her victory. But what victor hurries from the field? They were sorry winners, she and Iron Knife. Then she realized Iron Knife wouldn't have ridden out alone, or at the end of the day, with his tepee prepared for him here.

She sprang up, still half-disbelieving, and ran to find out.

Tearing back the door flap, she fell into the tepee on her knees, still sun blinded, and groped with both hands along the ground.

His bedroll was gone. So were the canvas cantinas that held their food and equipment. Flung against the far wall, where they had been lying since the first day, were two pairs of dusty saddlebags, still swollen fat and strapped tight.

"No!" she said through her teeth, and snatched up the bags, throwing them to one side. "No. No. No." She threw her blankets together and began to roll them into a pack, fumbling with the straps on the tarpaulin.

There was more activity outside. A number of horses, coming closer. She pushed her finished bedroll away and looked out the doorway for them. Blue coats and brown faces again, and two more who didn't match. They stopped at the edge of the camp as a young boy went forward to meet them. She couldn't hear what they said, but the boy pointed away across the river to the south, the way Jay and she had come. As he turned his profile to her, she saw that the boy was Johnny—no, Dream Speaker.

One of the two men not in uniform was Willard. The other she didn't know. She came out of the tepee slowly and stood up to watch them. The boy gestured back to her, and Willard saw her and dismounted, followed by the other man. The soldiers turned their horses' heads and made off for the river, leaving one behind to wait for the civilians.

Willard came to her hesitantly. She didn't move. She saw that he looked haggard and red eyed. He had cut himself shaving, in three places, and was patched haphazardly with court plaster. When he was in front of her he stopped, staring.

"God Almighty, Kate, is it you? You ought to see yourself. Are you all right? Can't you speak?" Then he put out his hands quickly to catch her as she slid to the ground unconscious.

# 18

HER FAINTNESS passed quickly, however much she might have wished to prolong it as a shield against questions. She looked up into a quartet of concerned blue eyes and one pair of brown. She was sitting on the ground, supported by Willard, while the stranger and the pony soldier hovered over them.

"Let me up," she complained, disgusted with her own weakness and her poor intuition. Of course he would leave at once. What was there to stay for? He would have remembered that the bluecoats were due to return that day. They had been more than polite to wait until so late before coming to confront the old chief on his own ground again. She should have remembered and been ready, instead of crawling away to feel sorry for herself, letting him think—what did he think? That she'd had enough; couldn't bear the truth Iron Knife had told? Couldn't he have waited one minute to call her, to see how she felt? No. He had known, when he found her gone.

"Mrs. Crocker, you've had a bad time of it, I guess," said the stranger, helping her to her feet. "But you're safe now. We'll take you back to the Fort to rest while we track Grobart. It won't take long now. You'll be home in a few days."

"Who are you?" she asked, and in her own ears her voice sounded as harsh as Jay's. Willard made the proper introductions at once, and she saw something between contempt and amusement flicker in the pale eyes of the man called

Harvey Lapchance as he did so. Willard was still gripping her arm in support, harder than she liked, and she shrugged away from him absently while studying Lapchance.

"Can you ride, Ma'am?" he asked. "If so, we can return to the Fort right away. The sooner you're rested and refreshed, the better it'll be for you. And then perhaps you can tell us what you know about Grobart's plans."

"I can tell you one thing, right now. The money you're looking for is in the tepee behind you."

He looked stunned. "You mean he intends to return here?" Harvey said incredulously. He whirled and ducked into the tepee to see for himself. Catherine saw the slight figure of Dream Speaker lingering within earshot of them. She stared at him bitterly for a long moment, then turned her face deliberately away.

Lapchance came out of the tepee with the bags. "It looks like he left it all," he said, hefting them. "He's full of surprises, old Jay is. But why did he leave it here?"

She frowned at the tone. "Do you know him?" she asked.

"In a manner of speaking, Ma'am. I brought him in for killing three men who most likely deserved it, some years ago. He laid my head open with a gun butt after I was forced to put a bullet in his leg. He could have done worse, and I always appreciated his restraint at the time. We mended together in the same boardinghouse until he went to trial." He looked off south after the pursuing pony soldiers. "Why do you suppose he left it here," he said again, "after going to so much trouble to get it?"

She shot another look at the listening boy. "He didn't care about the money. He wanted it to—buy something he couldn't buy. Even before he tried, he knew he was wrong to try it. After that it was just extra baggage." Like herself.

The slow, thoughtful look that Harvey Lapchance turned back her way made her flush and look down. It was as if he had read her last thought, and all the others that cried so wretchedly inside her head.

They returned to the Fort with her, taking along the money and, to her surprise, the boy. She rode, head down, trying to avoid as long as possible the reproach in Willard's face that was trying to masquerade as concern for her. She would have to face him soon enough.

When they arrived she was shown to a small room in the officers' quarters and given hot water and towels. Willard had even brought her a change of clothes, crammed into a small bag; terribly wrinkled, but clean. She wondered if it had been his idea to bring them for her comfort, or to dress her corpse for burial. She sighed wearily at her own injustice. Of course he had brought it for her comfort. He knew how particular she was about cleanliness and fresh clothes.

When she looked into a shaving mirror hanging over the commode, she saw why Willard had looked so stunned. There was no Catherine Crocker reflected there to whom fresh linen was a necessity. There was a starved-looking wild stranger, with enormous fierce eyes and a dirty face. She was deeply sun browned and creased with frown and sun-squint lines like an old squaw. Her hair was dull with dust and twisted into uneven braids.

She turned from the stranger's face and began to undress. As she did, she saw that her hands were calloused and embedded with grime in the knuckles. Her fingernails were broken and ragged. She remembered breaking one of them on Dawes, but couldn't account for the rest. Her body was pitifully thin and covered with bruises in all colors from black to fading yellow-green. She stank.

She bathed herself listlessly, and washed her hair. When it was rubbed more than half dry, she dressed, then braided and coiled it at the nape of her neck. Willard, in his amazing thoroughness, had even brought along a packet of hairpins. She would have to remember to thank him. She had no corset, but she was so thin now that it made no difference. Even without it the dress was loose on her. She walked to the door, feeling the strangeness of the swinging skirt and dust ruffle against her legs.

Willard and Lapchance were waiting for her in the officers' mess, with hot food and coffee. She couldn't eat, but she used the coffee as a diversion to keep her from having to look at them.

"Well, Mrs. Crocker, you have had an experience, no doubt about it. I wonder if you could tell us a little about it now, if you're not too tired." Lapchance was sipping at a cup of coffee as if it pained him. His tone was mild and conversational. Willard was staring at her, his mouth twitched down at the corners in the look of hurt anger she knew so well.

"How did you happen to be up by the railroad tracks when they stopped the train, Mrs. Crocker?"

"I was going to stop it myself, if I could."

"Where were you going?"

"I don't know. I didn't care. I was leaving my husband."

Willard drew in his breath over his teeth, and she gave him a dull look. It was too late for niceness, and they both must have known it anyway.

"Didn't you realize what they were up to, and try to avoid them?"

She told them about it, without enthusiasm. It was a part of the story that no longer seemed real or interesting to her. Billy, Captain Lightfoot, the offended young matron making her rash attempt to keep her property; they were all gone, and they had never been real.

She left out everything of importance to her, which was nearly everything about Jay and their mission inside the Reservation. She told about the renegade Indians and the death of Billy and Charlie, then sat looking at her hands around the cup.

"Did they hurt you in any way?" Lapchance asked. They waited.

"No," she said stolidly.

"Mrs. Crocker, in Atlantic City we ran across Coleman Dawes—"

She looked up sharply. "Did you get the money he had?"

"Most of it. He—"

"Then you've got it all, except what the Indians put in the fire. I hope you hanged him."

Harvey smiled at her fierceness. "I believe that's under consideration at the moment in Lander. It isn't the first robbery he's been involved in. Perhaps you'll get your wish as soon as we catch Jay Grobart." She tried to control her reaction to the words, but they both saw it. "I deduce you don't think Grobart is as worthy of the rope as Dawes."

"Coleman Dawes is a vicious animal! He killed Billy Bowan, and he tried to give me to those Indian drunkards to save the money, then ran away when there was fighting to do. He—" She stopped, then continued in a more controlled voice. "He was the worst of them. He would have left me in the desert to die, anywhere. He let me bribe him to help me get away, then caught me and kept the bribe. I hated him."

"You got a little revenge on him in the end, we heard." Lapchance smiled. She thought about Dawes bellowing at the pump and almost answered the smile, but caught herself. He thought he was being kind, and her friend, but however much she needed a friend, he was her enemy. If he hadn't come when he did, she would have been south beyond the river, following Jay.

"Jay Grobart behaved differently, then, did he?"

"He—yes, he did. He told me he couldn't let me go at first because I'd die alone. He could have left me. He didn't want me along, or want me for ransom. He saved my life at the miner's cabin. In his own way, he treated me very well."

"I'll bet he did," said Willard. "Lapchance, I don't know why you're asking these questions when you already know the answers, but I have a few I'd like to ask, myself. And I'd rather ask them in private, if you don't mind."

Harvey got up slowly, still watching her, and bowed to her slightly. "I have one or two messages to send, then, Mrs. Crocker, if you'll excuse me."

Willard watched him go, then turned back to her with a harsh laugh. "Treated you very well, did he? You bitch! Isn't it enough that you've dragged my name in the dirt through the length of Wyoming, without adding that piece of hypocrisy? He must be laughing his head off outside, right now. Don't you know that road agent you scalded told us everything about you and your murdering lover? He told us he tried to get you away, but you were stuck on Grobart from the first."

"That's a lie! He—"

"And that you were posing as his wife the day after the robbery, and sleeping with him three days after. Is that a lie too, Madam Blueblood?"

"Yes! It was four days!" she yelled.

He slapped her heavily across the face, twice. They glared at each other in rigid postures of threat and defiance until he slumped against the table, his angry face crumpling into harsh tears.

"That's why I left you in the first place, Willard. I remember now," she whispered.

He didn't hear her. "Katy. Goddamn it, Katy, why did you do this to me? I've tried to do the right thing by you and your father. I've given you everything you ever needed: clothes, money, a home that wasn't mortgaged. And all I've ever got for it was contempt and a cold shoulder when the lamp was out. No matter how hard I tried to please you, it was never enough."

"You didn't give me what I needed, Willard, you never—"

"I was never good enough for you. I was ignorant if I made a mistake in etiquette, and common if I tried to improve, and coarse when I tried to make you love me—"

"You never loved me, you never did! And you were afraid of me! How do you think that makes a woman feel? I never said I was a blueblood; that's what you thought! That's what you thought you were getting, and when you found out you were wrong you made me pay for it!"

"I loved you! I knew what your 'fortunes' were. I'd have been some kind of fool if I couldn't see through your old man by the time we were engaged. But I thought you were beautiful, wonderful; a real lady. Someone who'd make a better man out of me, if she loved me. If she didn't mind that I was a farmer's son who'd had to scratch in the dirt for everything he ever got! A lady!" He gave a sharp laugh. "You! You waited for years to get the kind of treatment you really wanted: coupling on the ground with some damned convict, like a bitch in heat! Did you tell *him* he was too rough and you were too tired? Did you count the calendar and tell him it was the wrong time of the moon?" Tears were running down his face, and making his red eyes bloodier.

"He didn't hit me," she countered, enraged by her own tears. "He didn't treat me like a gorgon one minute and belittle me the next. I caused him trouble from the beginning, but he didn't throw it up to me, ever. He didn't have to be, but he was gentle." She wiped at her eyes with the back of her hand, wishing she could control her voice, which was shaking badly.

"What I did, or what he did, doesn't make any difference between you and me, Will. I left you. Don't you understand that? You don't have to take any responsibility for me any more. You don't have to be concerned about me. Tell anybody who asks that you knew what I was and you threw me out. I'll never say anything different. Divorce me, and name any grounds you like."

"What the hell do you mean, I'm not concerned? You're my wife. You are my responsibility. If you behave like an alley cat, don't you think you're my disgrace? What do you think a divorce would do to my profession? Will my clients want to engage a man who dirties his name in a divorce suit? Who wants to control their money when he can't control his wife?"

"I said you weren't responsible! I ran away and threw myself at another man! No one will think the less of you for it when they hear the whole story. You'll have all the sympathy you could ever want."

"All the pity and all the laughs, you mean! Don't be such a fool, Catherine. There won't be a divorce. And you won't get the chance to tell everybody what a kind heart Grobart had. As far as the rest of the world is concerned, you were kidnapped by him and his gang, and abandoned when we got too hot on his trail. If anything else happened, I'll forgive it and you won't dare to mention it. Is that clear?"

She sagged back in her chair, seeing that it was going to be a long, sweet revenge for him.

"I'll divorce you, then," she said, knowing it was hopeless.

"You don't have any grounds. I'd contest the case, anyway. And when a husband contests, the suit is never granted."

"Then send me home to Papa. I'll stay out of your way."

"It will look better if you stay with me."

"Please, Will. I'm sorry I hurt you. I don't want to hurt you any more. Please let me go." Her voice was reduced to a whisper by her tears, and he answered it in kind.

" 'Please, Will'? That was never one of your phrases, Catherine. But I'm glad you've discovered it. It will make saying 'no' so much pleasanter."

He left her sitting there and followed Harvey's path, slamming the door behind him.

So he had loved her. So he said. Perhaps it was true. She was much better acquainted with the convolutions of loving and hating now than she had been before. She could see that it might well be true. But it made no difference now. It was all over. If she had ever been his passion, she would become his martyrdom. For the rest of their lives he would pretend in public to be her loving husband.

She thought that Jay had been kinder to his Cat Dancing, innocent or guilty, than anyone knew.

A slight noise behind her made her turn her head in a dull search for the source. The door at the rear of the mess hall was opened a crack. It closed, then opened again to show a thin strip of brown flesh on the other side.

"Have they given you your reward yet, for telling them which way your father went?" she asked. She wished she could put more sting into the words, but she was drained.

The door thought of closing again, but widened at last to expose Dream Speaker. He stared at her solemnly with Jay's light eyes in his copper face.

"Will you count a coup for that?" she finished nastily, hating him, and herself, because he looked stricken.

"What did you mean about the money?" he asked. "What did he come to buy? Me?"

"That's about it. He thought about you, and missed you until he was a little crazy from it, I suppose. He thought you were the only person in his life who had ever really loved him, and he loved you, very much. He stole the money to pay Iron Knife for you. He wanted to make up to you for what he'd done, and for leaving you to grow up alone."

"It was very foolish and dangerous."

"It was crazy."

"Iron Knife would never take it."

"He knew that too, when it was too late. So he didn't offer it, did he? He threw it in the tepee and forgot about it when it was no more use to him for what he wanted: his son. That's you: the big Shoshone brave, who can point out the way for the soldiers to go to kill his own father."

"But I did not tell them."

"I saw you! You needn't be so modest! Everybody will congratulate you when they bring him back. Will he be alive or dead, do you think? Maybe they'll have to—" But her voice failed her.

"I did not tell them," he said again. She let him see her disbelief and scorn. "It is true. I pointed the way to the south and told them he went as he came. But it was not so. He went west and north, to the home of the Ninambea. To the mountains."

They looked at each other in a long stillness.

"I'm sorry for what I said to you," she said at last.

He nodded. "You care much for him, my—my father?" She nodded in turn. "More than for this man who cries like a woman and hits you?" He sighed regretfully. "It is not lawful to enter the quarrel between a man and his wife, or to give the woman aid against the man. But—" She leaned forward, waiting. "I feel bad, that he should be guilty of that thing he did, partly because of me. Also, that he calls me to him and I cannot go. My blood is his blood; but Iron Knife is my father." He looked at her with puzzled, pain-filled eyes. "Yet I would not have him always alone. If you wish to follow him, I will show you the way he goes."

She made a movement of gratitude, as if she would rise and take him in her arms. But he stepped back.

"It cannot be now. There are too many people stirring. Go to bed. Take as much rest as you can. Eat. It will be a hard journey, and one we must make quickly. At midnight, come to the north gate, through that door. I will be waiting with food and two horses."

"What about the guards?"

"The man who will guard that gate tonight is very anxious to have Moon in Morning, my sister, for his wife. Iron Knife will never agree, but the soldier does not know that, yet."

"What about Iron Knife? What will you tell him?"

He looked more pained, then grinned sorrowfully at her and shook his head. She saw that Iron Knife would have to draw his own conclusions.

# 19

OVER THE rising foothills to the mountains in the west of Washakie's prison and refuge the straight-limbed cedars marched, in company with the white and yellow pine, lodgepole, whitebark, and the tall, bearded fir.

Jay Grobart had come to the tree country, and stopped to water and rest his weary horse at a threadlike watercourse falling out of the hills. He was, so far as he could see, still not being tracked. It puzzled him.

He knelt by the stream and drank with the pony, then filled his canteens. Again he found himself looking over his shoulder at some slight forest sound, until he gave up his intention to rest there and looked about for higher ground. Loosening the pony's girth straps, he led it after him up a well-clad, short-ridged hill with an eroded eastern face, and let it out to graze while he sat under a tree stretching his long legs and watching the empty slanting country in his wake.

He was still waiting for the ghost of Cat to come and confront him, but she was mute. While her brother spoke she had been real enough. He had clearly heard the swishing of her ample skirts across the bare floor, her little-girl laughter, and the confidential whisper, so moist, earnest, and loud against his ear. He saw again the black eyes sparkle with life, and the body, wide waisted, small breasted, smooth, with a clean animal smell. The old hurt and the hatred he once felt had tried to stir again too, but they had been beaten down by the double blows of Iron Knife's truth and the boy's hidden face. Iron Knife had made him believe. Now it was as if he had killed her again.

Cat Dancing. Cat, dying. Those darkening eyes, which he once thought he saw reflected for a moment in Catherine's, had not lied. Her last whisper had been the truth, and for that he had killed her. He could see that, now. She had been the only woman he had allowed to love him since he was seventeen. Yet her love had goaded his doubt, his resentment, his suspicion, until finally he had questioned her honesty and her innocence.

It was strange how he had believed Iron Knife at once, in spite of his denials. He had been bound as if with chains to stay and hear, from the first word. It was as if he had always known—but he had not!—and had come all that way, not to claim Johnny, but to claim his guilt at last.

Only, in coming, he had incurred another guilt. Because he came, the boy now knew his part in it. He had forgotten. Iron Knife had let him forget until Jay himself came to make him know.

So he had made a new ghost: the image of his own son hiding his face from him, unfolding his long body and darting away somewhere to hide like a terrified animal, to suffer his guilt and shame alone until Iron Knife, the surrogate, could find and comfort him. Even Catherine had to run, after that.

Well, that was the end of it. He had lost Johnny, lost him from the very beginning, and never known. If he had never killed the others, never suffered prison for it, if he had gone to find him the next day, the boy would have run from him. And he had murdered Cat for a fable, worse than a fable, a lie that struck some belief he had always carried in his heart: that she didn't love him because no one could.

Was he seeing the truth now, or just another excuse? He couldn't tell. But the fact of his life was clear. He had killed his son when he killed his wife. There was no Johnny. And Catherine was right. It was ten years done. If he needed damnation for it, there might be a hell that would take his enlistment, someday. But if he wanted to live a little longer, he had to put them both out of his mind.

He did still want to live, he discovered. Whatever the prospects, he wanted to get over the mountains, throw off his trackers, and survive to make old bones.

The sun was down and the light was fading fast. He had to put more distance between himself and the Fort before he could rest longer. There was a nearly full moon to light the way as long as he kept to the beaten trail. He didn't expect to find anyone on it who would stop him tonight.

He traveled at a moderate pace until midnight, stopping only twice to rest the pony. He had begun to worry a bit about his choice of it, wondering if it would be up to the demands he would have to make of it. He had taken one of Washakie's unshod, to make the tracking more difficult. But his own two crossbreeds, left behind in the corral, he thought had more stamina if only they hadn't been so much in need of a rest. He would have to be as sparing of this one as haste would permit, or he would find himself left on foot, a hundred miles from nowhere, straight up or sideways.

When he stopped to sleep, it was on a hill south of a long lake. He thought he could see fires glimmering through the trees on the far side of the water. He had already decided he would build no fires himself until he was well into the mountains.

He prepared for the short night, making a brief, unsatisfactory meal of dried meat and water. Food too would be a problem until he was away beyond the high rocks, where he might risk hunting. Here there was no time, and the noise of gunfire was unthinkable. He rolled himself into his blankets, dismissing the worry until tomorrow. Sleep came swift and dreamless, for a time. Then someone else came.

If he had thought to bury her with his regrets, forget her a second time without a struggle, she came and proved him the fool. How many ways she came, imprinting image after image on his brain. Smiling, black and amber under her flower-laden straw bonnet; the first one she had ever had. Standing at the front door in the warm evening with the child on her hip, or, big bellied in her long white muslin nightgown, before the child came, waiting for him to blow out the lamp and come to bed.

He dreamed her slim and ardent in his arms again, her girl's body learning to know its own hunger. Worst of all, he dreamed her struggling under him the last time; trying to fight both her fear and his merciless hands; whispering her denials and her love, even while he put the knife under her chin.

In the end, she had agreed to every accusation, nodded at every name he whispered, thinking him as mad as he was; hoping for life. And then, when he nearly relented, she had denied it all a last time and swore her love, and for that he had killed her.

She hovered over him with the blood on her throat, the little spot he had put there with the point of the knife. He could see the bruises on her from his hands, where he had stopped her whispering for all time. But it wasn't stopped. She was opening her mouth again; she would speak to him again; and if he heard her speak, he would die.

He struggled awake with a start that carried him up on one elbow, shaking and sweating in the cold darkness.

There were night-bird sounds, querulous and sleepy. Over him the moon was being swallowed by clouds and there was a damp, cool smell of imminent rain in the air.

He got up and found his pipe and the tobacco Washakie had given him, deciding to risk one brief flare of light in the blackness. Then he wrapped himself in the blankets, spreading the ground tarp over them, and propped himself against a tree to smoke. By this method he kept the ghost at bay until the rain began, softly pattering on the pine-needle floor of the woods behind him.

He pulled the tarp more securely around him and listened to the rain drum its fingers on it, until the sound put him to sleep sitting up, in the last hour before the gray wolf-dawn came that precedes the true day.

"But how can we follow him in the dark?" Catherine asked. "What if we should go the wrong way all night?"

The boy looked impatient. "He took the trail that leads to my own camp. It is an easy way. I think he will keep to it, once he has begun. There will be many tracks on it, to confuse the soldiers. I think he will know this, and keep to it at least for a while. If I am wrong—" He shrugged. "What else can we do? We must try to keep out ahead of the pony soldiers, and that means going tonight. By morning they will be tracking us."

"And him. They'll know he went this way instead of south."

"Then what would you do?" he asked. "If you would go to him, you must follow the way he goes! They will follow us, of course. We must be quicker! There will be little time for rest."

He had tethered the ponies some distance from the Fort to lessen the chance of immediate pursuit. They were lightly packed with blankets and water bottles. She didn't see food or think to ask about it.

When they were mounted he glanced at her clothes and asked, "Will you be warm enough? You have no jacket."

"I'm fine," she assured him. But she was already shivering a little. She had put on her secondhand pants and shirt again, but the controversial underwear had been left behind in the hotel at South Pass and her jacket, by mistake, in Washakie's camp. For the first time she regretted having abandoned the underwear.

They rode at the beginning under a bright moon that lit their path well. At the first point where a deviation from the trail was likely she waited, while he got down and searched the ground closely both ways, using his hands as well as his sharp eyes on the moon-silvered earth.

"There!" he said at last in quiet triumph. "It is as I said: he will take the easy way tonight. These marks are not deep, but they go over all tracks leading back the other way, made by my family yesterday."

When they had been some two hours on the way the moon sailed into a covering of clouds and didn't come out again. The air cooled sharply as a moist breeze sprang up, trundling the cloud mass along over their heads.

"Rain?" she asked. "I didn't think it ever rained out here." Rain would wash out his tracks. She mentioned this to Dream Speaker.

"Only if it is a hard rain. But in that case it will wash out our tracks as well." She tried to keep that in mind when the gentle drizzle turned into a downpour soaking her hair, shirt, and pants, until it ran down into her boots.

At least, she thought, the discomfort would keep her from falling off the pony asleep. She hadn't been able to get the rest that Dream Speaker had advised. Even after she found, to her relief, that Willard wouldn't be sharing her tiny room and bed, she couldn't loosen her knotted nerves enough to sleep.

She saw how they might be stopped a dozen times before they started. She worried that they would take the wrong way; that the boy might even betray her after second thoughts. She brooded on Jay, already captured or dead, by accident or at the hands of some late hunting party.

Worse, she foresaw finding him, only to be told unmistakably to turn back again. He didn't want her. If he had, he'd have taken her with him in the first place, wouldn't he?

The final worry was the practical one of how to tell when it was time to go. She didn't have a watch and there was no clock in the room. She could hardly ask to be notified when it was twelve o'clock by Willard or Mr. Lapchance. Twice, after hours of worry, she had drifted into a doze, only to jerk awake at the first sound, wondering if she had overslept; if the boy had waited for her, then gone home, supposing she had changed her mind.

When everything in the Fort was quiet, she had gotten up and dressed, putting on her old filthy clothes and carrying her boots as she crept out the door.

In the officers' mess she had found a clock, a heavy German import, ticking ponderously. Relieved, she had sunk into a chair to wait out the little time that was left.

But she hadn't slept, and now her bones shook almost as much for weariness as for the cold and wet.

In the early morning they came to the long lake where some of Washakie's people were camped. The fires were being rekindled by sleepy women who stood up, wondering, as they rode in.

Dream Speaker was among friends and relatives, so all the exchange of news and information was lost to her. He allowed her to warm herself at a fire while he traded ponies and talked earnestly to a young brave, still yawning and scratching himself awake.

It was too early for hot food. He gave her a cut of something that looked like a mating between a plug of tobacco and mincemeat and urged her to eat it on the way. He also offered her a blanket for warmth, for which she was grateful until she saw it was crawling with tiny gray insects: lice. She refused it quickly, letting it drop, and protested that she couldn't hold it about her and ride. She ached miserably in every sinew and muscle, and was beginning to feel the onset of a dull headache.

They retraced their trail for some distance back beyond the end of the lake. She saw he was looking for track. It took him an eternity of riding, casting back over his own trail until she couldn't see how he would be able to distinguish anything. He ranged over the hills above the lake, and was out of sight so long that once more she was visited by fear of being abandoned in the wilderness by him, as a piece of inscrutable Indian revenge.

But at last he appeared in the distance and waved her on to him. The sun was up by then, looking strangely wan in a muddled, cloudy sky.

"He climbed the hills and avoided the path when he saw the village. The rain spoiled the ground, but I found him—"

"Found him!"

"Found the way he went. He makes a path like a buffalo where there is grass. We must ride faster now. Already the soldiers at the Fort know you are gone, and why. They will not need to creep in the dark, or dally by fires and doze!"

"Do you think it's going to rain again?"

"It may, but that will not slow them much. And if my father, Iron Knife, is with them he will reason our trail as I have. And he will be very eager to catch us and put stripes on my back!" To her surprise, he grinned as he said it. Then he pounded at the pony's sides with his moccasined heels and started away from her, like some young centaur romping at play through the wet grass.

When the first scouting party returned empty handed from the south, Catherine and the boy had already been missed, and the beginnings of their plan laid bare. Iron Knife was at the tall gate, with a tearful Moon in Morning in tow behind him, to tell what she knew of her brother's departure.

In an hour Harvey Lapchance, Willard, Iron Knife, and a sergeant with six troopers were in the cavalry yard making ready to mount.

The rain had stopped, but they were all provided with yellow fishskin slickers, long skirted and split high up the back to fit over the saddle and cover their legs. Harvey buttoned and unbuttoned the neck of his several times, while pulling at it and resettling the shoulders, before he was finally satisfied with it.

The horse sensed his nervousness and began to champ and blow. Harvey hated horses. He never rode one when walking was possible or, on longer trips, when there was a train or a stage, no matter how badly sprung and slow. But now his unease was compounded by the appearance and mood of Willard Crocker.

That Crocker had been drinking again was not, in itself, alarming; merely disgusting. During their short, tedious association Willard had been more than half drunk every night. It was difficult to judge whether this was a common practice with him, or something brought on by the strain of his ordeal. He didn't carry his liquor well, or even toss it off with what Harvey would have called a practiced hand. But it wasn't necessary to develop a smooth technique in order to become merely drunk.

More seriously, he was drinking illegally on Indian territory, where liquor was forbidden. It was to be imagined that the several white officers had their private supply, but for a guest, and a civilian at that, it was another matter. He had already noticed the sergeant's nose twitching as he passed Willard, and he supposed everyone was as aware of the aura of raw alcohol as he.

It aggravated Crocker's worsening disposition. In Superior, he had been frightened; a little for his wife, a bit for himself. His earlier anger with her had run its course, and he was clearly bracing himself for the moment when he would be asked to identify her mangled corpse.

They had been delayed in Superior when the stage coming for them broke an axle in a washout and they had to wait an extra day for it to be replaced. Crocker began to get hold of himself there, and Harvey thought he might turn out to be some help after all.

On the way to South Pass and Atlantic City, Harvey thought Crocker had begun to enjoy himself, reveling a little in the romantic aspects of his chase through the wilderness to rescue his lady. If they had found Catherine in South Pass, Willard might have either fallen at her feet or swept her into his arms. Either action would have been appropriate to his mood then. Harvey realized now that they had missed her there by no more than half a day. The place had seemed deserted, so they had moved on.

But in Atlantic City Dawes had struck the blow that killed the romance. His wife was happy in her captivity, doted on her warden, in fact. Harvey had felt sorry for the man, then. He was childish and unstable, scarcely knowing what his own feelings about his errant wife were. But his bleak look had earned him Harvey's hard-won sympathy—until the drinking and the growing surliness throughout the frustrating four-day wait in Lander; waiting for permission to enter the territory; waiting for an absent sheriff to return and take over Coleman Dawes—until Harvey's sympathy withered and he settled down to steady dislike.

Last night there had been more tears. Harvey wanted very much to speak to the woman again, but she had gone to bed almost immediately after her conversation with Crocker. This morning she was gone, and there was an ugly sort of calm about her husband that was more unsettling than the tears.

He was carrying his fancy combination rifle-shotgun in the saddle boot. It was the first time Harvey had seen it out of its case since it had been exhibited so proudly in Point of Rocks.

He would almost have preferred two slightly drunk Sioux armed with repeating rifles to Willard, glum and ugly, with his custom-built freak.

"Mr. Crocker, do you think it's necessary to bring along your weapon? After all, we are well escorted and, inasmuch as neither your wife nor the boy is likely to prove dangerous—"

"I told you I know how to use it, Lapchance. Don't fret your policeman's mind about me. I'm not going to shoot the wrong person."

"I don't think it will be necessary to shoot anybody, right or wrong. Grobart's had a twelve-hour head start. If he gets into the mountains we'll never find him. And even if we did, he isn't likely to choose to shoot it out with nine men, seven of them professionals with a gun. He's still too much a professional himself, and too intelligent for such a thing."

"Well, *I'm* not entirely an amateur, *Mr.* Lapchance," Willard drawled with heavy courtesy. "I told you once before that I was considered an excellent shot by those who know me. I like to keep in practice with a little hunting when I can. You wouldn't object to a couple of sage hens or a rabbit for your dinner, would you?"

Harvey let it go. He wished he could find some excuse for demanding that the gun be left behind. He had even thought of asking the Fort's commander to keep Willard in custody for him. But he had no grounds for such a request, to the officer's way of thinking. On the face of things Willard was behaving properly. He might have exhibited gross lack of judgment in bringing his own supply of liquor onto the Reservation, but his right to join in the search for his wife and her abductor, even in the light of the morning's revelations, could not be questioned.

For the first time since he had scented trouble and gone out on the handcar to find it, Harvey Lapchance began to hope they would *not* catch up with Jay Grobart.

# 20

He had been very tired, and that perhaps accounted for his stupidity with the pony. Hobbling or tethering a horse was as habitual to him as breathing; as wearing a hat, cleaning a firearm after use, checking and caring for all his other personal equipment. Yet he had either forgotten to do it or had done it so carelessly that when he woke from a brief, unintended sleep the animal had strayed—was gone.

From now on he was on foot. The sleep he had managed to get did little to make up for all he had lost. Looking up beyond the sharpening ridges of the uplands to the ragged bareness of the mountain peaks, he felt his age—more than his age—for the first time. There was no possibility of reaching the upper passes alone and on foot with his present food and equipment.

Consulting his worn map, Jay cursed the cartographer again for all the ink wasted on border embellishments and calligraphy when there was so much blank space left unfilled in its heart.

To the north, and not too far away if he could believe his own estimate, was the Wind River. Beyond it, and the borders of the Reservation, was virtual emptiness when the map was made; cattle country now, maybe. It would not be an easy way to go on foot. But it was a possible way; the other was not.

Grimly, he began sorting out his equipment, taking the canvas cantinas apart and using one of them and the saddle straps to fashion a back pack. He rolled his bedroll tightly and twisted it into an inverted U around the pack, strapping it on. Neither food nor clothing was going to be a large item now. Matches, map, binoculars, ammunition, cleaning equipment went in with food and the extra shirt. Although instinct urged him to be off at once, he remained seated on his rock until he had examined both guns and their cartridges. They were supposed to be impervious to damp weather, unlike the old ones, but he was prepared to doubt everything now.

When he finished he strapped on his new pack at waist and shoulders, made some minor adjustments, then stood for a moment looking down at his castoff possessions: the compact kitchen gear in its tin box; the well-cared-for saddle, oiled to a shine; the rifle boot.

With a snort of impatience he left it, making long strides over the ground away from it. But in less than ten steps he stopped and returned to snatch up the boot and another strap. He wouldn't walk all the way to the border swinging a rifle in his hand like a damned farmer.

In the afternoon a hunting party drove him to a discovery he would not otherwise have made.

He saw them on an open slope below him as he was coming down, and took them for a band of Sheep Eaters, the despised mountain cousins of the Shoshone. There were four of them and, like him, they were on foot.

He was well protected from their view for the moment by the thickset growth of dark firs topping his ridge. But his easy path led down to a crossing with theirs. They were paused for a conference, expressive hands gesturing and pointing up his way, so that for a tense moment he thought they had seen him too.

While they argued he backed away cautiously, looking about for an alternative route. He could go back the way he had come, descending the ridge on the other side. But that would gain him little, and it would lose him the view he wanted of their own movements. West, behind him, was a narrow wooded hogback, its steep sides bristling with spikes of evergreen. It arched between two different levels of the submountain like a causeway. Above it, some recent landslide had sheared away the earth, exposing the gray rock face above a tumulus of ruined tree trunks, broken stone, and scree.

He did not want to climb again, and particularly he disliked the exposure of the bare cliff face and the treachery of the loose rubble beneath it. Only his dislike of yielding the high ground to them by retracing his steps was greater. So he climbed.

The heavy accumulation of dead pine needles and moss on the floor of the woods made a carpet that kept his feet almost as noiseless as the hunters'. By the time he reached the upper end of the hogback and came to the end of the trees he was far enough away from them to risk the sound of his leather heels on the bare stones.

He found he had an unexpected choice of directions. The bare northeastern face he had seen from below had a broad, uneven shelf at its base; rock strewn and broken, but wide enough for a wagon, now that he was level with it. And it led down.

But, angling to his left, the southwestern face of it narrowed to something less than four feet, and little more than two in places. The narrower shelf rose instead of descending, above a similar steep incline of fallen boulders and gravel. Below that was the way he had come before spotting the hunters.

He chose the southwestern face with the narrower ledge, because it kept the trees at his back a little longer, and looked firm. He did not relish starting a rockslide himself, and he was not an experienced climber.

And so he found the caves.

Some of them were not true caves but only wind-hollowed pocks in the cliff face. Others, like pockets, sloped downward and came to an abrupt, narrow end with a sinkhole or chimney crack. There were larger ones and longer ones that he would never explore, though the mountain people had, centuries before.

Some of them had been used as shelters by beast and man alike in the past, and they were decorated with the crude scratchings of the men and the refuse from the meals of the beasts. They were the tunnelings of subterranean streams that had steeped away before the land rose and split. Their visible parts were dissected and exposed by the falling of the hills, like the worm tunnels of a divided apple.

But those he never saw. The one he chose was of the pocket variety, with a slanting chute of an entrance that widened after four or five feet to a fairly level dry room roughly the size of a boxcar. The back of the "room" had experienced a fall of ceiling in the past and there was a narrow chimney hole opening to utter blackness above the debris.

There was no ammonia or rotten-meat smell to indicate that it was or had been recently occupied. He went in after unlashing his pack from around him and easing it from his strained shoulders.

It took little time to explore. The walls were nearly straight. It was high enough to stand up in, once he was past the chute. He was pleased with its dryness. After spending three matches inspecting it, he put his pack against the wall, took off his boots, and crawled back up the chute, stretching out belly down on the slope at the entrance to listen for the hunters.

After approximately twenty minutes of silence he crawled out to the mouth cautiously and looked about. The sun was far past the zenith, so that no light fell beyond the threshold that would show him in it to anyone below. Only the dimmest twilight inside let him see where he had left his white pack.

Below him, visible above the ledge, was the way he had come from Washakie's camp. The lessening hills, green with pine and fir, gave way to rolling, less densely wooded poplar country. The world beyond the ledge shaded from darkest green to blue-green, blue, and shadowed purple in the farthest distance. He could see that in the east the low-hanging clouds still trailed gray skirts of rain.

A disturbed crackling of the forest floor below him made him start, then risk a closer look from just outside the cave when he heard a shout.

The hunters had flushed their quarry; not the bighorn

mountain sheep, but a white-tailed mule deer. He saw the flash of its rump as it dashed out of cover, confused and quick, facing this way and that with bounding leaps before they brought it down. They cried congratulations on one another as they swept down on it and cut its throat.

He was almost as pleased about it as they, because now they would go home with their prize and leave him in peace in his eyrie.

They gutted the beast first and left the entrails for the mountain spirits, and to lighten the load. Then they lashed its feet together and passed a lance between its legs for a carrying pole.

He watched them out of sight with approval, then gave them another half hour to be well gone while he sunned, or, rather, aired himself, on the ledge. The sun was over the higher peaks behind him.

He thought he would prefer to take his meager dinner on the ledge rather than in the night-dark cave. When he returned from groping through the pack his eyes were arrested by two tiny moving figures in the distance. He watched them while he ate, but they scarcely seemed to come any closer. Yet they were close enough that he could see they were mounted and traveling at a purposeful canter over the rising ground. Soon they were lost to him behind an interposing hill.

One part of his mind had been considering the natural chimney in his shelter, and when he finished eating he left his watch for the hidden riders to feel his way in to the rear of the cave and scratch a match on the back wall.

When he held the flame under the chimney hole, it shook and flickered, then stretched up long and blue until it burned to his finger ends and he dropped it.

With the hatchet he'd bought in South Pass he foraged through the wooded ridge looking for dropped branches and other dead wood. He hauled as much as he could carry back up to the cave, using his jacket, its arms knotted around the load, as a carrier.

When he reached his shelf again he glanced down across

the treetops to check on the travelers, and stopped. A third moving figure had joined the two. In the distance and lessening light he couldn't quite see it, but experience told him, by its lighter, freer movements, that it was an unmounted horse.

He slid into his hole, pulling the firewood after him, and spent the next ten minutes carefully sorting and arranging his fuel and laying the base for a fire. It would be cold in the cave at night. The pocketful of dry needles he had scooped up made good tinder and the resinous, aromatic wood kindled readily. When it was going well he laid his hatchet neatly in place beside the woodpile and shook the bark and needles out of his jacket. Then he fished out his field glasses and went outside again.

He had resisted the urge to use them until now, because he was cautious of signaling his whereabouts with an unintentional heliographic flash from the lenses when the sun was high. Then too, the constant watch on the pursuers, if he sighted them, would be as debilitating as the ghost watch he endured at night.

Safe from the declining sun, he focused on the intruders. They had come to a stop. One sat motionless, while the other had dismounted and was moving slowly toward the third, unmounted, horse. He let his breath out through his teeth, a wordless hiss of exasperation.

As he had suspected, the evasive, shifty animal, adroitly courting and resisting capture down there, was his own pony.

"Is it his?" cried Catherine, to the boy in the distance, when he had at last caught the dragging reins. He flung himself onto it and succeeded in bringing it back to some semblance of its duty, after a few bucks and snorts.

"It is one of the chief's. It has his mark on it. I think it must be the one Washakie let the whi—my—father take."

"What does it mean? Is he dead?"

The boy rode up frowning, still gentling the pony. "I don't know." He searched the hills with narrowed eyes reflecting the red sun, while the subdued animal dropped its head to graze with the other two. "If you mean, is he dead—

killed by men—I think, no. They would have taken a pony with a saddle; but the saddle is gone. If you mean, is he dead by accident—it would be the same. The pony would run away from the fallen man still with a saddle, and the other things too."

She shifted irritably in her own saddle, because he was enjoying his own rumination, while she was anxious and miserable.

She was reaping the wages of too little food and sleep, too much strain and anguish, too many hours of chill from her rain-soaked clothes. Her head was crowned with pain, her eyes hurt, her chest ached and labored for breath. The tireless boy had let her sleep only two hours at a time, while the horses grazed and rested.

She had not thought of complaining, because reaching Jay was more important to her than all her aches. But while the boy, with all the resilience of his age, was enjoying the rigors of his quest, she had moved through the last twenty-four hours in a haze of interrupted sleep and pain.

"Could someone have stolen him?" she asked.

He nodded, then shook his head. "Maybe. But why not the saddle and other things? Again, the saddle is the thing of mystery. No thief or murderer would leave it behind. I think—" he nodded his certainty—"I think he has unpacked it for the night—and let it stray. It could happen if he tied it and it took fright at something. Or maybe he forgot. He must be very tired by now," he mused, making a long, thoughtful face like his elders.

Tired? Oh God, yes. My poor old Jay, what are we two doing out here, tormenting our weary bones to stay alive? She suppressed a groan. Such mad rides without rest are for the Billy Bowans of the world, and this boy.

"How will we find him? If he's still alive and on foot he could be anywhere. Would he go north or south, or what?"

Dream Speaker shrugged one of his fine, dismissing shrugs. "We will have to look."

"It will be dark soon."

"All the better then, if we're under the trees. The others can't be far behind us."

She couldn't understand his reasoning, but she followed him dejectedly over the next hill. Later, when he found blood on the ground, she could hardly breathe out her question. But he relieved her, after casting back and forth along the ground several times.

"There are no boot heels stamping the grass. It is pressed by many feet; see the double track? Hunters, carrying their kill."

When she could speak she said, "We'd better hurry." The looming mountains hid most of what seemed to be a brilliant sunset. Almost to the meridian the buttermilk sky glowed with tints of pink, peach, and salmon.

"Let us divide our search here and each look on a side of this ridge before it is dark. Then we will rest and eat. We can do no more until tomorrow, I think. You are very tired."

"But how will we find each other again?" she said, alarmed by the thought of being lost in these black wooded hills at night.

"Why, we will each return along our own path and meet here!"

"You say that as if we'd be leaving a trail of bread crumbs along the way." He looked puzzled. "What if I can't remember what my path looked like?"

"Then I would find you. Do you know how to call?"

"Call? You mean it's all right to call him? Then why didn't you tell me? We should have been calling him all the time. He's much more likely to be in shouting range than in sight." Even the mild scolding voice made her head throb, but she drew in a breath to shout. He cut her short with his urgency.

"No! No! Don't call his name. It would be bad for all of us! And the Ninambea would hear it and know who he is!" It was her turn to look puzzled. But he didn't explain.

"Do you know how to call like a bird?" He demonstrated.

"Well, I can whistle. Nothing fancy." She piped thinly.

"Very good." He laughed. "You go that way, and come back here. Or perhaps we will meet on the other side. If you are lost, you whistle and I will call. When I call, you whistle. Good?"

"Good."

"Don't whistle to the bears. Just to me." He grinned.

He left her there, and she was terrified. Common sense urged that the remark about the bears had been a joke. Surely he wouldn't ride away with such a jaunty wave if he really thought there were bears around. She urged her pony forward into the dusk.

She would have called out for Jay anyway, except that she hadn't found out who the Ninambea were. He had mentioned them before and she had thought he meant the mountains. Perhaps he did, but it was more likely to be a tribe, like the hunters who had splashed the blood on the grass. Would he have left her alone if he thought the hunters were still about?

Oppressed by her fatigue and her fears of bears, listening enemies, and being lost in spite of all his calls and whistles, she rode through the darkening declivity in a stupor of weariness and numb dread.

At the sound of movement on the hill above her, she froze, hands tight on the reins. The pony reacted accordingly, just as Captain Lightfoot had on another occasion, backing and blowing nervously. Even when she saw the figure coming through the close-set trees she didn't know. He might have been man, bear, or unimaginable mountain spirit called up by her tired mind or Irish blood.

When she heard his voice commanding the pony with a businesslike "Hoa. Ho, there. Ho," she tried to speak to him, and couldn't. She had reached her destination and the end of her strength at the same moment.

As he reached up to take the reins from her she slid off the saddle into his arms.

# 21

"CAN YOU STAND? I can't afford to lose another horse." She nodded slightly and he let her go, to tether the animal to a scrubby juniper. She stood with closed eyes, swaying, waiting for his return. When he took her arms again she leaned on him, pressing herself into him, too tired to speak.

He held her that way tightly for a moment. Then he said in a ragged voice, "What are you trying to do, kill yourself? What are you doing out here, anyway?"

"Looking for you," she whispered.

"You must be crazy. You'd have played hell finding me if I hadn't been watching you for the last couple of hours."

"When we found the horse, I thought you were dead." He swore softly into her ear, thinking about the animal. "That's very vulgar," she complained, "and all those esses tickle."

"Who's that with you?"

"Your son." He pushed her back so he could see her face. "He offered to bring me to you. He's a wonderful boy. He never gets tired."

"Where is he now? I lost track of him when I came down for you."

"On the other side of this hill someplace, looking for you. I'm supposed to whistle like a bird if I get lost."

"Well, let's find him. Can you go a little longer?"

"I think if you let go of me I'll fall flat on the ground."

He picked her up and carried her a little way up the slope to a grassy spot. She seemed to weigh nothing, yet his own arms were cramping with fatigue when he put her down and wrapped his jacket around her. He supported her, half-sitting, half-lying against him. Her forehead pressed against his throat and he realized she had a fever.

"Goddamn it, Catherine," he said angrily, "you must be out of your mind to do a thing like this. Your head is hotter than a stove! What's the matter with that damned husband of yours? Why didn't he knock you down and lock you up?"

"We talked it over," she whispered, "and he decided to make do with just keeping me on a leash for the rest of my life. I thought it would be better if you had a dried-up, jealous bitch around to nag you. Keep you on your toes."

He raised her face with his hand in time to see her faint smile. "Shut up," he muttered.

"Shut me up."

He did, kissing her dry lips, and her closed eyes, while he wondered about the seriousness of the fever. She seemed to sleep. When the boy's birdcall came he answered it, and in a few minutes he could see the shadow shapes of his son and the two ponies coming through the dusk. He stood up, after easing Catherine to the ground, and went down to meet them.

"Here is your pony, although it would be better if you took mine instead. He is saddled, and there is food in the pouch. I see you found your woman."

"It was a mistake to bring her. She's sick. And you've brought more company behind you. I could see them from up above. But thank you for coming anyway, son." He could barely see the boy's face, but the embarrassment and stiffness suddenly in his voice were plain.

"I did not come to stay. Only to bring her. And the others would have come soon enough."

"I know. It's all right. Thanks."

"She could have stayed, but she chose you, as—as I did Iron Knife. It was wrong to help her run from her man, but sometimes the right way—" His shoulders lifted like Iron

Knife's. "I didn't want you to think we must be enemies because I must stay with Iron Knife."

"Yes," said Jay. "Tell Iron Knife I thank him for his pony. And the help of his son."

The boy chuckled softly. "I'll tell him that before he beats me, or there might be two beatings."

"He won't beat you very hard; only enough to show that he's glad to have you back, just as I would myself. Now, you better get out of here. You'll be able to see their fire when you get back to that first rise where you chased the pony."

"What about the ponies?"

"I'll leave them here. They'll be no use to me tonight."

"I'll hobble them for you." He did, then leaped on the back of the unsaddled one. "They'll be there when you want them this time, unless a bear or a big cat comes along."

"I'll have to risk it."

They looked at one another's shapes in the darkness.

"Good-bye, John Grobart. If I were two people, as you said—but I must be Dream Speaker. Take care of your life, and your woman's."

"Good-bye, boy."

When the sound of the pony's feet could no longer be heard, Jay stirred from where he had been standing and returned to Catherine, slinging the leather food pouch over his head and shoulder.

He shook her gently and pulled her to her feet to partly walk, partly carry her up the ridge to his shelter. She stumbled repeatedly, but by the time they reached the ledge she was moving well enough for him to push her along in front of him. He had been wondering if he would be able to carry her along it without spilling them both over the edge.

The cave was cold. He had knocked his fire apart to save some of the wood when he decided to intercept her. He built it up again from the embers while she sat in a trance, watching. After it was blazing he held a blanket near it until it was warmed, and wrapped her in it. When he had the bedroll smoothed out in front of the fire, he put her on it and lay down beside her, covering them both with another blanket.

Neither of them had spoken since he waked her. They were both too tired for speech. They fell asleep nested together, the first undisturbed rest either had had in a week. She dreamed bright fever dreams of falling, leaflike things and drifting colors, imageless and soothing.

And even for him, Cat Dancing did not come that night.

In the first light, Harvey's company left their camp and took up their search again. Dream Speaker had not ridden to meet them, having chosen to slip around them and make his way home to await his foster father's wrath.

But the evidence of the two horsemen who met a third, chased him, and joined him to their train was not lost completely on the grass when Iron Knife came to look at it.

They followed the triple track into the hills through all its turnings until one of the troopers found the hobbled ponies.

"Two of them aren't far away, then," said Harvey. "But which two?"

"These are my own ponies," said Iron Knife. "The one that is gone was Washakie's. Grobart has escaped."

"So she went running out here after him and he wouldn't have her," sneered Willard behind them. "He wasn't so damn stupid, after all!"

Harvey gave him a brief look of dislike and turned back to Iron Knife. "Where do you think the other two could be, without their horses? Catching a little breakfast in the hills, maybe?"

"That would seem likely. They have made no cooking fires along the way. They will be hungry, and small game must be hunted quietly on foot."

"Then we'll spread out and look for them," Harvey said. Willard dismounted and unsheathed his gun. "Put that damned piece away, Crocker," Harvey told him. "This is a woman and a boy who haven't done anything. You don't have any use for it now."

Willard put it back sullenly after measuring the size and

mood of the two men staring at him. "Just what do I have your permission to do?" he asked.

"Just get back on that horse and start looking for them. Take any hill you like. There are enough to go around."

"Since the old man didn't want her any more, she's probably bedded down cozily someplace, letting his boy use her for practice."

Harvey felt a twinge of hatred that made his stomach cramp. He looked quickly at Iron Knife, but the other man only turned away from Crocker, as from the sight of carrion.

"Get out of here, Crocker. You make the air stink. And if I hear that gun of yours go off, it'll be the last time you ever use it."

When he was out of earshot Harvey sighed, one hand flat against his ribs. "I never killed a man in my life, not even in the line of duty. But if I have to pick one to start on, by God, I'd like for it to be him. I wish old Jay had stuck around to put a hole in him. I believe if he had, I'd buy him a stage ticket to California and shake his hand."

"Should he be allowed to keep the gun?"

"Well, I took the shells out of the rifle while he was sleeping off his liquor, so he isn't going to make any quick shots. I don't think he's checked it since. The best he could do, if he's got a wad up that second barrel, is blow the bark off a tree, or blow up the gun and himself with it, which wouldn't be a bad idea. Only a blowhard would want a damn crazy gun like that. It's all show. He'd have to get right up on it to hit the broad side of a buffalo with it. It's got no range." He knew he was protesting too much. He'd feel better if he had taken the damned thing and wrapped its barrels around a tree trunk.

He was right about two things. Willard had not checked the gun since loading it. And there was a charge in the muzzle-loaded second barrel. It had been in there for several years, and was nearly solidified.

The sound of her breathing alarmed Jay when he woke. He put his hand on her head and she was hot, though not so hot, he thought, as the night before. She opened her eyes while he was testing, and smiled.

"Good morning," she said. "This is a very unusual hotel you've picked. Our room was full of glowworms and butterflies all night."

"That's your fever working on you. You need a doctor."

"You make a very good doctor for what I need." She covered her mouth in mock shame. "Isn't that awful? I'm turning into a low woman. Are you going to marry me and bring me out of it?" She giggled. "Or shall we just stay here and live in sin?"

"You're out of your head."

She sat up with a look of injured dignity. "I am not out of my head. And I'm not sick. I have a chest cold; I often get them, and I've felt a hundred times worse than this with them before. I was only trying to be—jocular. How do you like that? Could a sick woman even think of a word like jocular?" He didn't smile. "I'm trying to tell you how much I'm pleased to have you scowling at me and ordering me about again, that's all." Her breath was quick and shallow as she sat surveying the cave. "I may have just a touch of pleurisy," she admitted.

"Cat—Catherine, you've got pneumonia, from the sound of you."

"You did that once before. Called me by her name." Her overbright eyes stared accusingly. "I suppose it's slipped your mind, what a jealous bitch I am."

He shook his head, forced to smile, in spite of his concern. "No, I haven't forgotten it for a minute. It was a slip of the tongue. My apologies. Do you want some water?"

She drank thirstily, then poured some in her palm and patted it on her face and throat. "That feels good," she murmured, but she shivered.

He got up to make a new fire. The cave seemed cool to him, and to her it must feel cold. Yet when he turned his head to ask, she was pulling her shirt off over her head. With a sharp exclamation of dismay he grabbed the tail of it and jerked it down again, only to find himself tangled up in her arms and pulled down on her.

"What in the hell do you want to do, die, stripping down for one of your goddamn baths in a cold cave with a fever?" he snarled. "If you're hot I'll make a cold cloth for your head, but keep your clothes on!"

She lay looking at him with her hands locked behind his head. Slowly, her eyes filled with tears. The tears made him angrier, because they increased his feeling of helplessness for her, and his certainty that she was delirious with fever. She couldn't travel, and she couldn't stay where they were and live. The only help for her was to find her a doctor, and there probably wasn't a doctor this side of Lander.

"I wanted you to make love to me," she said reproachfully. He couldn't speak. "Oh, now you're shocked. Let's blame it on my fever. You know, I think a little fever must be like a little whiskey. It lets you say all sorts of things you wouldn't have the nerve to say otherwise, and it gets all the blame."

"Kate—" She pulled his head down until their lips touched. In spite of himself he responded, pressing her down as he caught the fever in her mouth and felt the rapid shaking of her heart under his hand. She made a small sound and her hands slipped away from his neck. He raised his head, reluctantly, realizing he must be smothering her. She had fainted.

He laid her down guiltily and covered her again with both blankets. For a while he sat watching her. Her breathing was shallow and rapid, but even. There was a gray light coming through the cave mouth now. He felt for his watch to see how much time he had, and found that he'd forgotten to wind it and it had stopped. He eased away from her and went to the hole to look and listen.

He couldn't hear anything below, but from the degree of light he judged it was about a half hour before sunup. If they weren't down there yet, they'd be there soon. He didn't think about what to do, because there were only two things to do. Stay here with her until they went away, and then hope she'd live. Or take her down the mountain and see that whoever was in charge down there sent for a doctor, if it meant killing one or two of them for an incentive. Even an Indian medicine man would be all right. They had herbs for fevers as good as anybody's. Getting away afterward was going to pose a problem. After winding his watch and setting it arbitrarily for five o'clock, he went back to Catherine.

Her faint seemed to have passed into an ordinary sleep, so he stretched out cautiously beside her again. After a while he gave up reconstructing the prison cell in which he had lived so many years, and in which he would someday die. He too slept again.

Below the ledge, Willard Crocker passed the rubble bank for the second time, and only then looked up and saw the holes in the cliff face. For a moment he blinked at them, because he was certain he had looked up there before and had seen nothing. His eyes felt like two throbbing sores in his head now, from putting himself to sleep with the gin the last two nights, and from not eating any food this morning.

He dismounted with care and let the pony stray while he examined the incline to see if it was climbable. But the pounding in his head and the dryness of his throat, which was slightly sore, discouraged him from trying right away.

He sat down on part of the rockslide that had fetched up against an ancient tree, putting his gun across his lap so he could open his canteen. When he could swallow better, he closed the canteen and got out a flat silver flask from his inside coat pocket. The liquor both burned and soothed the soreness in his throat. He leaned back against the tree with his eyes closed, waiting for it to dull the pain in his head.

That goddamned, holier-than-a-virgin Catherine, who had once hit him in the nose and made it bleed like a stuck pig, because he tried to pull her nightgown all the way off one Sunday morning! She was up there in one of those holes, he bet. She had to be, because she sure as hell wasn't anywhere down here.

He was glad he'd been the one to spot the holes. When she got through letting herself be worked over by a dirty, hot-handed, half-breed kid, he'd have a little surprise for them both. But, oh God, how his head hurt. He wasn't used to swilling liquor like this. He didn't see how Catherine's old man could live on it like he did. Well, there wasn't much danger of him becoming a drunk like that, the way it hit him. He'd only started drinking to stop the self-blame and worry about her in the beginning. Now he drank to stop the pain in his head that he got because he drank. But when he was home again it would be different. He wouldn't need it then. Jesus, would he?

"Did I miss something?" she asked, when she woke and found him sitting up watching her.

His mouth made a half-smile. "You missed about a week's sleep, and a few hot meals. You've caught up a little on the one. Are you hungry?" He thought she looked better. Her face didn't seem so flushed. She shook her head at the offer of food, but took more water.

There wasn't much water left, but that didn't make any difference now. She noticed that he was dressed, including gun belt and hat. All the minor items of his equipment were out of sight, presumably in the pack.

"Are we going someplace?"

"If you feel up to it."

"Wouldn't we be safer, staying here for a while? They must be close, looking for us, by now. Let's stay here until they get tired and go away. It can't be for long."

"No, we have to move out now."

She searched his face carefully in the dim light. "What is it? There's something, I can tell. You weren't thinking of leaving me up here while I was asleep? Did I wake up too soon?"

"Now, that's a hell of a thing to think, even of me," he said heatedly because, inevitably, it had occurred to him while he was trying to look at all angles of the problem objectively.

She put her hand out to him. "You know I didn't really think it. What I really think is that you're still convinced that I'm dying or something, and you might be planning to give yourself up, because of me."

"Wrong again. I'm thinking that I haven't heard a sound out of anybody down there, and that they're probably off trying to run Johnny down. And that if we're smart, we'll get on those ponies and ride the hell out of here as quick as we can while they're busy. If you feel up to it."

"I told you, there isn't anything wrong with me but a cold and a little pleurisy." She pushed herself to her feet, determined not to stagger, although his image was coming to her in blue and red pulses with the beat of her heart.

He stood up too. "All right, then. You roll up the blankets and wait for me here. I'll go down and get the horses and bring them around to this side of the hill. I think we can get you down that bank without taking off too much skin, and it'll be easier on you to slide a little than to walk half a mile over the ridge."

"But why wait? Look, I'm ready to go. See? Just let me pick up the bed and I'll come with you."

"Will you, for God's sake, ever learn to shut up and do as I tell you?" He took her by the shoulders and shook her a little, partly to confirm his suspicion that she was quivering like an aspen just from the effort to stand up.

"There's one thing you might tell me, if you could, and then I'd do anything you'd say. With no arguments." He waited, frowning when she faltered. "Tell me whether you love me or—or not."

He looked at her, mute. His hand left her shoulder and caught the nape of her neck, pulling her against him. Once he started to speak, but thought better of it. The truth was like a pain in his throat now, and it would only hurt her, afterward.

"You must be the craziest damn woman in the world," he said helplessly, before letting go of her. "You stay here until I come around down below and whistle. Now don't come tottering out on the ledge and break your neck while I'm gone. Understand? I'll be about thirty minutes, so don't get in a panic." He touched her face and was gone, climbing quickly up the chute with a scraping of boots and pulling himself through the sunlit hole.

The sound that burst into the cave seemed so loud it was directionless. She was stunned, clapping her hands to her ears; thinking landslide, earthquake, cannon fire. Then she knew what it was and her scream shattered against the walls of the cave and sent a thousand shrilling echoes racing into madness.

Before they had half run their course she was scrambling up the slope on hands and boot toes into the blind brightness after him.

He was already dying when she reached him. He had not fallen off the ledge but, slammed against the cliff by the force of the clustered shot, he lay across the entrance in her way.

On her knees she pulled at him, trying to gather him up, and saw that his lips moved. "What? What?" she begged. "Oh God, Jay, please try," until his face changed and she saw that she would never get her answer now.

She sank down howling. Her face and hair were dabbled with his blood and she pressed against him. With one hand she blindly touched his face imploringly; petted and caressed his body, until she reached the heavy leather flap of his holster. Sightlessly, she pulled it open and felt the slick-oiled weight of the old Remington inside.

She raised her head as she drew it out: rustless, unpitted, cared for; fourteen inches of death from blue steel muzzle to worn walnut grips, weighing more than four pounds loaded. It was more than her one hand could manage. She withdrew the other, bloodier, hand from beneath him so she could put both thumbs on the hammer, forcing it back until it clicked, twice.

Below her, Willard labored up the incline, clutching at half-buried stones that gave way under his weight. He ignored the rage of the mail shuffler just now riding up behind him.

"Goddamn you, Crocker! I told you if you fired that gun I'd kill you!"

Willard laughed, panting with his exertion. "And I promised her I'd have a little surprise for her when she came out of there! Up in that hole with that damned half-breed—" He came near enough to the top to see Catherine's blank, bloodied face staring at him. He was taken aback to see her still alive. He just had time to notice what she held between her hands when she pulled the trigger.

The second explosion sent Harvey leaping from his horse, clawing at his pocket for his own small pistol. He fired a warning shot and broke into a stumbling run. But he was too late.

As he reached the rocks Willard Crocker's body, arms stretched upward as if in appeal, came sliding face down—slowly—leaving a thin red smear in its wake the length of the rough bank, until it stopped at his feet. A moment later a large revolver, spinning butt over barrel, followed it and lay near the dead man's head, winking at the sun.

Overhead, there was the sound of a woman crying.

Harvey stood quietly, looking at the old gun and listening to the voice of her pain. He had no idea even how to begin to ease her, but he knew that it was the most important thing left for him to do now: to try.

He went up to comfort her.